d. E. ROGERS

The Dark Side of

MONEY

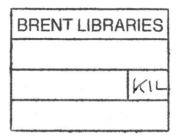
Published by REGI Books, a Subsidiary of Rogers Entertainment Group International.

For information, please contact:
d. E. Rogers at: dERogers@thedarksideofmoney.com.
www.thedarksideofmoney.com

ISBN: (10 digit) 0-9700880-6-3 and (13 digit) 978-0-9708808-6-4

Printed in the United States of America
Cover Design by Jason Alexander at Expert Subjects

Edited by John Paine

This book is dedicated to the people who have been there for me since day one. With or without blood, you are my family. Thanks for all the inspiration and guidance you have given me. Without you, I might not have even finished one book.

PROLOGUE

New York, 1983

"**I**s this really what you want?" Jack yelled at his daughter. "I love her. Whether you like it or not, she is my wife." He shoved the papers in his hand back at her.

His daughter, Gloria, was a dark-skinned beautiful woman, and as she glared at the papers she had drawn up, she couldn't help but think how much she was like him. Her father was trying to get her to accept his new wife, who was just thirty years old—only three years older than Gloria.

She rolled her eyes at his declaration. No matter what her father was saying, she wasn't listening. She wanted it her way or no way. "This is business. No place for soft hearts in the money game. Isn't that your motto, Daddy?" she said sarcastically.

Jack Dean, the patriarch of the Dean family, was in his late forties. A brown- skinned handsome man, he stood six foot three with a very athletic build. He was successful and loved to be stylish, as if he was still posing for a magazine cover. With his late wife, they had built their fashion business from the ground up. The Gloria Dean Company, named after their daughter, had been making clothes since the start of the civil rights movement. He had been a tailor and shoemaker, and his wife was a seamstress. The company had stood the test of time, producing clothes, accessories, and nowadays cosmetics. Not only was it a market leader among black people, the Gloria Dean Company had expanded worldwide in a time when black people couldn't even shop in white stores.

Gloria had fought many battles with his new wife, and she knew he was tired of them. On his face at the moment was total disgust. As he had told her repeatedly, he expected Gloria to be the bigger person. Yet she wanted things to return to the way they were. The six years since her mother's passing had been rough on her, yet at the same time she learned to be the partner her father lacked. For a mid-twenties model type, Gloria's looks seemed innocent, but underneath her perfect skin, her father had created a family-first, business-minded, driven woman. And she was willing to do whatever it took to keep her family, and its business, the way she thought it should be.

"Just sign it," Gloria pleaded. "This solution is best for us all."

"Why don't you like her?" he asked, trying to get Gloria to directly face him.

Gloria tilted her head a little, not afraid to meet him dead on. "Where should I start?"

"You haven't given her a chance."

Gloria went over to her desk, picked up a magazine and handed it over to her father. "That bitch said on page forty-nine, paragraph three, that she was now running the Gloria Dean Company, and that I report to her. Is she crazy?" Gloria's bottom lip trembled. Confronting her father about anything had always been tough for her. Anyone else would have gotten a tongue-lashing.

"You can't believe everything you read," Jack said, though he frowned at what his wife had written.

"She even said I should call her *Mother*. Ugh! That bitch is the same age as me. I want her gone!"

"That's not going to happen."

"One way or another it will!" Gloria said, her eyes blazing. That remark by her father's new wife about running the company was the last straw.

"Do you want your family business in the street?"

Gloria smirked. "We ain't family!" She fumed that her father was not seeing the evil power play by his new wife.

"Why are you acting this way?" Jack was beginning to lose his cool as well. "Is it the money? The power?"

For a moment there was silence as the two combatants just stared each other down. The answer was her father's love. Gloria hated sharing her father, especially with a woman who was taking advantage of her father's weakness to please beautiful women.

"Just sign the damn paper," Gloria demanded.

Insulted by her attempt at intimidation, Jack grabbed his daughter by the shoulders and shoved her against the wall.

"You're not disrespecting me," Jack said, breathing heavily into her face. "I built this! Everything you got is because of my work! Don't you forget that!"

Behind Jack, a young black man about Gloria's age opened the door. Seeing Gloria pinned up against the wall, the man started to rush to her aide.

"Leave now, Richard!" Jack shouted, halfway turning to him.

The grave fear he had for his father-in law stopped Richard dead in his tracks. He looked over at Gloria. She nodded at him to go. He paused for a second, thinking of what he should really do—but one more dark look from Jack sent him scurrying on his way.

"Daddy, she's not Momma!"

"No one said she was." Jack eyes watered up a little, but no tears fell.

"This is my momma's company too!" Gloria said, wincing with pain. The grip her father had on her was hurting, but she knew not to speak on it. Weaknesses were frowned upon in their family.

"Your mother and I built this!" he said sternly. "Not you!"

"And not Alexis!" Gloria shot back, trying to not appear afraid. "This is my mother's legacy. No one will destroy that."

"I never thought we would reach this impasse," Jack said sadly.

"I never thought you would marry some slut and call it love." Gloria had to dig the knife in a little more for her cause. "If she had it her way, you and I would be removed from the picture entirely. You thought you were marrying a catwalker, but she's a streetwalker."

"Gloria, Alexis is my wife now. We're married."

"Is that supposed to change my feelings?" she challenged. "Huh, if you married her a thousand times, that would just mean I hate her a thousand times more."

Jack raised his hand up to slap the taste out of her mouth. Yet as his hand was descending downward, he saw the fear in her eyes. The fear of the little girl he had raised. He stopped short and just walked away from her.

Gloria stayed against the wall, trying to figure out why her father didn't slap her.

Jack went over to her desk and picked up the contract papers he had thrown at Gloria earlier. "Where is she at now?"

"You don't know?" Gloria said. "She's using the company jet again! Supposedly going to see her sick mother. She must be the sickest person in Puerto Rico. It's going on four years now. Shouldn't she be dying soon?"

"We fought about the same thing yesterday. We got to make this family work!" Jack pleaded.

A little girl in pigtails, about four years old, strolled through the door. She was cute as could be. Jack and Gloria both smiled at her.

"Hey, Mommy!" the little girl said as Jack went over to her. "Hey, Poppa Jack."

"Jasmine, where is Jaymee at?" Gloria asked.

"Sleeping as usual. I want to play," little Jasmine replied.

Jack hugged the little girl. "Jazzy, you know Poppa Jack loves you."

Jasmine's eyes lit up as he dug in his pants pocket. "What is it,

Poppa Jack?"

Jack handed her two silver dollars with Benjamin Franklins on them. "One is for you and the other is for Jaymee."

Gloria took a deep breath. "Jasmine, go find your father. Mommy's not finished working yet."

"Okay," Jasmine said as she sailed out the door, gleaming at the coins in her hand.

Jack went back over to the desk and started signing the contract. Gloria had hoped that they could come up with another option. But with her father unwilling to disconnect his new wife from the business, she was left with no choice but to seize sole control.

"Are you sure?" she asked with bittersweet regret in her voice. She really hated the position she was putting her father in.

"Isn't this what you wanted?"

"Not exactly!" Gloria checked her watch again. This time Jack saw her.

"Going somewhere?" he asked, curious. He knew his daughter was very calculating and probably up to something.

"Just don't want to miss our reservation." She smiled. "It's our anniversary. Richard and I have been married for five years."

Jack rolled his eyes. She knew that he didn't think much of Richard, but he did at least accept him. Gloria walked over to her desk and pushed the intercom button.

"Margaret, send Ralph in here."

"Okay, Mrs. Dean," the secretary replied.

Gloria glanced over to her father. "Got to make it official. Ralph will be our witness."

Jack nodded. He wanted to get it all over with.

Ralph ran through the doorway. "You need me?" he asked, trying to catch his breath.

"I need you to witness our agreement," Gloria said.

"Yes. Sure." Ralph looked at Jack and Gloria cautiously. Gloria knew that the intense anger they both felt was not masked by their phony smiles. Jack pointed at the document on the desk. Ralph came over and started reading through it. After finishing, he glanced at Gloria, then at Jack. They both nodded at him. Ralph signed the document as the witness. "I'll file this for you. Mr. Dean, I'll leave you a copy in your office," he said quickly, walking out the door.

"I know you will do wonders here. Just don't make the mistakes I made." Jack mustered up a small smile, which surprised Gloria. She didn't expect well wishes from him.

"If things ever change, you have a place back at the top." Gloria couldn't look her father in the eye. She knew him signing over total control of the company to her signaled the transition from teacher to pupil. Her relationship with her father would never be the same again.

Jack stared out the window, looking over Manhattan. "I love you, Gloria. Be strong—and wise," he said.

Just then a beautiful Puerto Rican woman poked her head inside the door.

Gloria saw her first. "Excuse me!" she said with disdain.

The woman ignored Gloria's remark and walked in. "Jack, we need to talk."

Jack turned around. "Alexis dear, what's going on?"

Gloria rolled her eyes. "Yeah, you two do need to talk."

"What's your problem?" Alexis asked, growling at Gloria.

"Only you."

"Not now!" Jack jumped in the middle.

"Not never," Gloria said, wanting to get the last word in.

"How much money? How much power do you need? You're the evil one," Alexis said, staring Gloria down to the floor.

Gloria couldn't believe her audacity of trying to play innocent. "Oh, that's a great question, how much money do YOU need?"

"It's my money too," Alexis shouted, annoyed by Gloria's perception that she was only with her father for the money.

Gloria saw the clueless look on her father's face. She knew he was missing a couple of pieces to the conversation.

"Tell my father about the hundred million dollars you took."

Alexis rolled her eyes. "Why do you hate me so much?"

Gloria couldn't believe her avoidance of the question. She looked toward her father to see what his response might be.

"I know about the money," Jack said, glaring at Alexis.

Gloria knew he was just lying for her.

"Jack, can we please just go?"

"I do want the money back." Gloria looked dead at Jack.

"You will get it. I will make sure you get every cent."

Gloria gritted her teeth. "Enjoy your trip."

"Bye," Alexis said as she pulled Jack toward the door. She wanted out in a big way.

"I love you, Daddy. Always will."

Jack smiled at his daughter. "I love you too. I'll see you later."

Before he went out the door, Gloria rushed over and hugged him. Alexis turned away from them.

"Don't be a stranger. You are still my hero." Gloria kissed him on the cheek.

"Bye, Angel," Jack said as he walked out of the door.

Outside, beyond earshot of Gloria, Jack stopped Alexis in her tracks.

"What did you do with the money?"

"Relax, Jack. It's our money, dear."

Jack huffed. "It's the company's money."

"Why does she always get her way? I don't think you love me."

Jack rubbed his head. "Come on, you know that's not the case."

"Jack, I love you but I can't live like this. We're partners, right? Who was there when you truly needed someone? "

Jack deeply sighed. "What do you want from me?"

"I just want you to be on my side. You are my husband."

"I'm always on your side."

"I can't tell!" she pouted.

"Alexis, I love you with all my heart."

"Gloria will always make sure we're never happy. Your daughter wants me dead. I refuse to live like this."

"Forget Gloria."

"I can, but can you?"

Jack was confused by the question. "She's my daughter."

"And she hates me. Probably plotting to kill me as we speak."

"Come on. Not today. Are you still leaving tonight?" he asked, trying to change the conversation.

"Yeah, are you coming with me?"

Jack looked back toward Gloria's closed office door and remarked, "I don't see why not."

Later that evening, after Gloria and Richard had dinner celebrating their anniversary at Le Cirque, they were headed home in the back of their limousine. As they sipped champagne, Gloria suddenly burst into tears.

"What's wrong, babe?" Richard asked.

Gloria wiped away the tears. "I can't believe what I did to my daddy today. I'm an animal. A greedy, filthy animal."

"Don't beat yourself up so hard. Alexis is evil and she can't be trusted. You did what's best for everyone."

Gloria wanted to believe what Richard was saying was true, but deep down the guilt weighed a ton. She knew she had no right in kicking her father out of the company that he had built or telling him who he should be married to. Her father had been her Rock of Gibraltar from the very beginning.

"I can't do this," she said sadly. "I have to make this right. I have to work this out with Alexis."

"Are you sure?" Richard asked, baffled by her change in attitude.

Gloria opened the window separating them from the limo driver. "Take us to our hangar at Teterboro."

"Yes, ma'am," the limo driver replied.

Gloria grabbed the phone in the back of the limo and called the pilot. "Hey, Sam, I need to speak with my father."

"Okay, I'll go get him on the phone," Sam replied. "Hold on for a minute."

Sam got off the phone and went out to where the plane was located in the hangar. The first person he ran into was Alexis.

"Sam, when are we taking off?" she asked sharply. It was obvious she was ready to take off.

"Where's Mr. Dean?"

"What is it, Sam?" she asked.

"Mrs. Dean wanted to speak with him."

"Oh, really! About what?" Alexis asked.

"I don't know, ma'am. She just wanted me to get him."

"Well, tell her that you tried, but he was unavailable. I want you to get this plane in the air within the next half hour. I'm tired of waiting."

"Ma'am..."

"Ma'am, my ass, Sam, let's get this show on the road."

"Sorry, but wouldn't Mr. Dean like to speak with her?"

Alexis roared at him, "Get the plane in the air now!"

"Okay."

Sam returned to his office and got on the phone. "Mrs. Dean, we're taking off very shortly."

"What did my father say?" she asked. That was the whole point of the call.

"Your stepmother ordered me to take off as soon as possible. Sorry."

"What's the big rush?"

"Your stepmother had some extra passengers join her," Sam said sarcastically.

"Who?" Gloria asked.

"Your father's sister and her husband."

Gloria couldn't understand why. Alexis couldn't stand them for the same reason she couldn't stand Gloria. They thought she was a gold digger. "Stop the flight!" she demanded.

"It's your father's plane."

"Stall them! I've got to talk to my father. No matter what, make sure he knows I want to talk to him. They can't leave. Tell Alexis I said I'm sorry."

"I'll try."

"Do it! Stall them! I don't care if you have to wreck the plane. Make sure it stays grounded," she yelled as she hung up the phone.

Richard stared at her. "What's going on?"

"That damn Alexis! She wouldn't let my father talk to me. I hate her."

She looked at Richard's watch and prayed. "I hope we make it."

Traffic was light heading out to Teterboro Airport in New Jersey, where their plane fleet was based. Still, Gloria knew that she was racing against time. At last they turned into the entrance to the small airport. As she approached their hangar, she spotted the plane out on the runway, readying for takeoff. She had the limo driver drive onto the tarmac, but she was too late.

As the plane lifted off the ground, she pressed her lips together in anger. She couldn't believe Alexis was so evil to not let her speak to her father before they left.

Gloria was watching as the plane ascended up to the clouds—when the aircraft exploded into pieces.

"Dad! Oh, my God, Dad!" Gloria jumped out of the car and dropped to her knees. "How could this happen? All I wanted was to tell him to come back!"

CHAPTER **ONE**

30 Years Later

The size sixteen boot hit the door like a hand grenade exploding. The blast shook the floor of the entire penthouse. Bursting into the apartment, the assailants sprinted toward Jasmine. By the time she could react, a bright shining light was blinding her. The black-gloved hand that smothered her mouth told her this wasn't a friendly visit. The cold steel of a 9mm barrel pressed up against her temple. She couldn't move. She couldn't believe this was happening. Her penthouse was in one of the upscale neighborhoods of Baltimore, so a break-in was highly unusual.

Jasmine Dean, former supermodel and daughter of Gloria Dean, sweated profusely as the gun's trigger cocked back. At the same time, she and the gunman covering her mouth saw the scissors on her dresser.

"Be a good girl and you might live," the gunman said sarcastically as he removed his hand from her mouth.

She slowly looked up at the masked intruder, but the light was still blinding her. The gunman started stroking her hair. Though it violated her to have his grimy hands on her body, she was in no position to stop him.

"I swear I don't have any money," Jasmine pleaded. "You can take whatever I have."

The gunman laughed. "Well, we know Tommy don't have it …" The diamonds on his teeth and the onions on his breath were a bad mix. It made her want to puke.

Jasmine tried to make him see reason. "Tommy doesn't live here anymore."

The gunman's response was to tighten his grip on the gun. It was obvious that he had come to collect someone's money, and that he meant to do it.

"Man, let's get this over with," said the gruff-voiced man holding the light. "If she don't have the money, shoot the bitch, so we can go!"

"Nigga, don't be my excuse for killing two people tonight," the gunman yelled back at his partner.

"Man, I'm just sayin' —" the light holder began.

"When my lips part, yours stay shut!" the gunman warned his partner.

"Tommy and I are separated," Jasmine said, interrupting them.

Jasmine felt the gun barrel nudge between her eyes. She ceased any movement, anticipating her end was near.

"We just want the money."

"I haven't seen him in months," Jasmine cried, hoping he would understand her position.

Without warning, the gunman fired off the pistol into the floor. Jasmine screamed, thinking she had been shot. He slapped her across the jaw and grabbed her by the neck. Blood began to trickle out of her mouth.

"Why'd you do that?" his partner cried. "Now everyone in the neighborhood knows we're here!"

Jasmine put her fingers to her mouth as she attempted to feel the bleeding. This is what came of a colossal mistake in picking her husband. Tommy was in rehab for the fifth time in three years. Though she hadn't seen him in over a year, Jasmine had up to now paid off his debts so that he could have a fresh start whenever he turned his life around. Yet this sweeping up after him couldn't go on forever.

A police siren could be faintly heard from the outside.

"Hey, dummy, turn off that bright light!" the gunman snarled at his partner. By the way he squinted his eyes, it was obvious that the light was bothering him too.

Quickly the light was shut off. Jasmine's eyes went back and forth, trying to get a read on what the men were going to do.

The gunman's partner went to the bedroom window and noticed that the police had arrived. He signaled to his partner to hurry up. The gunman looked like he wanted to hit her again, but he hurried out the door after his accomplice.

She heard racing footsteps up the stairs, and two uniformed men charged into the apartment.

"Are you okay, ma'am?" Two officers, one white and one black, asked as they cautiously looked around.

Jasmine raced to the window and saw nothing. It was as if the criminals had vanished into thin air.

"Are you sure you're okay?" the black officer asked. "Ma'am, what happened here tonight?"

Jasmine turned around and looked at the two officers with fear. She then focused on the front door, wondering whether or not the crooks were really gone.

"Nothing. They were two goons looking for my former husband," she answered.

"What about your face?" the white officer asked.

Jasmine felt for blood on her lips once again. "Let's say they weren't gentlemen."

"You should have that looked at," the officer replied.

"I'll be fine," she said. Suddenly the enormity of what had happened washed over her. She had nearly been killed. "Thanks for coming out here so quickly. It's much appreciated."

"We're going to keep looking through the building," said the black officer, and the two men retreated out the door.

As they left her penthouse, she wiggled her jaw, testing it to see if it was broken. When she licked her lips, she tasted the blood. Jasmine ran to the mirror in the bathroom. Seeing her bloodied and bruised face was hard to take. After mulling over her next move, she walked into her bedroom and went into the closet, taking out her biggest suitcase.

As she opened the suitcase across the bed, a feeling of despair came over her. Jasmine had thought when she left that all of the issues with her mother would remain in New York. She had started her own fashion brand named Jazzie. She did everything from design to production, but her distribution was still through the Gloria Dean Company.

Jasmine's siblings wanted her to fail. They felt their mother should have cut off the distribution deal she maintained with Jasmine and buried her business. To them, Jasmine had become a traitor who jumped ship. They wanted her to pay. But Gloria left her alone. The family did cut off communication with her, and after months of trying Jasmine got the point and stopped trying herself. It was now almost five years since they had spoken a word to each other.

But today none of that mattered. Jasmine had to escape the vicious cycle of men coming after her former husband. This time she had almost been killed. She picked up her cell phone and scrolled through her address book until she reached the entry "Gloria Dean." All it would take was one call.

CHAPTER **TWO**

At the Manhattan headquarters of the multibillion-dollar Gloria Dean Company, its CEO, over fifty and still remarkably beautiful, was sitting back in her lofty, cushioned leather chair, contemplating what to say to the young lady sitting across from her. The ugly frown on Gloria's face showed that it wasn't the first time this had happened.

On every wall was pieces of artwork she had collected on her worldwide travels. Her office was reminiscent of the Oval Office of the president of the United States. It was apparent that Gloria was very wealthy *and* a stately woman. Her clothes were hand-made from the finest fabrics in the world. Her jewelry was priceless. Behind her was a huge portrait of herself hanging on the wall. Some estimated her net worth to be twenty-five billion. Most of her money was in real estate, stocks and bonds, and medical technology, but her heart stayed with her fashion business.

Being an only child, Gloria enjoyed the spoils of luxury provided by the family business. Still, she was the consummate businesswoman. No man intimidated her, and no woman outclassed her. No one ever imagined that she could take the family empire and turn it into a dynasty, but she had. Legend has it that she had something to do with the plane crash that killed her father, Jack Dean, and his wife, Alexis.

Though questioned by the police, no evidence was found, nor were formal charges ever brought against anyone. To this day it remained an unsolved case. For several years Gloria had demanded that the police find out who did it, but with the passage of time her desire for revenge had faded. All she felt now was the dull ache of loss for her beloved father.

Gloria leaned forward and rested her elbows on her hundred-thousand-dollar Egyptian desk. She put her chin on top of her fists. The young lady across from her winced. She could tell that a scolding was about to commence.

"Jaymee, what am I going to do with you? You cannot keep making deals that are not approved by me."

"But, Momma, I—"

"Who told you to speak?"

Jaymee Dean, the middle child—a beautiful woman in her early thirties—stood five feet seven inches tall. If she had been a little taller, she would have been a knockout model. Though she often tried her best to impress her mother, it always seemed like she didn't think her plans all the way through. Several of her mistakes had cost the company millions. Yet she would never admit to any mistakes. She always blamed them on her mother having it out for her.

The thing that hurt Gloria the most was that she had had such high hopes for Jaymee once her older sister, Jasmine, left. She took Jaymee under her wing and taught her everything she knew. The advice, though, seemed to go in one ear and out the other. In actuality, since Jasmine had taken off on her own, Gloria hadn't been the same. Jasmine was her heart, and it broke the day she left. Even though they fought all the time, the fire she saw in her oldest child was equivalent to her own. For the past five years, she had lived in regret, hoping that Jasmine would return home, but her pride wouldn't bring her to go and ask her daughter to come back.

"Momma, I'm sorry. I'm not perfect," Jaymee cried.

Gloria hated seeing emotions and business mixed together. Coming from her daughter only made the situation worse. She threw up her arms out of frustration. Never let anyone see weakness was her golden rule. The first rule she taught her children.

"Perfect," Gloria yelled. "You blew a hundred-million-dollar deal because you didn't feel like the brand represented the urban market. For God's sakes, he's the hottest rapper on the planet. People would buy his shit if he sold it from his mother's basement."

"All he ever does is cuss."

Gloria looked at her with her head slanted. "And you fuckin' don't! We're the third largest merchandiser in the world. I'm trying to grow this business, not destroy it. We have over seventy-five thousand employees counting on us to make smart decisions. I need you to be a lot smarter."

"What about our image?" Jaymee shot back at her mother.

"Our image is about making money. The motto is simple enough even for a first grader. Make the deal and get the money. Can you remember that?"

"I think we have to draw the line somewhere."

"Huh, and you want to run this company? You are not ready for the throne, my child. No matter what you think, it's nothing compared to what you go through sitting in this chair." Gloria wished she could tell Jaymee the truth of everything she had done over the years to remain on top, but she knew Jaymee couldn't stomach the evil parts. Gloria was a master at shielding her family from the pain she had inflicted on others.

"I'm not Jasmine," Jaymee said angrily. "Just because I'm the middle child, you treat me like shit!"

Silence filled the room. Gloria wanted so bad to strangle Jaymee and beat some sense into her, but she restrained herself from jumping across the desk.

Instead she sighed. "Is that what this is about?"

Jaymee didn't respond. She defiantly looked across at her mother.

Anyone questioning her parenting skills irked Gloria. She prided herself on being a good parent as well a business magnate.

"You have to grow up and fast. You're my daughter. I love you all the same. But when you blow it, I'm going to call you on it."

Jaymee scoffed. "Are you done?"

"No! I'm sorry to say this, but I don't pay you to think about what's right for this company. That's my job." She pointed out a former issue that Jaymee had handled badly. "Look at that Maxwell Kennedy. What's his line called…Maximus, right? You turned him away four years ago, and look at him now. He has one of the hottest clothing lines around."

Jaymee sulked in shame. She knew very well that she had blown a couple of big deals. "Why don't you talk to Ricky like that? He's messed up too."

"This isn't about pointing fingers," Gloria said, pointing her finger at her daughter.

Jaymee snorted. "Sho'nuff seems that way to me."

Gloria threw up her arms. "Unbelievable. You still don't get it."

"Get what?" she asked, clueless as ever.

"This is about the future. When I'm not here anymore, I want to make sure that this company doesn't die right after me."

Jaymee thought, *If that were only today, we would all be blessed.*

"So you understand that I have to make sure that you're ready," Gloria said, trying to get through to her.

Jaymee's eyes lit up. "I'm sure you'll live forever. Uncle T thinks you're strong as an ox."

"Oh, really, does he?" Gloria replied with one eyebrow raised. She had her suspicions about the comment. "Where is he at now?"

"I think in his office."

"I think I'm going to—" Gloria stopped in mid-sentence as her phone rang. She indicated that Jaymee should be gone. "We'll finish our discussion later. If you see your brother, tell him I want to talk."

"Who knows what Ricky is doing—or who?" Jaymee said, walking toward the door.

Gloria answered the phone. "Hello."

Jaymee tried to find out who was on the phone by lingering at the door. Gloria saw how slow she was moving, and with her hand, she signaled for her to get out. Once Jaymee closed the door, Gloria put the phone back up to her ear.

"Do you have the information I need?" she asked impatiently. "What? I don't care what you have to do—I need to know what they really know or—"

Teddy, aka Uncle T, stuck his head in the door. She gave him a look that would have melted stone. "Just do whatever it takes. I have to handle another problem here," she said, hanging up the phone. She looked at Teddy. "Come on in. We need to talk right now!"

"I can come back," Teddy replied back with a hint of sarcasm.

His arrogant attitude only got her hotter under the collar. "Don't you go anywhere. We are going to talk."

Teddy Hicks, a sixty-year-old white man, had once been very handsome, but smoking and drinking had soured those attributes. Never married, he was a career womanizer. He dressed like an attorney or a Wall Street trader, and he enjoyed the fashion business because it gave him the opportunity to meet sexy young women willing to sleep with him to advance their careers.

Teddy was also Gloria's business partner. Thanks to his father, he owned thirty percent of the company. After she gained control of the company, she needed money to stay competitive. Teddy's father was a Wall Street tycoon who had a huge fortune. He provided the investment Gloria needed and stayed out of her way as she made both of them wealthy beyond belief. But after Teddy's father died, Teddy inherited his ownership and immediately became Gloria's thorn in her side. He was always up to no good, but she kept him around because his backstabbing kept her on her toes, ready for real threats to her throne.

"Yes, my queen," Teddy said only to irritate her further. Still, he remained by the door, scared to come closer.

"Sit down!" Gloria roared.

Teddy slowly walked over to the chair in front of her desk.

"Don't play with me, Teddy."

He rolled his eyes. "What did I do now?"

Gloria hated when people played dumb. She was more willing to reason with a person who just admitted their wrongs. "How dare you tell Amancio that we should merge with Inditex?"

"I didn't say that!"

She stared him dead in the eye. "You're lying through your teeth. Amancio wouldn't lie to me. We go way back." Gloria was getting disgusted just sitting across from him. "Just name your price and this will end well for all of us."

"I'm not selling," Teddy said, getting up to leave.

"You can sit back down. This discussion is far from over."

Teddy remained standing. "No matter what you offer me, I'm not selling."

"Teddy, we can't continue like this," she said, once again trying to make him see reason. "I told your father I would look out after you. I love you as a person, but you are tying my hands."

"What are you saying?" Teddy asked, concerned by what Gloria was implying.

"I'm making some re-org changes."

"Like what?"

"You are cut off from daily operations."

"But I run the Europe office!" he shouted. Teddy started to see where this was going and he didn't like it.

"*Did* run the Europe office," she said smoothly. She was enjoying this. "I hired someone this morning to run the design, production, and distribution over there. So, you won't be needed."

Teddy looked as if he was about to cry. "I own thirty percent of this company. You can't treat me like dog shit!"

"I offered you a respectable way out, but you didn't want that."

"This isn't legal," he cried.

Gloria was growing tired of his whining. "How long have you known me, Teddy? Over twenty years? When have I ever made a decision that was illegal? Never. Your father's investment never had anything to do with running any part of my company."

He shook his head, disagreeing. "This isn't fair. I don't think you want to go through with this."

Gloria chuckled. "A threat. Now that's funny."

Teddy put on his best threatening face. "You need to rethink this choice."

"Teddy, we have gone down this road before. Your double-dealing ways have come to an end. The name on the side of this building says the Gloria Dean Company. It's my knowledge of the fashion business that keeps us profitable. And don't think you're going to go around me. Jaymee and Ricky might be fooled by your act, but I'm five steps ahead of you."

"But I helped build this company," Teddy said boastfully.

Gloria placed her face in her hands, holding back her first reply. He had said the words she hated most. In her mind only four people could ever take credit for building the Gloria Dean Company and that was her mother, her father, Teddy's father, and herself. The audacity of him saying that irked her deeply.

"You're really pushing it!"

"I gave you a lot of money when you had nothing. All this expansion came about because of my money. You had only a thousand stores when I met you. Look at us now, over four thousand stores."

"Teddy, let's make a few things clear. It was your father who invested with me. A man that is three times the person you could be. If he hadn't died so suddenly, we wouldn't be having this discussion."

Teddy came right back with, "We have that in common. Fathers who died early." He smiled grimly. "It's kind of ironic."

"You really want to go there?" Gloria knew he was alluding to her own father's death. "Say one more word."

"Just an observation."

"You don't want to go to war against me."

"I'm not afraid of Jackie," Teddy said, referring to her longtime aide. "Or you."

Gloria pointed her finger at him. She wished it was a sword. "Your new office is on the forty-fourth floor."

He gritted his teeth. "That's six floors down."

"Sorta like a grave," Gloria said, grimacing. "Now, go die."

"Gloria, I—"

"Say it walking out the door."

Teddy looked like he wanted to get the last word, but he was too afraid of what Gloria might do to him, so he left. She did hear him mumble, "I got to stop her."

CHAPTER **THREE**

Later that same day, Gloria left the office in a hurry, heading for her attorney's office. Ralph Berkowitz, Esq., was the best money could buy. Long ago, when he had first started out, Gloria took a chance on him mainly because she wanted a lawyer she could control. But as the years went by, they had developed a special bond of love and trust without sex being involved.

With her special client status, she walked right through his door without being announced. Gloria went over to his couch and laid down as if she was at a shrink's office.

Sitting behind his desk, Ralph just chuckled at her dramatics. He continued to read some papers on his desk. He knew that when she was ready to talk, she would.

"Ehhhhhhhh," she said, sounding like she was clearing her throat. She glanced over at Ralph to see if he was paying attention.

He ignored her.

"I'm dying over here," she said. "Aren't you going to save me? You're my only friend."

He looked at her and grinned. "I'm a lawyer, not a doctor." Still, he put the papers he had been reading to the side.

"Did you get the papers I sent?" she asked.

He nodded.

She sat up on the couch. "What do you think?"

Their attraction was nearly palpable. Ralph looking like Tom Selleck didn't hurt the situation either. Ralph had desired to be with Gloria for the longest. Back when they'd met, it was not acceptable for a white man, let alone a Jewish white man, to be with a black woman. Plus, she had been married back then, to her children's father. Now that times had changed, he wanted to express to her the love he felt, but every time she said *friend*, it killed his momentum.

"I've been telling you for years that Teddy Hicks is a liability. His father was a saint for us in the eighties, but Teddy is pure evil."

"But I do owe his father. He was such a good man."

"He was, but Teddy has always had his own agenda, and that includes taking over your company."

She knew he was right. But just like Ralph, Teddy had been around for the longest time. If there was one chink in her armor, it was her love and loyalty for family. Though she and Teddy didn't see eye to eye on many issues, she never forgot the promise she had made to Teddy's father about helping his son out to be a better man.

"Maybe I shouldn't go through with it." Gloria rubbed her forehead.

"It's a good insurance policy," Ralph said. "Shocking, but definitely good. I hated that other clause you insisted on having."

"Well, Jaymee and Ricky were younger then, and I wasn't sure who could run my interests in my absence. I thought initially that they might be able to work together equally, with each obtaining twenty percent, but with Jaymee and Ricky's attitudes, they would fight Jasmine on every single issue. So now I figure on giving the control to the eldest, then giving Jaymee, Ricky, and my cousin Jackie ten percent each, and giving you and Richard five."

"But that leaves Jasmine with thirty percent ownership."

"I can't have Teddy with his thirty percent being the majority. He might pull off a scam to sell my company."

Ralph could see the sense in this idea. Yet one question had been bothering him. He asked her, "Then why the change now?"

"Is that a real question?"

"Yes," Ralph quipped back.

"Well, Teddy has a talent for persuasion. I just don't want Ricky and Jaymee to fall prey to it," Gloria said, rolling her eyes.

"Yes, he does."

"That's why I chose who I chose to run it in the future."

"But why her?" Ralph asked, curious about her decision.

"I've known all along, ever since she was a child, that Jasmine was something special. She's the only one who will try to keep this family business together. Plus, she's done wonders with her Jazzie brand."

Ralph wasn't surprised that Gloria could make such an astute decision, despite being estranged from her eldest daughter. "You are going to make everybody mad."

"Life isn't perfect." She smirked. "And you and I know that I have made a lot of mistakes."

He wasn't so sure of that. "If your father could see you today, he would be so proud of you."

Gloria ground her fists into his leather couch. She hated all conversations regarding her father, because she could never overcome her tremendous guilt about his death. It ate at her soul that she wasn't able to make peace with him before he died. "I can't . . ."

"Can't what?" Ralph asked.

Yet she only sat there staring at the carpet, overcome with dark emotions.

"Okay," he said, not sure of the reason for her change in mood, "so, what about your will?"

She looked at him like she didn't know what he was talking about.

"You sent that as well. I saw the changes. Are you sure about that?"

Gloria straightened up again. Her decision was final. She was confident in what she wanted done.

"Done," he said. Ralph brought the paperwork over to her to sign. She grabbed his pen and quickly scribbled her name. After she finished signing the documents, she handed the pen and papers over to him. On the exchange of the pen, she grabbed Ralph's hand.

"It's a shame our timing was never quite right. You would have been perfect for me," she said with a twinkle in her eye.

Ralph tried for an easy tone. "I see you have been drinking."

She playfully pushed his hand away. "I still love you, Ralph."

"And I you," he replied back with his bedroom eyes searching hers. "Now, Gloria, what is really going on? Are you getting threats again?"

She didn't want to answer that question. "Maybe we can buy an island and live out our lives there. Just you and I."

He smiled. "That would be nice if you were serious."

"I'm being serious." Yet she couldn't hide the look of fear on her face.

"What's wrong?" he asked.

She ignored his question. "What do you have to drink in this place? I know you have something. Later this week I'll be updating more documents."

"Okay."

Though Ralph knew there was more to why she wanted these documents updated, he knew she wouldn't tell him anything that she didn't want to. So he did what he had done a thousand times before, just didn't say anything.

"I've got your favorite!" he said with a smile. Ralph walked over to his cabinet and opened it up. It was filled with an assortment of high-priced liquor and wines. He held up a bottle at her.

"You remembered," she gasped.

"All I drink is Bowmore," Ralph said. "It reminds me of you."

"Because it's aged for twenty-five years." She laughed.

He chuckled. "By the way, when is your cousin Jackie O getting back?"

"Now, you know, that's the part of the business I keep you away from. I know you hate it, but it's for the best."

"I hear you, but…"

"But nothing. Jackie is the most trusted associate I have. He will do whatever it takes to protect me."

"And I wouldn't?"

Gloria smiled. "It's not a matter of whether or not you would. You could never go the depths that Jackie has. He is extremely gifted at what he does."

"Being a ghost?" Ralph frowned.

Gloria knew he was jealous. "That ghost has saved our lives many times."

"Where is his brother?" Ralph asked.

"Stepbrother. He's around. He's Jackie's responsibility," Gloria said with disdain. She wasn't fond of Jackie's stepbrother.

Although his name was Billy Fox, he was nicknamed Bronco. He was an older special services officer dismissed for bad behavior. Gloria just didn't like his erratic style in handling delicate situations for her.

Ralph glanced over at her. "By the way, Randolph James made another offer." She slit her eyes at Ralph, and he waved off the notion. "I know you're not selling. I just thought you might like to know."

"Who is this Randolph James character anyway?" Gloria asked suspiciously. "And why does he want to buy my company?"

Ralph was puzzled as well, and he had done his due diligence. "Nobody seems to know anything about him or what he even looks like. Kind of an obscure fellow. I did uncover that he entered the fashion world around twenty years ago. He has basically been like a holding company, absorbing all the small fashion entities en route to becoming one of your main competitors."

"If that's the case, why does he want my business?"

Ralph shrugged his shoulders and poured the drinks.

"I'll put Jackie on him. He'll find out who this Randolph James is," Gloria said.

***

The sun was beginning to dive into the sea as the *abras* came into dock. The night lights gave a beautiful yet serene feel to Dubai. Sitting on one of these boats was Jackie O. Fox. A rugged, dark-skinned man, Jackie stood six-three and weighed 220 pounds. Though he was in his forties, his physique was impeccable. Still wearing his sunglasses, Jackie surreptitiously kept his eye on a bearded, European-looking white man seated near the bow of the boat.

Jackie had been Gloria's most trusted sidekick since Jasmine left. Their bond had been formed after Jackie's parents died and Gloria took him in like a son. He wasn't on the business side. Jackie was the problem fixer. Every problem Gloria faced, he eliminated the obstacle for her so that she could wreak havoc on her competition. He gained his special skills from being in special forces for over ten years.

When the boat finally docked, the man Jackie had been watching got off with a woman friend and walked away. Casually, Jackie stepped out of the boat and followed in the same direction. As the couple strolled through Deira Gold Souq, he kept a good distance behind. He kept glancing at his watch and his frown grew deeper as the afternoon passed into evening.

After they exited the Al Bahai Jewellers, the man noticed Jackie behind them. The next time he glanced back, though, it was like Jackie had disappeared into thin air. Still nervous about being followed, the man picked up his pace and hurried the woman down the street. They made several turns until they found themselves alone on a dark, isolated stretch of road. Up ahead, they noticed a bar and hurried toward it. Once inside, they surveyed the crowd of people. The loud music and dancing crowd put the man at ease. Feeling like a drink, they headed to the bar.

Out of nowhere, Jackie jumped in front of them.

"What took you so long?" he asked with the smile of a cat that had cornered the mouse.

The man gave him a pissed-off look. "Gloria Dean doesn't scare me! She's just a pathetic woman whose bag of secrets is about to be made public. I don't know what the statute of limitations are on murder, but she may end up doing twenty-five to life."

"Who's your source?" Jackie demanded.

"A good reporter never tells, and I'm the best."

"You can put a stop to the story. I want the source, not you," Jackie replied, hoping the reporter would reason with him.

"I'm not through digging up her skeletons," the reporter gloated. "She's going to need an army to stop me from running the story."

"You know, when you go digging, it's normally for graves." Jackie glanced at his watch again. "I tried to make a deal with you…"

"The answer is still no!"

Jackie laughed. "I said 'tried.'"

"Is that supposed to be some kind of threat?"

"Let's just say I'm glad you purchased two cemetery plots," Jackie said, beaming down at the man.

"I'm a *New York Times* reporter and you're threatening me. You're only giving me more material. I'm going to bury Gloria Dean."

Jackie shook his head. "Not in this lifetime. This is one story you'll never write."

Before the man could get another word out, he and the woman were shot two times in the chest. When their bodies were found on the dance floor, not a hundred feet from the bar, Jackie had already vanished.

An hour and half later, a helicopter landed on the helipad of the Burj Al Arab hotel. Out came Jackie, dressed in all white, a shirt and pants outfit, with shades covering his eyes. On his arms were two Arabian women, whom he escorted into the hotel.

As they approached the Royal Suite on the twenty-fifth floor, they could hear people inside partying. When the door was flung open, it was full of naked women running around drinking, some guys watching the scene, and a group of men sitting around a poker table. The suite was magnificent. The luxurious accommodations were only for the people who had big bucks to throw around. The suite's view of the ocean was breathtaking, but with beautiful, exotic women running around naked, nobody cared to look out to sea. Everyone did stop once they saw Jackie enter.

"Mr. Fox, sorry we started without you," a plump Italian man sucking on a cigar said from the poker table.

"My home is your home. Next hand I'm in with five hundred thousand. It's time for the big boys to play."

Instantly, some of the players got up from the table, shaking their heads. The amount was too high for them. As Jackie made his way over to the table, his cell phone rang. As big and bad as he was, his face revealed that he feared the person on the phone.

"Hey, go ahead and start the game. I got to take this call," he said as he ducked off into the bedroom. "Hello, cuz."

"Don't 'cuz' me. You did take care of that situation?" Gloria demanded.

"Yes, ma'am. But no dice on the source."

Gloria was silent on the other end. It was obvious she was affected by Jackie not having the information on the source.

"I need you back here tomorrow. We have to take care of something else. You know you're the only person I trust in these situations, so don't disappoint me."

"I'm there. I've always been there for you."

"I know. Jackie, if anything happens to me, I need for you to protect the family," she said with fear cracking her voice. "I don't know how much longer I'm going to be around."

Jackie was taken aback. He could tell whatever her issue was, it had to be serious for her to sound so afraid. Gloria was his role model, mentor, and closest living relative. She had taken him in as a teenager when his mother and father died in the plane explosion with her father. There wasn't anything in the world they wouldn't do for each other.

"Glo, ain't nothing gonna happen to you. If something happens, then that must mean I'm dead," he said with certainty.

"I'm just saying, if it happens, Jasmine…"

"What?"

"I didn't stutter. Jasmine…will run the company."

"The whole company, including your other holdings?" he asked in shock.

"Don't question me!"

"I'm sorry. I'm not."

A long pause followed. The silence made Jackie start to think she hung up. Gloria was just pondering her fate and feeling sorry for the things she had made Jackie do for her.

"Glo, are you still there?"

"Jackie, don't rush back. Forget about what I said," Gloria said in a nonchalant tone. "I'll take care of it on my own."

"What's going on?" he asked, concerned about his cousin. She wasn't a wishy-washy person. "Talk to me!"

"When you get back, let's sit down and discuss the idea of you doing more on the business side. I've been unfair to you."

"You've been great to me."

"We'll talk when you get back. I love you like you were my own child, Jackie. I mean that."

"I love you too. Are you going to be okay?"

"Bye," she said, hanging up before he could respond.

"Bye," Jackie said to a dial tone. He slowly sat down on the bed, staring at the phone. Without warning, he found himself bursting into tears. The last time he had cried was when his parents died. Gloria was the closest thing to a parent he had. Jackie worshiped the ground she walked on. "I gotta go home."

***

The next morning, the clouds stretched out for miles. The frost and fog made it a difficult day to jog, but Gloria stepped out unbothered by the weather. On her back was a large, filled backpack. The agelessly dark-skinned beauty carefully looked around, nervous and guarded. As Gloria slowly sauntered by the four antique Rolls-Royce automobiles parked in her circular driveway, her cell phone rang. She saw that it was Jackie and hesitated for a moment, then cut her phone off.

When Gloria reached the front gate, she gazed up at the sky. The gloom reflected her mood. She frowned but continued on her journey.

The groundskeeper waved at her, but Gloria paid him no attention as she ran through the steel gateway that surrounded her mansion. The groundskeeper looked over at one of the security guards. They both shrugged their shoulders, surprised that she was running over to the park, near the lake. Both men watched her until she disappeared into the fog.

Gloria ran close to the lake at a steady pace. She often looked over her shoulder. When she noticed something rumbling in the bushes, she took off running as fast as possible. She was on edge and jumpy as she jogged to the other side of the lake. She came to a screeching halt when she saw a stop sign. Gloria glanced down at her watch. She looked both ways, then dashed across the street. A streaking noise got her attention before she reached the other side. With no time to react, she froze as a black Acura TL loomed hugely out of the fog rammed into her. The pain felt like every bone in her body were breaking at the same time. Gloria's body flew through the air and dropped heavily onto the pavement. The car raced off down the street.

As her body lay in the middle of the street, a masked man rushed over to her and grabbed the backpack. The man looked inside and saw nothing but hundred-dollar bills. Gloria looked at him dully before going into shock.

"Rest in peace," the masked man mumbled as he ran off into the fog with the money.

CHAPTER **FOUR**

On the Upper East Side, in a swanky penthouse suite, Ricky Dean grinded on a woman's butt as a soft love song played in the background. The white woman, a sexy swimsuit model with an exquisite body, was trying to sleep. His plan was to wake her up. After enough of his poking and grabbing, she did.

"What do you want?" the woman asked, half asleep.

"I'm not here for nothing." He gave her a look, then glanced down at his private part.

"Not now," she said, turning over. She peeked at her wall clock. "They start towing cars early around here."

He laughed. "I'm not leaving until I get my second helping."

She pulled the bedsheets over her head. "You're gonna have to wait."

Ricky rolled out of bed. "That's more like it. I'm willing to wait. A brother got all day."

He went over to her kitchen and looked in the refrigerator. Ricky took out some grapes and went to the sink. While he washed them, he glanced out the window. It shocked him to see his new Bentley coupe getting tied to a tow truck. He dropped everything. Ricky grabbed his clothes and headed out the door.

When he got outside, the tow truck was already heading down the street. Ricky ran down an alley to catch up with it but had little luck.

He stopped and sat on the curb. One look at his watch made his stomach turn.

"She is going to kill me. Damn!" He bowed his head to the ground and ran his fingers through his medium-size afro. "Fuck it."

He pulled out his cell phone and dialed.

"Uncle T…" he said with a frown. "I need your help. They towed my car." He sounded depressed.

"Again?" Teddy chuckled. "How many times have I saved you?"

"I know. You think I like calling you? You're the only one I can trust these days."

"I'll have Tony call you. You can give him directions. I'll send your mother an e-mail saying you're doing work for me on an ad." Teddy chuckled. "I'm sure she'll eat that up."

Ricky smiled. "Thanks."

"I hope you know when I'm running the company, you won't be treated like a child."

Ricky smirked. "Uncle T, please, Momma is not going anywhere."

"Really!" Teddy said, sounding shocked by Ricky's impression that his mother would be around forever. "Are you sure?"

Ricky's other line clicked in. He looked at the caller ID. "Damn, it's my mother."

"What?" Teddy asked.

"She's calling. I'll talk to you later."

Ricky hung up and clicked over. "Yes, Momma."

"Mr. Dean, this is James, the security guard."

"What's going on, James?" Ricky asked, knowing something wasn't right. He had never received a call from security before.

"Your mother is in the hospital."

"How bad?" Ricky asked figuring that James was not going to give him a good answer.

James paused not knowing what he should actually say.

"How bad?" Ricky demanded.

"Bad!"

Ricky hung up the phone and started running up the street toward a double-parked cab.

***

Later that morning, Teddy sat in his den clicking the remote to different channels. He was waiting to hear some good news. His patience was wearing thin. His fingers punched the channel buttons on the TV remote ferociously. With each channel, his disappointment increased.

His clothes were disheveled, being the same clothes he'd worn the previous day. On the table in front of him were several bottles of scotch.

The ringing of his phone at first fell on deaf ears. Teddy didn't have time to talk to anyone, nor did he want to. He just wanted to watch the news. Every time the reporters mentioned what was coming up next, he huffed with displeasure. By the fourth call, he noticed and directed his anger at the phone.

"You better be important." He leaned over to grab the phone. "Hello, did I win the lottery?"

"Momma's in the hospital. I don't think she's gonna make it," Ricky said mournfully. "I'm at the hospital now."

Teddy shut off the TV. She wasn't supposed to be in the hospital. She was supposed to be dead.

"Do the doctors think she's gonna make it?"

"I don't know," Ricky replied.

"What do you actually know?" Teddy asked, raising his voice.

"I don't know! Damn! My mom is here dying and you're asking all these damn questions. I gotta go."

"I'll be there as soon as possible," Teddy said before hanging up the phone.

He went over to a mirror on the wall and looked at himself with annoyance. He was definitely bothered by Gloria being in the hospital.

"Damn, she's alive." In a burst of frustration, he punched the mirror with his fist. It shattered into a rain of strangely angled, sharp pieces. He looked down at his bloody knuckles.

"Add that seven years to all the others," he growled. "Why won't that bitch just die?"

***

In the crowded operating room, doctors had Gloria cut wide open, trying to fix her internal injuries. Blood seeped out everywhere as her body lay there hanging on by a thread. Suddenly, Gloria's heart stopped beating and she flatlined. The doctors went into overdrive to get her heart pumping again. Nothing worked. Everyone stopped when the doctor pulled his hands out of her body.

The doctor said, "The time of death…"

The nurse replied, "Eleven thirty a.m."

The doctor had started to walk out when Gloria's heart miraculously started pumping again. Everyone looked at one another. It was really a miracle, how she came back to life. The doctor hurried back to the operating table. Though he still didn't believe Gloria had a chance for survival, he wasn't going to let the richest patient he'd ever treated die without a maximum effort.

***

Outside of the Mount Sinai Medical Center, a black Porsche Cayenne with dark-tinted windows pulled up in front of the emergency room entrance. As EMTs escorted other patients inside, a hospital staffer directed the driver to move. The driver ignored his directions.

Jaymee jumped out of the SUV and checked herself in the driver's side window. She frowned at her undone hair and mismatched clothes.

Jaymee ran inside and up to the ER counter, where Ricky was engaged in a confrontation with a nurse. His fists were balled and primed for fighting. Being the male child, he always felt like he had to protect his sisters and mother.

"Ricky, what's going on? How's Momma?" Jaymee asked in a panic.

Ricky turned to the nurse. "If this bitch gets off the phone, I'll find out."

The nurse ignored both of them by turning around. She did a wonderful job acting like they weren't there.

"Excuse me!" Jaymee yelled, getting the attention of everyone in the emergency room. "Don't play me...bitch!"

When the nurse continued to act as if she and Ricky were invisible, Jaymee reached over the counter, grabbed the phone, and hung it up. The nurse turned in outrage.

Jaymee stood there, silently daring the nurse to say something. The nurse saw the intense anger in her face and sensed she would become violence any moment.

"What do you think you're doing?" the nurse asked in an angry tone.

"Bringing you back from break!"

Ricky stepped in front of her. "All we want to know is, how our mother is doing? You're taking this the wrong way." He pleaded to the nurse. "As far as I know, my mom could be dead right now!"

The hospital security rushed to the scene. They grabbed Ricky and Jaymee. At the same moment, a doctor came out of ER. He stepped in.

"What's going on here?" the doctor asked. "This is a hospital!"

"These people—" the nurse started to say before Jaymee interrupted.

"We just want to know how our mother, Gloria Dean, is doing. This bitch is getting on my nerves. Whatever happened to customer service?"

"What is your mother's name again?" the doctor asked.

The nurse couldn't believe the doctor didn't have them kicked out.

The security officers released their grip, and Ricky and Jaymee pushed them away.

"Gloria Dean," Ricky said.

The doctor paused and his face became grave. Ricky grabbed Jaymee by the arm. They both feared the worst.

"She's not dead?" Jaymee asked with a trembling voice.

"Come with me," the doctor said.

He led them into the Intensive Care Unit waiting area. Jaymee and Ricky tried to prepare themselves for bad news. Neither one wanted to appear weak.

The doctor stopped in a quiet, unoccupied corner so no one could hear what he was going to say. "Please take—"

"We ain't taking shit until you tell us what the hell is going on. Where's my mother at?" Jaymee asked, losing her patience.

The doctor looked at both of them. "Your mother is in a coma."

"What?" Ricky asked, stunned by the news.

"She's fighting for her life. I would be lying to you if I said she's out of the woods. We almost lost her."

"Do you know who my mother is?" Jaymee asked forcefully. Name-dropping was her specialty. She loved throwing the Dean name around to get an advantage over others.

"Yes, I do."

"I don't think so. I want the best doctors to attend to her. I don't want any first-year interns," Jaymee said disdainfully. "My mother is one of the richest people in the world."

"Believe me, she is getting the best care possible. You can bring in any doctors you want, but I promise you there's nothing they could have done differently. Your mother suffered serious internal injuries. Most people might not have made it."

Up to this point, Jaymee had held her pain in pretty well. Yet the thought of her mother being dead crushed her. They had their problems, but everything she had learned came under Gloria's tutelage. She turned to the window as tears welled up in her eyes.

Ricky wanted to break down as well, but he felt somebody had to stay strong. "I want to see her," he said. "Right now!"

"Not right now," the doctor said with regret.

Jaymee folded her arms. "So, she's gonna make it?"

The doctor gently put his hand on her shoulder and pretended to look out the window too. "I don't know. I wish I had a better answer, but I don't. I promise you we are doing the best possible."

Ricky couldn't take it any longer. "This is bullshit!" he said before he rushed out of the room so no one saw his tears.

"When can we see her?" Jaymee asked.

"Let me find out, and I'll personally get back to you."

As the doctor walked off, Jaymee hit the window with her palm several times while tears raced down her face.

The people in the ICU waiting room stared at her. She felt their eyes burning the back of her neck. Jaymee turned to them, wanting to scratch their eyes out.

"Do you all have a fuckin' problem?" she yelled.

Jaymee found Ricky in front of a window, crying on his phone. He saw her reflection in the window as she approached. Ricky quickly wiped his eyes as she approached. Jaymee turned him around and hugged him.

"Are you doing okay?" she asked.

Ricky pulled away from her. He was torn apart by what he had learned during the phone conversation that just ended.

He gritted his teeth in pain. "The fuckin' driver got away."

"I only care about Momma," Jaymee said.

Ricky nodded his head in agreement. "What was she doing running in that park anyway?"

Jaymee scrunched up her face, not understanding. "She hates that park. Momma always talks about how dirty it is. Hell, her property is just as big as that park."

"Daddy's on his way," Ricky said with one eye on Jaymee.

Jaymee gave him a dirty look, and Ricky immediately added, "He had to know. He is our father. What do you want from me?" Then, more to himself, "He's our father…"

She turned away from him, shaking her head in anger. The riff between she and her father went back to when their parents had got divorced. Even though Gloria took the blame for her marriage, Jaymee took her side, calculating that she had more to gain from her mother's power and financial clout.

"Why are you trippin'? He's our father," Ricky went on, getting pissed. For him, Jaymee knew, it was different. He had remained neutral throughout his parents' divorce, and it was hard to be around his mother, let alone be married to her.

"Are you still talkin' to me?" she asked snidely.

"Fuck you!" Ricky said, putting up both of his middle fingers in her face.

***

Back in the ICU, Gloria's heart rate and oxygen levels decreased rapidly. Fearing the worst, the doctors rushed in and revived her by shocking her heart with a defibrillator. They feverishly worked to save her, all were now well aware of Gloria's status. A few had seen all of the media coverage during their breaks. The number of reporters and cameras made it seem like a president had been shot.

***

For the next few hours Jaymee would periodically glance at Ricky from across the room. But they were both doing their best to ignore each other. She tried to listen to his phone conversations, not wanting any more surprises, and his changing expressions left her speculating on whom he could be talking with. When he did bother to notice her, Ricky would stare back, occasionally putting up his middle finger. Finally, he hung up his phone and stormed over to her.

"Is there something you want to say?"

Yet Jaymee touched his forearm gently. With the situation bordering on volatile, she knew strong-arming him would only backfire.

"We need to talk," she said endearingly.

From his shrew look she knew he wasn't fooled. He figured by her kindness that she had something up her sleeve. Jaymee was never the one to care about her brother's feelings. She might not have been the best business person, but she did have a cutthroat mentality like her mother. The only difference lay in the fact that Jaymee was reckless in doing things whereas her mother was a pure master.

"What?" he asked defensively.

"This means the company is in trouble. Somebody has to run it." She put her arm around his shoulders.

Ricky threw up his hands and stepped away from her. He was appalled by her timing.

"I ain't trying to hear that shit right now! Damn! You are something else!"

Jaymee got in his face, trying to intimidate him. "It's only us now," she whispered. "We have to stick together."

"Momma ain't dead," he said, raising his voice a little.

"Shhh. I just want you to know that I will always have a position for you in the company. We're family."

Ricky giggled. "You ain't shit in the company. You better pray I keep *you* around."

His comment hurt her. Normally, she would have cussed him out, but he was integral to the plan she'd been dreaming up over the past hour. The one thing she knew about her little brother is that he always was loyal to the family. Over the years, that usually had meant he went along with what she said. With Ricky, there would be no stopping her.

"It's only right that I take over," she said nonchalantly. "I've worked with Momma for twelve years now. Nobody knows the business better than me."

"Jasmine, Daddy, and Jackie all know the business better than you!"

She brushed off his comment. "Please—a traitor, a no-good father, and the family flunky?"

Ricky motioned as if he was playing a violin. It only added to her anger. It took everything in her to keep her hands from strangling him.

"Tell me when I'm supposed to care," he said, shaking his head. "I'm not supporting you on that. Sorry."

"Yeah, and what about you? You just graduated from fashion school in France. I don't think that qualifies you to run a major company. You think?" She smiled meanly. "Don't think you didn't get special treatment over there. I saw the donations. Earth to Ricky—you're no fuckin' Einstein, bitch-type nigga."

He rolled his eyes, but they both knew that his treatment was way better than most. His designs did not rank even in the top half of his class, but he still *finished* the program at the top of his class.

"I see you had a full breakfast of yourself this morning…two scoops of bullshit. Get out of my face." He fanned her away.

She didn't move. She was determined to make her pitch. "You never listen with that hard head of yours. Did you consider this? I don't want Uncle T to try and pit us against one another. Bottom line, you're my little brother and I'm here to protect you."

"Jaymee, I love you, but if you think I'm going to sit by and watch you run Momma's company into the ground, you're crazy." He extended his hand toward her. "Look at how you're dressed. You think you know what's in this season? Please!"

A dapper-looking Teddy, wearing a dark suit with a red tie, approached from behind. He was dressed for a board meeting rather than a hospital visit. "Uncle T," Jaymee said, drawing Ricky's attention to him.

"Hell n'all. He can't—" Ricky stopped when he felt someone's arm wrapping around his shoulders. "What?" He turned to see who it was.

"How's your mother doing?" Teddy asked.

Teddy gave Jaymee a hug. It seemed sincere, and her defenses broke down.

"All we know is that she is in a coma," Jaymee said, getting emotional. "It doesn't look good."

"What happened?" Teddy asked, looking toward Ricky.

"It was a hit-and-run," Ricky said, frowning. "I want to kill the person who did it."

"The police don't have any leads?" Teddy asked, unabashed curiosity in his eyes.

Jaymee noticed the peculiar look. He seemed desperate to know.

"No. He or she got away," Ricky said, punching the palm of his hand. The smacking sound he made got the attention of all the people in the waiting area. For them it was a big spectacle: a real-life soap opera unfolding in front of their eyes.

"What happened to Jackie?" Teddy asked.

"Why would you ask that?" Jaymee asked, staring at him. It was common knowledge that Teddy hated Jackie. Why would he ask about him? Teddy instantly became a prime suspect in her mind.

Teddy said logically, "Your mother doesn't make a move without him. If he's not here, then where is he?" Teddy raised an eyebrow to imply that Jackie had something to do with her being in the hospital.

Ricky picked up on the insinuation. "That's a good point! That muthafucka got some explaining to do!"

"I don't want to talk about that right now," Jaymee said.

Ricky glanced at her. "What do you suggest we talk about?"

Jaymee rolled her eyes at him. "Not that!"

"Well, here is something we should talk about. Somebody needs to get in contact with Jasmine," Ricky said, staring at his sister.

If he wanted to get her full attention, he succeeded. Neither of them had spoken to her in five years. Jasmine had called to explain why she left and to maintain their relationships, but Ricky and Jaymee had fallen in line with Gloria's stubborn ways and ignored their older sister. But they were always puzzled by why their mother continued to allow Jasmine to distribute her clothing line through her company.

"Hell, no! Why?" Jaymee shouted.

"Jaymee, are you serious?" Ricky asked in disbelief.

Teddy cringed. "That's a bad idea. Your mother and Jasmine hate each other."

Ricky slit his eyes at the both of them like they were crazy. "That's Momma's firstborn you're talking about. Jasmine is just as much a part of this family as any of us." He started to back away from them. "You'll see. Jasmine ain't going to be staying in no Baltimore once she hears the news."

CHAPTER **FIVE**

At the Shore Club in Miami Beach, Jasmine sat slumped in her chair on the terrace, staring at the pool across from her bungalow. She had on old jeans, a white tee shirt, and a black scarf tied around her head. She fidgeted every time someone by the pool moved. Being on the run had her nerves running on high. She couldn't stop herself from thinking that everyone was watching her.

When her cell phone rang, she jumped. She stopped the ringing but didn't answer it. She eyed the display window in disbelief.

"What does she want?"

She took a deep breath and pushed the talk button.

"Savannah, how are you?" she asked.

Savannah Worthington, a beautiful, powerful white woman in the business world, was once one of her closest friends. They had lost touch, though, over the years. Savannah still considered her a close friend, and she kept tabs on Jasmine through mutual associates. Savannah in recent years had also come to be one of Gloria's friends, though strictly because of their business deals.

"Everybody's been trying to reach you." Savannah's voice cracked with emotion. "Where are you?"

"Why?" Jasmine asked. "Nobody cared before. Why now?"

"Jasmine, someone tried to run your mother over. Ricky said it doesn't look good. She might not make it."

Jasmine thought Savannah was being overdramatic. She whispered to herself, "What has Mother done now?"

"Where are you?" Savannah asked again.

"Chicago," she said, glancing out at the pool. Jasmine didn't want to reveal her location to anyone.

"I have a plane at O'Hare. It'll bring you home."

Jasmine hesitated. The last place on earth she wanted to go was back home. "I'm not coming back there. Nobody wants to see me."

"No matter what you and your mother went through in the past, she is your mother. She loves you."

Jasmine fought off a sudden wave of tears. She did love her mother. What wore on her soul was the constant fighting, not to mention her mother's conniving actions. When she left home the last time, she made a promise to herself to never return, no matter what happened. In her mind, Gloria was indestructible and would outlive them all.

She kept thinking Savannah was making this accident out to be worse than it actually was. As they talked, a call came in from her father, Richard Dean. She answered it.

"Jasmine, have you heard the news?"

"Yes, Daddy, Savannah just called me—"

"You have to come home right away!"

"But, Daddy, what makes you think she would want to see me?"

Richard sounded almost amazed that she would ask. "Jasmine, if your mother was incapacitated, for whatever reason, who do you think she would want to run the company?"

***

Later that evening, the doors to the ICU waiting area were flung open. Richard Dean burst inside like a madman on the loose. Heads turned as he passed. His eyes had a glassy look to them, like he'd been crying for a long time.

Ricky saw his father and went to him. They shared a hug. Jaymee noticed Richard too but turned her back on him.

"Dad, I'm glad you're here," Ricky said, almost in tears.

Richard Dean was the same age as Teddy. No matter where he went, he always had a cigar in his mouth. He was a charismatic man with charm and sophistication. A born hustler, he had attached himself to Gloria's star and rode it to the top. In a world where men demanded that women take their name, he actually took her name and became a Dean. He told people that he did it so that their children would always be associated with the company. Even though they had been divorced for five years, his love for her never faded.

"How's your mother?" he asked.

Jaymee glanced over. "He's the reason Momma's here in the first place."

"Some people just smell money." Teddy smirked.

Richard heard what Teddy said and stormed over to him, focusing on his fist and Teddy's face. Teddy saw him coming and defensively stood up to protect himself. Just as Richard got within swinging distance, Ricky jumped between the two combatants.

"Now, Richard, let's not show our true colors," Teddy said with a slight grin.

Richard wanted to punch his lights out but didn't. He and Teddy at one time had run the streets together. Since neither one of them back then had worked at the Gloria Dean Company, they had plenty of time to golf, drink, and flirt with the high society women of New York. Around the same time as his divorce from Gloria was occurring, something happened that ruined their friendship. But Teddy and Richard never spoke about it, but Richard always avoided Teddy after that.

Ricky tried to calm his father down. "Daddy, the doctor said that Momma is getting better."

"What does that mean?" Richard asked. He slowly backed away from Teddy.

"She's still in a coma, but he said her heart is getting stronger. She's gonna make it." Ricky mustered up some enthusiasm to make the situation seem improved. The truth was, the doctor never told him anything like that.

Richard saw Jaymee sitting by the window and smiled over at her.

"Jaymee, how are you doing?" he asked. "Where's my grandchild Brittany?"

Jaymee ignored him. She had nothing to say to him. She hadn't really talked to her father since he divorced Gloria. They had been amicable, but that was only when Gloria was around.

Richard turned red in the face with anger. He pointed his finger at her.

"Little girl, I know you hear me. I don't care where we are. Don't have me act a fool," he said, anger rising in his voice.

She glanced at him for a brief second, then rolled her eyes. That was absolutely the wrong move to make. Instead of attacking, though, he waited to see how far she would take her childish act.

"Were you talking to me?" she asked. Jaymee wanted to show him that he meant nothing to her, and he got her drift.

"I called Jasmine," Richard told her.

Jaymee whipped back around to face him. "You did? Now, that's a surprise!"

Richard took a deep breath to calm his temper. He was really close to slapping Jaymee into next week. His relationship with his children had been strained since the divorce, but disrespecting him was the one thing he never accepted. Jaymee was pushing him to a territory they had never ventured to before. His kids knew him to be a nice, gentle man who stayed calm and relaxed at all times. They never saw the street side of him, the Richard who used to knock guys out for just staring at him the wrong way.

"Call your sister," he said in a demanding tone.

Irritated, Jaymee glanced over at Teddy. "Richard, you stopped being my daddy a long time ago. And what kind of sister is she anyway?" Jaymee asked with disdain. "She should already be here if she cared."

Richard reached his boiling point. He went over to where Jaymee was seated. She stood up, brave as could be, but she looked scared. Without hesitation, Richard slapped her down in her seat. As she held her face, crying, Richard held his hand up in the air, waiting for her to say something else smart. They stared at each other. Cowed, she tearfully bowed her head.

"I don't care how old you get. You'll show me respect!"

"Daddy, I'll do it. I'll call her again," Ricky said, intervening before the situation got out of control.

The anger Richard felt made his eyes red and bloodshot. He hated that feeling. Getting control of himself, Richard walked across the room and sat down. He kept his eyes on Jaymee, though.

Jaymee turned to Ricky and whispered, "She doesn't even like Momma."

Teddy came over. "At some point, we need to discuss who's going to run the business in your mother's absence," Teddy said in a fatherly tone.

Everyone looked at one another. No one said anything. Then the doctor came out. Their attention turned to him.

Richard stepped in front of everyone. "When can we see her?"

Jaymee and Teddy looked at one another with hatred in their eyes for Richard.

Richard looked at Ricky. "Where's Jackie at? It's not like him to not be here."

Ricky shrugged his shoulders. "I called him but got no answer."

***

Over at his swanky penthouse in the Village, Jackie sat on his couch doing lines of cocaine and drinking Jack Daniels straight from the bottle. His face showed the pain he felt as he watched CNN report on what had happened to Gloria. Today was the worst day of his life. Though Gloria didn't want him involved, Jackie felt like he should have been there to protect her. Feeling like he failed her, Jackie didn't want to face anyone.

His cell phone rang, and simultaneously someone started pounding on his door. He acted as if he had earplugs in. All he kept repeating was, "I should have been there."

After a few minutes, his front door opened and a caramel-skinned woman walked in, slowly. He pulled out his gun and held it between his legs.

"Jackie," the woman called out.

Without turning around, he put his gun back in his shoulder holster and snorted up another line of coke.

"Clairesa, I told you I was coming home later," he said, still not looking at her.

Clairesa walked over to the back of the couch and gently touched his shoulders. "Everyone's calling, wondering where you are."

"It's my fault," he cried out.

"Don't blame yourself. You can't be everywhere."

"I should have been there," he said, shaking his head.

"She's gonna make it."

"What if she doesn't? Then everyone will hang this on me. I can't live with that." A single tear raced down his face. Quickly, he covered his eyes to stop more of them from coming.

"Jackie, you have me and your son to live for. Who cares what others think? I know you didn't have anything to do with what happened."

A fire grew in his eyes. "I got to find out who did this. They have to pay."

"Don't do anything stupid. The police are working on it right now," she replied gently.

He turned around and faced her. "What do you mean?"

"They came by the house asking questions and looking for you."

He grimaced. "Ricky gave them our address. That—"

"I didn't tell them anything. I know the drill." She smiled. "But you should go to the hospital. That is your family."

"I don't do hospitals," he said stubbornly. Then another thought occurred to him. "Did anyone contact Jasmine?"

"I don't know. I thought she deserted the family," Clairesa said.

Jackie picked up the phone and dialed. "She has to know."

CHAPTER SIX

In the heart of midtown Manhattan, ten floors up, Jaymee glared out the window of her high-priced lawyer's office. Her mood was gloomy as she watched two little girls skipping down the street. The scene reminded her of times she had shared with Jasmine. They had a notorious love/hate relationship, filled with more hate than love. Being the younger one, Jaymee always tried to outperform Jasmine at everything. She felt she had to beat her in order to earn her mother's love. Her highly competitive, deceitful nature was what drove her and Jasmine apart.

As her attorney, Michael Lawrence, came back into the office, she forced a smile. He slammed the files he had on his desk. His face was red with frustration.

Jaymee raised a brow at him. His actions said it all. The news he was about to deliver wasn't going to be good. Jaymee contemplated taking a seat to brace herself for the bad news.

"Michael, what is it?"

"All three of you have an equal share of her sixty percent," Michael huffed.

"So, I have to run the company with Ricky and my father?"

Michael gave her a peculiar look. He knew Jaymee would not take the news he was about to deliver well.

"Actually, Ricky and Jasmine are the other two. Richard and Jackie only have five percent. And of course, Teddy has his thirty percent."

She was astonished. "Didn't my mother write her out of the will?" she asked, trying to figure out what was going on. Her mother always said that Jasmine was disowned and would get nothing when she died. Yet she didn't want to put the family "business" out there, and she stayed quiet.

"No. Only Ralph would know that information," Michael said. "Take a seat."

She kept standing. Michael started touching his pens and pencils on his desk. He was trying to muster up the confidence to say something.

Jaymee noticed his fidgeting out of the corner of her eye. "What is it?" she asked, irritated. "Just spit it out!"

"Well, I did receive a call from Mr. Hicks," he said hesitantly.

"What does he want?"

"He offered to give you the presidency if you joined him with your twenty percent. That would make you two the majority." Michael smiled. "His thirty and your twenty. Unless you want to make the call to Jasmine. You know Ricky will cave with her on your side."

The latter choice was not a viable option. She rolled her eyes just thinking about it. She and Jasmine working together would be impossible. And the last thing Jaymee wanted was to repeat the subordinate role she had with her mother.

She turned back to the window. Though she loved Teddy like an uncle, she didn't trust him. The comments her mother had made in the past about him wanting to steal the company out from under her rang clear in her head. She also thought about what Ricky had said at the hospital about her qualifications. If she didn't make some kind of power play, she would be left out in the cold.

"Draw up the papers," she said with a grin on her lovely face. Hungry for the top spot, she had no qualms about putting Gloria's survival on the back burner while she attended to her own ambitions.

"All hail, Madame President," Michael joked as Jaymee turned back to staring out the window. But inside, she was rejoicing, knowing that she was so close to achieving her dream.

***

Over the next couple of days, Ricky, Jaymee, and Teddy turned their attention to positioning themselves in the best situation to seize control. There were a lot of secret meetings and negotiating between attorneys. Lost in the shuffle was Gloria as she fought for her life. Though none of them spoke openly about running the company, it was obvious everyone had their own agenda. The happiest of the three was, without a doubt, Teddy. He knew that his thirty percent was paramount in any takeover scenario by the sister or brother. With his chest pushed out, he made his way around the office as if he was already crowned the new king. All his hard work was about to pay off with the special board meeting he called to settle the chaos.

In the massive boardroom on the fiftieth floor, most of the heads of the different divisions and other business interests waited patiently to hear whatever announcement was going to be made. Some of the attendees overseas were video conferenced in on the four hundred-inch TV screens around the room. On the walls of the massive room were the top clothing designs made by the company throughout the years. Smug, Teddy sat comfortably at the head of the table. Everyone could tell that he had pulled off a major coup.

Jaymee took a seat next to Teddy. She glowed as she waited to hear what Teddy had to announce.

Teddy peeked at his watch and stood up. The clock showed exactly two o'clock.

"Hello, everyone," he said. "I called this emergency meeting to discuss how we are going to operate while Mrs. Dean is out. I know the past few days have been rough, but I thank you all for keeping things afloat. I want everyone to know my prayers are with her and her family…"

Jaymee smiled as Ricky gave her a cold stare. She turned her attention back to Teddy as he continued.

"Our bylaws call for the person with majority stake in the company to assume the role of chief executive officer during these times. In this case, I have thirty percent ownership, of which you all are aware, and with twenty percent from …"

Teddy dropped his head for a moment. The pause had nothing to do with the rift created between Ricky and Jaymee, but for dramatic effect. He prided himself as being a good actor. Truth be told, he enjoyed seeing them backstab each other. Both of them were perfect pawns in his chess game.

Jaymee placed her hands on top of the table. She tried not to smile, but this was the moment she had waited for her whole life.

Teddy lifted his head. He looked at everyone in the room one by one, then said, "The new president is Richard Dean the Second."

It was like everyone stopped breathing or even blinking. The faces of the executives froze. No one knew how to react. Disappointment floated through the room while Jaymee sat paralyzed. She grabbed her pen tightly in her hand. Her first thought was to jab it in Teddy's throat. Her lawyer had told her the deal was sealed. She tried to play it cool, to not seem embarrassed by the news.

Teddy saw Jaymee fuming. She was known to go off the deep end at times. And it was anybody's guess what she might do.

Ricky stood up joyously and shook hands with well-wishers. He glanced at Jaymee and gave her a big wink.

"You bastard," Jaymee said to Teddy as she threw her papers back in her folder. She had prepared a speech, highlighting her accomplishments and her vision for the company.

Ricky came over to Jaymee, almost as if he was gliding. "'There will always be a position for you.'" Ricky laughed. "You thought you had beat me, didn't you?"

Without any warning, the boardroom doors were flung open. Gloria's personal lawyer, Ralph, strolled in, followed slowly by Jackie and then, to everyone's surprise, Jasmine Dean. The room fell utterly silent. Ricky and Teddy looked at one another, wondering what the hell was happening.

Jasmine radiated confidence as she came forward. Her persona shouted money, power, and success. The designer business suit tailored to accentuate her fabulous figure made her appear graceful but strong. And with her stunning natural beauty, she got the attention of all in the room.

"Why is she here?" Jaymee asked, eyeing Ralph with disgust.

"I hate to interrupt," Ralph said, focused on Teddy. The devilish grin on his face told Teddy that he was going to avenge all the bad history they'd had together.

Ralph noticed everyone in the boardroom and on the TV screens. "Good. Everyone's here, so I don't have to repeat myself. What I have to say will change any plans stated before our arrival."

"What's going on?" Teddy asked, confused by the interruption.

"After a thorough review of the bylaws and provisions set forth by Mrs. Dean, I'm here to inform you that until she is released from the hospital and is able to return to work at full capacity, the person who will run the company is Jasmine Dean, the eldest child. She will personally oversee the flagship entity, the Gloria Dean Company."

"Oh, hell naw!" Ricky cried.

"This is crazy," Jaymee said, turning away from Jasmine. "She can't run this company."

"She's a deserter. A traitor. She hates her own mother." Teddy laughed. "This is a joke."

Jasmine advanced on Teddy and raised her hand to slap the taste out of his mouth. Yet she stopped herself. Jasmine and her mother were at odds about many things—except for their distrust of Teddy. Jasmine knew she needed to make a strong statement for everyone to respect her new position. Seeing the fear in Teddy's eyes were satisfying to a small degree. But Jasmine knew that the war was just beginning.

"I'm not my younger sister or brother," she sternly said. "And you best remember that."

"Good day," Ralph said as he grabbed Jasmine by the arm. The three of them walked out, not even once looking back at the angry faces.

Once they had left, Ricky picked up a coffee cup from the table and threw it against the wall. It shattered everywhere.

Jaymee smiled, pleased by the new plan. "I guess you two got screwed also." She laughed as she strolled out of the room.

Humiliation filled Teddy's face and his anger exploded. This was supposed to have been his big moment. He lifted his head and saw that the executives were still present, stunned by everything that had just transpired. For a man who normally was full of colorful words, he was now speechless.

"Meeting adjourned." Teddy grimaced as he took a seat.

"Uncle T, can they do that?" Ricky asked in a panic.

Teddy nodded his head grimly, and Ricky rushed out of the room.

Many of the executives had questions about the new leadership, but one look at Teddy's pissed-off face, and they decided to save those questions for later. After the room cleared, Teddy pounded the table with his fist. He couldn't believe Gloria had undercut him once again.

CHAPTER **SEVEN**

The next morning, when Jasmine opened the door to her mother's office, its emptiness gave her an eerie feeling. It was the same as she remembered it being when she left. Her eyes scoped the room, taking the many photos of the company's long history. It touched her deeply when she saw a picture of herself hugging her mother after she'd won the Miss New York Pageant. She walked over to the picture and gazed at it. It was one of the rare happy moments they'd shared. But when she turned toward the chair behind the desk, the huge portrait of Gloria seemed like it was glowering at her. Jasmine felt out of place.

"Momma. Oh, Momma." She shook her head. "Why am I here?"

Out of the corner of her eye, she spotted a family photo of all of them—Ricky, Jaymee, Jackie, Richard, her mother, and herself. She chuckled grimly.

"You have never made my life easy."

Ricky busted in the office without knocking. She faced him. Instead of being upset, she smiled. Jasmine felt this was a time for their family to reunite, but his face told a different story. He was still simmering from his failed takeover bid with Teddy the day before.

"Ricky, how are you doing? I missed you guys so much."

He frowned at her. "Don't get too comfortable."

"Let me remind you, I didn't ask to be here," Jasmine said.

"Then leave," he replied harshly. His face was filled with hateful thoughts. "Don't nobody want you here! Just leave like you did before."

She sighed and plopped down in her mother's chair. She didn't take too kindly to her baby brother huffing at her, but thought maybe after he let out some steam, things would change.

"I don't want to fight you. We're family. I love you guys," she said, giving him the opportunity to return the gesture. It was an opportunity she had hoped he would accept graciously.

She could tell that he didn't care what she had to say. She was in his way of running the company. In reality, Ricky didn't know Jasmine as well as she knew him. During his formative years, Jasmine had taken care of him and Jaymee. Not until her modeling career blossomed had she left for the road. And of course, Jaymee never told him about all the things Jasmine did for them because she wanted to be the one he admired.

"I don't even know you," he said with a disgusted look.

"You don't remember all the things we used to do when you were little? You were my little man."

Ricky yawned at the attempt for reconciliation. "Why don't you just go back to that rock you crawled out from? From supermodel to super traitor. How can we even trust that you'll be here tomorrow?"

Jasmine turned away from him, trying to gain control of her emotions. Of all people, she never would have imagined Ricky saying something so hateful to her. He was the little angel who always supported everybody in the family. She expected venom from Teddy and maybe Jaymee, but Ricky was almost like her own child. Jasmine felt like letting the tears roll down her face—before she caught a glimpse of the smile on his face. Her pain quickly turned to anger. She whipped back around and pushed herself up from the desk to stare at him dead on.

Ricky's jaws tightened. She knew the look she gave him reminded him of his mother. He was instantly intimidated as a lump formed in his throat.

"Whether or not you like it, I'm here and you best get used to it. Once Momma gets better, I'm gone. You can have this damn place. But right now I have a business to run, so get out of my office, Mr. Dean, and next time, make an appointment."

"You're jokin', right?" he asked.

She placed one hand on her hip and slit her eyes at him. "I'm not smiling. And let me make something very clear to you from this point forward. If you ever say anything negative about me again... and try to bring me down, I swear I will hurt you. And that's a promise. Ricky, ask yourself—do you really want to go to war with me?"

Ricky surrendered without saying a word. Upon leaving, he slammed the door. It brought a slight grin to Jasmine's face, knowing she had won the exchange.

That wouldn't help her in the long run, though. She sat down in her mother's chair and put her head on the desk. With Ricky against her as well, the uphill battle in front of her seemed unwinnable. She started to question whether coming back was really worth it. But then she remembered what Jackie had said to convince her to return: *Your love for your mother is greater than your hate. Ask yourself, what would Momma do?* And Jasmine knew that her mother, no matter how much they fought, would have her back in any situation if she needed her.

"God, give me strength," she begged.

***

In her office, Jaymee was typing up her leave-of-absence letter. Feeling spurned by Teddy, Ricky, and her mother, Jaymee felt she could not possibly stay and work under Jasmine. "Yeah," she said, reading what she had just written. "My leave is effective immediately. I will return to the Gloria Dean Company full-time when Gloria Dean returns to the company." She reread the letter over and over. "Yeah, take that, Jasmine!"

As she pushed the print button, her cell phone rang. She glanced at it. The number was blocked, but she still decided to answer it.

"Hello," Jaymee said.

"Jaymee," someone whispered through the phone. It was so low Jaymee could hardly hear the person.

"Hello, who is this?" she asked, trying to figure out the voice on the other end of the phone.

"It's me!" the person said a little louder.

Jaymee still couldn't make out the voice, but she knew it was a man and their were only two men who would call her like this: Ricky and Teddy. And she knew the person definitely was not Ricky, so she took an educated guess. "Uncle T?"

"We need to talk."

She laughed. "Just come to my office and quit playing on the phone."

"We can't meet in the office. I can't trust Ricky or Jasmine with what I have to tell you."

"Why not Ricky?" she asked, a bit confused. Ricky was always in Teddy's corner.

"We can still take over the company."

Jaymee rolled her eyes. "That ship has sailed."

"The ship is still docked. I'm in contact with Randolph James's people, and they want you involved in the takeover."

"Why me?"

"I guess they want a Dean and a woman when we take over. But they did specifically ask for you."

"Hold on, what do you mean by takeover?" Jaymee asked, concerned about where this conversation might be heading.

"Jaymee, this is a very delicate conversation. Let's meet and discuss the details."

"I don't know about this. That is our competition."

Teddy huffed through the phone. "Jaymee, I understand you want to be loyal to your family, but what do you think is going to happen if your mother dies? You think Jasmine is going to give you power?"

She and everyone else could bear witness to Randolph James's fast rise in the fashion industry. Her curiosity grew. "Where?"

"Right around the corner in our favorite coffee shop."

They hung up the phone, and Jaymee sat back, wondering. She couldn't figure out what exactly Teddy had planned with Randolph James, but the intrigue and the possible power shift had her interest on high.

***

Later that evening, Jasmine broke down crying while she sat next to her mother in her ICU room. She held her mother's hand as her gaze shifted back and forth between the heart monitor and the lifeless look on her mother's face. She admired her mother's courage, drive and passion, even if she hated the way she sometimes accomplished her goals. Not seeing any fight in Gloria only depressed her more.

"I don't want to fail you again. You built this company with your own two hands, and I don't want this responsibility. I just want you well again."

Jasmine's eyes followed the tubes going in and out of her mother's body. It saddened her even more.

"I hate everything we've been through. How am I supposed to coordinate for the fashion show next week?"

Yet when she saw the same family photo from the office on the table next to her bed, she smiled.

"You know, I never wanted to come back." She motioned with her hands. "I can't trust my own sister or brother. They're turning people against me. How do I make it right with them when they don't even want me here?"

Jasmine slumped down in her seat. The situation killed her spirit. It seemed like a no-win situation. If she stayed, her brother and sister would wage war, and if she left, her brother and sister, with the help of Teddy, would tear the business apart.

A voice came from behind her. "They might not like you, but you have to make them respect you."

She turned to see her father.

He emerged as if from the dark, like a superhero. "I know you got it in you. Just put the past in the trash." He smiled at her.

She jumped up and gave him a hug. "I love you, Daddy."

Jasmine and her father had always had a close relationship, to the point that it angered her siblings. As the oldest child, she knew of all the secrets between her parents, even the reason why they split up. Though Ricky and Jaymee blamed Richard, Jasmine knew where the blame should be placed. Being the man that he was, Richard made her promise never to tell her brother or sister the truth. He didn't want them to look at their mother any differently.

Richard held tightly to his precious daughter. He kissed her on the cheek and looked into her face.

"I'm always here for you. Don't you forget that. Remember Team Dean. I got your back."

She nodded. If there was anyone in her corner, she knew it was Richard. As his firstborn they had a special bond. No matter what the occasion or circumstance, her father had always protected her. And Jasmine loved him deeply for it.

"Okay, we're going to keep Gloria Dean's company great even without Gloria Dean."

CHAPTER **EIGHT**

Times Square never seemed brighter, except of course on New Year's Eve. Tonight was a special occasion. Movie, music, and fashion stars strolled by the bright lights and cameras, heading into the W Hotel on 47th Street. The occasion was the Mahala Fashion Show, a yearly event that brought out the who's who of the fashion industry. All the top designers, from Italy to California, attended this prestigious event, in hopes of praise, money, and the right to brag for the coming year. Outside of the normal Fashion Week events, Gloria had set up this gala to raise money for breast cancer research in honor of Mahala, her mother. The deadly disease had taken her mother's life.

When Gloria Dean's silver stretch limousine pulled up to the red carpet, the paparazzi ran and waited to see who would step out. Surprisingly, Jasmine and Ricky emerged from opposite doors.

The ride had been a cold one. Ricky immediately walked off the carpet into the crowd and brought some of his women friends, standing behind the ropes, over with him, leaving Jasmine to fend for herself. When the reporters caught up with him, he hurried inside with his friends.

"Jasmine, Jasmine, can I get a minute with you?" one of the reporters asked, barging past his colleagues.

Jasmine stopped hesitantly. Talking to reporters was one of the functions she hated. During her departure from the Gloria Dean Company, they had burned her with negative press, saying that she had been fired. The press was also the reason she had stayed out of the public eye while building her Jazzie brand. But she remembered that her mother always said there was no such thing as bad press. As Gloria would say, the game was all about keeping your name in the news.

Jasmine looked into the camera and smiled.

"I'm here with a blast from the past...You guessed it, Jasmine Dean, the former fabulous supermodel," the reporter said to the crowd by the red carpet.

The reporter shoved the microphone in her face. Everything seemed blurry as she looked at the crowd of onlookers waiting outside the roped-off area. She opened her mouth, but nothing came out. It seemed like she had forgotten why she had even come.

"Jazzy, it's been a long time since we've seen you at an industry event. How does it feel to be back?" the reporter asked, interrupting the awkward pause.

She cleared her throat. The magnitude of the event had overwhelmed her, and taking a few deep breaths calmed her down.

A fan yelled out, "We still love you, Jazzy."

Jasmine grinned. What she had prepared to say came back to her.

"I love you too," she said to the camera and to the crowd. "First, I want to thank all the fans for sending their love to my mother while she's been in the hospital. The prayers are working. To answer your question, I'm back for my mother. She has been such an icon in the industry that I feel lucky to step into her gigantic shoes for the moment. Even with four pairs of tube socks I couldn't fill them, but I'm trying." She shyly laughed.

"We all wish your mother 'get well soon.' I know I miss the Queen of the Night." The reporter smiled.

"Thank you," Jasmine replied. "All the prayers count. But please remember that tonight is about finding a cure for breast cancer. Mahala, my grandmother, the true matriarch of the Dean family—this disease took her life at such a young age. I hope and pray that in my lifetime a cure is found."

"So Jasmine, with you now running the Gloria Dean Company, what does this mean for your Jazzie brand? Is it finished?"

Jasmine smiled. "Of course not. My Jazzie brand is still owned by me. Currently, Mikhael Thornton is running the company until I come back."

"You have a great night, Ms. Dean."

"I will." She waved at the crowd, then turned to walk into the W.

Before she could get through the doors, another reporter stuck his microphone in her face. It came within inches of hitting her. Irritated by the near miss, Jasmine glared at him.

"Please, just a couple of questions," the reporter begged. "You're so beautiful."

She didn't want to answer any more questions, but the guy's innocent demeanor made her feel guilty. Plus, the "beautiful" remark won her over.

"Okay," she said with a smile.

"So, where have you been for the last five years? Rumors have it that you were kicked out of your mother's company. Can you comment on that?"

Jasmine gritted her teeth. She wanted to choke the reporter for that remark, but with the camera on her, she realized she had to handle the situation professionally. She brushed off his comments and looked into the camera with a big smile.

"God is good. I love you all. Support the Gloria Dean line. It's hotter than ever. Thanks." Jasmine waved at the crowd again as she waltzed into the show.

The first reporter turned to the second one. "Is it true?" the reporter asked.

"I'll tell you all the dirt on that diva when we get inside," the second reporter whispered. "She's worse than J Lo."

"That's nothing. Wait until she sees that she and Tyra have on identical dresses. Now, that's a screamer."

The two reporters laughed.

"Can you say *catfight*!" the second reporter exclaimed.

In one of the unused dressing rooms at the show, Ricky and Dee, a model from the show, were having wild, passionate sex. They tore up the room going at each other. In midstroke, someone knocked on the door. They got quiet, hoping whoever was there would leave. Ricky focused on the table he had set up to block the door. He prayed it was good enough to keep people out. After the person left, he tiptoed over to the door, naked, and turned off the lights.

Backstage at the fashion show was a madhouse. The beautiful women were incandescent, but things were moving at a rapid pace all around them. Many of the designers were pulling their hair out trying to gather their models together to coordinate their turn on the catwalk.

With such a torrid pace, a normal person would have cracked under pressure. Jasmine seemed unnerved by the yelling and screaming as she and her assistant, Sasha, got their models lined up for the catwalk. Looking at the roll call sheet, Jasmine found a discrepancy. Appalled, she went through her list of models until she realized that some people were missing. She looked at the other designers and their models. Noticing that they were ready to take the stage angered her immensely. This was the Gloria Dean Company event, and no way did she want to be outshined by anyone there. At first, Jasmine glared over at Sasha, but before she said a word she walked back in the dressing room where the models had gotten dressed. With no one in the room, she stormed back out to Sasha.

"Didn't we have fifteen models for this show? I only count thirteen," she asked Sasha.

"Remember, I told you Sherry is sick."

Jasmine gave Sasha a crazy look.

Sasha hadn't told her any such thing, but hoped that Jasmine believed her anyway.

"Like I said, I only count thirteen models. Someone's missing."

"Kisha, Michaela, Stephanie, Renee. Dee—that's who's missing. I saw her earlier," Sasha said like the problem was solved.

"I need her now!" Jasmine demanded.

The other designers in the crowded backstage noticed the tension in Jasmine's face. They started to gossip among themselves about how poorly organized Jasmine and her team seemed to be. Jasmine caught a glimpse of them and knew by their facial expressions that they were expecting her to fail. This was her gut-check moment.

As Jasmine checked her watch, a bead of sweat dropped onto it. The last thing she needed was a hiccup at the show her mother made famous. Jasmine knew that everyone wanted to see how the company would function without its fearless leader.

"Have you seen Ricky or Jaymee?" she asked Sasha.

Sasha didn't want to lie, but she flinched. Jasmine knew very well that her loyalty was more with Ricky and Jaymee since she had known them a lot longer. Jasmine also guessed that she had been told that Jasmine's reign would be short-lived, and listening to her was not necessary.

In any case, Jasmine saw her hesitation. She huffed under her breath at Sasha's evasions. She wasn't about to accept a mole sabotaging her work for the greater good of Ricky and Jaymee. Jasmine got as close as she could, to avoid drawing any attention.

"You like working here?" Jasmine whispered sternly in her ear.

Sasha buckled. "I saw Jaymee talking to Maxwell Kennedy about a position in his company. But I haven't seen Ricky. I promise."

"This shit is going to stop. Make sure that the models are in place and ready to go when it's our time. Have Nelson come fix a couple of the girls' makeup so that they don't look like clowns." Jasmine looked around. "It may look like a circus, but it's not. Calm down and get it done."

The stage manager came over to Jasmine. "Are you ready to go?" he asked.

Jasmine looked at Sasha, then responded. "Give us ten minutes. I promise that's all the time I need."

Jasmine headed off at a rapid pace. Behind her back, Sasha gave her the middle finger. In a distant mirror, Jasmine saw her. For the moment she decided to ignore it for the sake of the show. Her reputation, and the company's, were riding on how well everything turned out. Reprimanding Sasha was last on her list for tonight, but tomorrow was a different day, and she would be dealt with.

In the auditorium, some people were already seated while some were standing and mingling. Jaymee was one of the latter, flirting with Maxwell Kennedy as if she didn't have a care in the world. Every time she laughed, she rubbed his arm affectionately.

Maxwell Kennedy was one of the biggest designers in the industry. His clothes were tailored to the hip-hop generation. Maxwell's success stemmed from his record label, the Kennedy Administration. He was known as a player in the music and fashion industry, and the eye of almost every woman at the show was upon him. He was the type of guy, though, who chased money, not women. Being young, brash, handsome, and very rich kept his name in the mix of gossip.

Being flirtatious himself, Maxwell frequently looked off at other women who arrived at the show while Jaymee was talking his ear off. To regain his attention, Jaymee would rub his arm even more.

"You know, I can do wonders with your line. I hate to toot my own horn, but I'm the reason for all of our recent success. We can blend hip-hop with elegance. We'll call it Hip-Elegance the Fusion." She giggled.

He looked sideways at her. "Now you want to be on my team?"

"Hey, that was my mother who passed on your line. I am with the hip-hop movement. I always knew you would be hot."

He stopped in mid-sip to give her his full attention. "Does your sister know?"

Jaymee became upset. "She doesn't run me!"

At that moment Jasmine strolled up from behind. Jaymee turned and glared at her with total disgust.

"Quit breathing down my neck," Jaymee growled.

Jasmine returned her look with one of contempt. Jaymee's childish antics were wearing thin, but she held her composure.

"Where is Ricky?" Jasmine asked.

Jaymee smiled. "Do I look like MapQuest?"

Jasmine started to walk off, but Maxwell stopped her by touching her arm. She gave him a look like *what are you doing?* Startled, he looked at her with undisguised admiration. Like most men during her heyday, Jasmine had sexy on lockdown. Every guy wanted to be hooked up with her.

"Jasmine Dean. I have been trying to meet you for years. I can't believe this," he said, grinning. "I'm a true fan."

Fuming with jealousy, Jaymee stomped off. All through their childhood, everyone had fallen head-over-heels for Jasmine.

"Do I know you?" Jasmine asked, trying to think where she might have seen him before.

"I grew up with your posters all over my room. You were my *it* girl."

She glanced at her watch, hoping he would get the hint. He didn't. Maxwell stood there looking into her eyes, like a baby amazed at seeing a ceiling fan turn clockwise.

"Nice meeting you, but I have to go," she said politely. "Enjoy the show."

He came out of his temporary spell. "Don't be so formal. Maybe I can buy you a drink."

"I don't drink," she said as she walked off.

"I got to get a piece of that," Maxwell laughed. "Damn, in person she's a hottie."

Going backstage again, Jasmine was on a rampage trying to locate Ricky. Weaving through all of the models and backstage crew, she went in and out of every room. Noticing the time, she was about to quit and get back to the staging area, but then noticed a door she hadn't tried. Jasmine turned the knob and it turned, but something was blocking it from opening. On the inside, Ricky and Dee got quiet. Jasmine started to walk off, but she heard something move. Using her shoulder, she pushed the door open and flicked on the lights. Lying on top of some cardboard boxes were Ricky and Dee, completely naked. Jasmine glared at them. They scrambled to put their clothes on in a hurry, but the damage was already done. Dee jumped behind Ricky for protection. He and Jasmine locked eyes. Jasmine shook her head in disbelief and disappointment.

"So," Ricky said, feeling guilty. "You don't know me, so don't judge me."

"What do I need to know? That you're a spoiled brat who wet his pants till he was fifteen?"

"Fuck you," he said, giving her the middle finger.

What is it with everybody and their finger? she wondered. Jasmine rolled her eyes. "Why do you think we're here, so you can get your freak on? I tell you what. Don't come to work tomorrow if you don't want to work tonight."

"I'm sorry, we got carried away. I'll be right there," Dee said remorsefully.

Jasmine smirked. "Don't be sorry. You're fired. When I'm done with you, you'll be lucky to flip burgers."

Jasmine glanced at her watch, then dashed off. The show would be starting in minutes, and this nonsense was not worth her time.

"We got a contract," Dee yelled, hoping Jasmine would reconsider her decision.

"Sue me, bitch," Jasmine yelled from down the hallway.

When Jasmine got back to her models, they were lined up and ready to hit the catwalk. She didn't take kindly to seeing Sasha take directions from Jaymee, who had come backstage at the last minute. Once again, she ignored it.

As the Gloria Dean models pranced out onto the runway, Jasmine reminisced about when she used to help her mother get the models ready for the show. The fashion shows were the crown jewels of her calendar. It was the only time she ever saw her mother's vulnerable side. Being a control freak, Gloria could always dictate how life played out on a normal day, but during the fashion events, she couldn't predict what might go wrong. During those moments Gloria shared her deepest feelings with her.

By the sound of the continuous loud applause, the audience loved the fall clothing line. The models did a superb job in making the designs seem flawless. Hearing the reactions brightened Jasmine's spirits. Pulling this event off in such a short time made her feel proud. She hugged each and every model as they came off the stage for the last time.

"These fashions are brought to you by the legendary Gloria Dean Company," the announcer said as the last model sauntered out of view, dazzling the crowd.

Jasmine was hesitant to walk out on the catwalk. Though she had much success as a model, it cost her everything. She lost her childhood, her mother, and friends—and it all started on that long runway. If the models hadn't physically been pushing her out toward the catwalk, she probably wouldn't have gone.

Upon seeing her beauty at the beginning of the catwalk, the attendees all stood up and clapped for her. For them and for Jasmine, it was her homecoming. Her legs shook so much that she had a hard time moving a muscle. She stood still, praying that this would be enough for the crowd. The announcer signaled for her to walk the catwalk, but she didn't budge. With the room being dark and the catwalk lit up, the runway seemed endless. The camera flashes were blinding. Her heart pounded fast, as if it was her first time.

"And presenting the Gloria Dean Company fall line is no other than the great Jasmine Dean, former supermodel and diva. We still love Jazzy," the announcer said, waving at her.

She took a deep breath and slowly walked to the T of the runway, feeling as though her feet were bricks. Jasmine took a bow as she looked into the crowd. Then her emotions got the best of her. She began to cry as she turned to head off stage. Within a matter of seconds, the heel on her shoe broke off and sent her flying off the stage and into Maxwell Kennedy's lap. Her head dropped right near his crotch. Jasmine looked up at him.

"Now I know who you are," she said, trying to conceal her embarrassment.

The photographers raced over to get a picture. While the bulbs flashed, Maxwell looked at his white suit. He saw some red lipstick stains on his pant leg.

"You got lipstick all over my pants. Now can I buy you dinner?" He laughed.

Shielding her face the best way possible from the cameras, Jasmine smiled at Maxwell before hopping off backstage.

***

The memory of last night's event stayed on Jasmine's mind. Thinking no one was paying attention, she tried to discreetly walk past the design team to get into her other office on the design floor. It was so quiet that it appeared that no one was at work. She couldn't believe that the hundred cubicles outside her office were empty. As she passed the last set of cubes, she glanced back and still saw no one or heard anything. She shrugged her shoulders at the oddity and continued to her door. But as she fumbled with her office door keys, she heard people snickering. She unlocked the office door, then suddenly stopped when she noticed the picture from the fashion show of her falling into Maxwell's crotch posted on the door. It brought a smile to her face. Jasmine sensed eyes upon her. When Jasmine went back to the design area, the staff put their heads down. They pretended to be hard at work.

"It's okay. I think it was funny myself." She laughed.

The team breathed a sigh of relief.

"Thank you all for your endless efforts. Besides my show-stealing act, we did a phenomenal job last night."

The team clapped.

"The new designs are superb. I think this is going to be a banner year for us," she said enthusiastically.

One of the team members yelled out, "What about a bonus?"

Jasmine smiled. "If everything goes well, we all will get bonuses."

The design team roared in enthusiasm.

When Ricky walked in with Sasha, laughing at the newspaper, though, Jasmine was not as lighthearted. Thoughts of last night resurfaced, and the image of Sasha giving her the finger was vivid in her mind. One glance at the clock showed that it was after eight o'clock. The way Sasha strolled in, it was apparent she saw no rush, and that was what pissed Jasmine off the most.

"And, I will try not to get in your way…that much," Jasmine said with her eyes fixed on Sasha. It was like a bald eagle eyeing a field mouse before the kill.

Not wanting to face them at that moment, Jasmine quickly retreated into her office. Jasmine sat heavily in her chair and started to take deep breaths. Confrontations had always been her Achilles' heel. She turned around to face the window and mumbled a calming chant to herself. The chant was similar to a Buddhist mantra.

After a few minutes, Sasha knocked on her door and poked her head inside.

"I just checked my messages. Do you still want to see me?" she asked, smiling.

Jasmine spun around to face her. Her cheeks jumped because of her nerves.

Sasha noticed the strange way she looked at her. "Jasmine, are you okay?"

Jasmine snapped out of it. Her demeanor quickly changed. A harder, take-no-prisoners look overcame her beautiful face. The memory of Sasha giving the middle finger to her wouldn't fade away.

"Have a seat," Jasmine said in a hard voice.

Sasha couldn't bring herself to even move. "What's wrong?" she asked. "I'm sorry for being late, but Ricky said it was okay."

"I regretfully have to terminate you from the company, effective immediately."

Sasha was stunned. "What did I do?"

Jasmine tightened her jaw. She had no sympathy for people who dis-respected her. With Ricky, Jaymee, and Teddy already being a load to handle, there was no room for Sasha or anyone like her who wouldn't change.

"Let's just say that what I expect from you, you cannot deliver."

Sasha stepped closer to her. "This is bullshit. If you don't like me, then that's fine, but I didn't do anything wrong," she said tearfully. "Everything was fine with your mother."

Jasmine leaned back in her chair confidently. "Last night, I saw you give me the middle finger."

Sasha got quiet as they stared at one another. Slowly Sasha's eyes hit the floor in regret. "I didn't mean it." She squirmed. "You can't fire me for that."

Jasmine rolled her eyes. "You should have thought about that last night."

Sasha's tears had no effect on her. Even when she got down on her knees, Jasmine paid no attention to her.

"I need this job. I have two kids to support. Haven't you ever made a mistake that you regretted?"

Jasmine thought about what she said. Though she had made many mistakes herself, none of them involved disrespecting someone who didn't deserve it.

"Get up from the floor. I'm not changing my mind," she said coldly.

"Please, don't do this," Sasha cried.

Jasmine didn't respond. Sasha knew by the icy glare in her eyes that she wouldn't change her stance. Being on her knees made her feel like she had hit rock bottom. And when she saw Jasmine look at her calendar, she felt ignored. Sasha quietly got up from her knees and left the office.

Moments after Sasha had left, Ricky came rushing in, mad as the devil. "How dare you fire Sasha?" he yelled.

Jasmine gave him an evil look. She wanted him to know she was tired of the games. "Were you screwing her too?" Jasmine asked, staring him down into the ground.

Ricky didn't know how to respond. Jasmine guessed that in fact he was sleeping with Sasha.

"This is a business, Ricky. Not your own personal brothel. Grow up! I want you to help me run this company."

He stood pissed, wanting to debate what she had just said. Yet in the end he left her office. Jasmine had two victories, over Sasha and her brother, that she didn't want.

CHAPTER **NINE**

I n a dark, isolated Brooklyn alley, near three a.m., Teddy sat in a beat-up car with a scruffy thirty-something man named Kyle. By the weird look the man displayed, Teddy had clearly agitated him. The man often raised his voice to express his point. Teddy, on the other hand, remained nice and relaxed. A smile was stuck on his face. He barely paid attention to Kyle's erratic behavior until he pulled out a gun.

"I want my money!" Kyle said.

"You didn't complete the job," Teddy said, still calm as could be. The gun really didn't put any fear in him. Teddy knew that, more than anything, Kyle wanted to be paid.

"I got the money from her."

"But you didn't finish the job. The money was just to throw her off my trail."

"You expect me to kill someone who's dying?"

Teddy smirked. "She's still alive."

Kyle was amazed. For a moment, he just stared off in space, reflecting back on that foggy morning when Gloria was hit. All he remembered was how gruesome she looked with blood splattered everywhere.

"Damn. That old lady is tough as nails, but that doesn't change our deal."

"The mere fact that she's still alive changes it." Teddy frowned at Kyle's ignorance.

"Blame that shit on advancements in medicine. I still want my cut," Kyle said as he gave Teddy the evil eye. "You said run her over, and that's what I did."

Growing tiresome of the conversation, Teddy reached inside his suit jacket and pulled out one of the two sealed envelopes he had.

Kyle snatched it out of his hands, keeping the gun directed at Teddy's chest. Teddy was focused on the envelope, though. Something about the envelope made him uneasy.

"That should be all that you need," he said with a sly, nervous grin.

Kyle started to open the envelope. Teddy's eyes looked nervous, shifty.

"When have I not paid you? You gonna embarrass me in front of my face?"

Kyle put the gun away and looked at Teddy. "We still need to talk about the other arrangements. I'm not satisfied. It's my neck on the line."

Teddy sighed. "We discussed this over the phone. A deal is a deal. You're not thinking of crossing me, are you?"

Even though he had a gun, he was the one scared. Teddy was intimidating.

"Of course not. Who loves you, baby?" Kyle said jokingly. He hoped that their relationship could return to what it was before he pulled out his gun.

Teddy glanced at him. Kyle put his hand out for them to shake.

Teddy was hesitant in obliging. "If you fuck me on this…I swear, your children's children will be feeling my wrath."

Kyle's hand started to tremble a little. He felt apologetic.

"I didn't mean...I just thought since I did a great job on that other thing that maybe you would give me a little extra scratch. I deserve it. We go way back."

Teddy chuckled. "Greed. It's a funny thing. It's the reason men make money and the reason they die for it."

He abruptly got out of the car and slammed the door. Teddy walked down the gritty, stinky alley, whistling like he was strolling through a park on a Sunday afternoon.

Kyle grabbed the envelope and opened it. He saw only blank sheets of paper in it. He looked angrily at Teddy. The thought of running him down entered his mind.

"You trying to fuck me? I don't care who you are."

He gripped his gun and placed it on the passenger seat. Kyle started up the car, shifted it in drive, and pushed all the way down on the gas pedal. His car stormed down the alley toward Teddy.

Teddy heard the car roaring behind him. He pulled a remote device out of his pocket and pushed a button. Instantly, the car exploded into a fireball. Not once did Teddy turn around or even flinch. While the car and Kyle burned, he kept his stride and whistled to a steady beat until he disappeared in the darkness.

CHAPTER **TEN**

With Fashion Week only a month away, Jasmine kept her crew working their butts off, trying to find some hot and fresh designs. Riffling through the designs provided by her staff became frustrating, as the designs kept disappointing her. Locked up in her office for most of the day, she had to attend to the bulk of the Gloria Dean Corporation's business, which was outside of the fashion industry. Not to mention keeping the three-headed monster off her back: her sister, her brother, and Teddy.

She examined the latest sketches with a frown. None of the designs came close to the top quality that people were accustomed to seeing. She glanced at her desk calendar and shook her head when she saw that the new ad for the upcoming spring/summer season was due in two weeks. Jasmine turned and faced the window. Looking out over Manhattan made jumping seem like a great idea. The stress of being in her mother's shoes was not what she had bargained for. She wanted nothing more than to leave it all behind, but she knew that Teddy would swallow up Ricky and Jaymee with ease. Not that they understood that, because the inner fighting and plotting continued. Jasmine just prayed that her mother would wake up and once again take over the reins of the company.

She was startled when her new assistant, Karen, knocked on her door. "It better be good," she said, irritation written across her face.

Karen, a timid young white girl from Idaho came in as if walking on eggshells. Under her arm, she held a poster-size framed picture that was wrapped in brown paper.

Jasmine stared at Karen, hoping that she would give her a clue as to what it was. All Karen did was shrug her shoulders.

"Do I have anything on my schedule of great importance?" Jasmine asked.

"At four you have a meeting with—"

"The Donald. Damn. He's just like all the other vultures trying to capitalize on my mother's accident. Tell him I'll have to reschedule for next week."

"Okay."

"Don't just stand there. Bring whatever it is over here."

Jasmine's curiosity grew as the picture was dragged over to her. She eyed the packaging and stood up, curious to open it.

Karen stopped in her tracks, misreading Jasmine's look. "I really didn't mean to disturb you, but this came for you. The messenger said it was urgent."

Jasmine smiled. "They always say that. What is the picture of?"

Karen once more shrugged her shoulders. Jasmine saw the fear in Karen's face and remarked, "Don't be so timid. All the stories about me being a shark aren't true." She laughed. "Well, maybe some of it."

Her comment didn't go over so well with Karen. She got a huge lump in her throat.

"Lighten up, girl." Jasmine nudged her on the arm. "You're doing a fine job. Don't believe everything you hear. Work hard and be honest, and you'll go far here."

"I'm sorry. I just want to make sure I do a great job for you. I need my job."

Jasmine grabbed the picture. "Now, let's see what the surprise is all about."

She ripped off the paper and smiled. The picture was of her and Maxwell at the fashion show. She picked up the little card taped to the frame and opened it.

"Anytime, any place, I'll be there to catch you, Maxwell. Call me so we can do dinner."

She paused to think about it. Maxwell was a fine-looking man, and he could definitely take her to the places she was accustomed to dining. The fact that he was in the same business didn't appeal to her, though. Every man she had ever been involved with was in the fashion business, and every one of those relationships ended badly. Seeing his smile in the picture gave her a glimpse of hope that it would be different. *Just maybe*, she thought. Then the thought that she hadn't had sex in about a year came to mind. Her hormones raced. She gently rubbed the top of her chest bone. Always the romantic, Jasmine envisioned true love, but as she stared at Maxwell's face, only hot steamy sex came to mind.

"Is everything okay?" Karen asked.

Jasmine giggled like a schoolgirl. She hoped that might break the ice with Karen. It did, but in a different kind of way. Karen now thought she was weird.

"It couldn't be better," Jasmine answered. "Have you seen my brother, sister, or Teddy?"

"They've been cooped up in Ricky's office since lunch."

"Figures!" Jasmine smirked.

Karen slowly walked out the office door. "I'll go finish up that labeling you needed."

Jasmine paid her no mind. Maxwell's smile captivated her attention while she contemplated whether or not to sleep with him. That was the only dinner she really wanted: him on a platter.

***

The venetian blinds in Ricky's office blocked out much of the fading sunlight. The room still illuminated with the candles he had burning around the room. It was his way of adding an aura to his office whenever a model came in to audition with him. On the walls were poster-size pictures of him and all the famous people he had partied with, from J.Lo to Jay-Z and Denzel to Angelina Jolie. He called it his wall of fame. The centerpiece amongst his pictures was his hundred-inch plasma TV mounted on the wall.

Entrenched in his alligator-skin chair, Ricky looked as though he was doing his best to stay awake as Jaymee and Teddy sat across from him.

"We have to do something. I can't continue to work with her rules," Jaymee said as she stared at Ricky.

He felt her eyes upon him and sat up straight.

"Are we on the same page?" she asked the two men.

Jaymee didn't trust either of them, but they were both useful to a certain degree. She just didn't know which one better served her purpose for running the company. Their last attempt to screw her was stained on her brain. Even though, she was working on something new with Teddy, she didn't see it going anywhere. With Teddy's past history of failed plans, she assumed that it would turn out the same. Still, she had kept her word and did not mention a word of it to Ricky. The thing that did keep her curiosity going was the Randolph James connection and why they wanted her involved.

"You on deck?" Teddy asked. "We can't do this without you."

Ricky smirked. "How do I know I can even trust the two of you?"

Jaymee took offense. "I have only two words for the both of you. *Last time*," she said sternly. Jaymee glared at both of them.

Teddy put his hands up in a calling-timeout position. "Hold on. This is not about fighting each other. This is the time for us to reunite. I take total blame for what happened, but this is more about preserving your mother's legacy than anything else. I know she never wanted Jasmine back in the family, let alone running her precious company. That's idiotic!" Teddy said as smooth as silk. "You have my word on that."

Though his word was as good as a condom with a hole in it, Jaymee was willing to buy into what he was presenting. She remembered her conversation with her mother before the accident about her one day being in charge. Running the company was her destiny, and now was the time. No matter what it took, she was going to fulfill that dream.

Ricky stared at Teddy with fire in his eyes. "She's still family. No matter how I may feel, she's still my big sister. Whether she and Momma liked each other or not is not up for discussion. Jasmine is always welcome back into this family. Removing her from power is one thing. Removing her from this family is not an option."

"I'm just stating the obvious. They fought all the time," Teddy said, hoping to regain Ricky's support.

"You know Teddy is right. They were always at each other's throats," Jaymee chimed in, trying to help get Ricky back on their side.

"Then why did Momma put it in writing for her to be in charge? You don't think that's a little strange? She did it days before someone ran her down like a dog."

"She definitely wasn't in her right mind at the time," Jaymee said sarcastically. "Jasmine hasn't been around the business for over five years. This shit is foul."

"Exactly. You don't find it strange?" Teddy directed his question at Ricky.

"All I know is that Momma must have known she was in danger. Why else would she put that clause in writing prior to the accident happening? Answer that Chinese riddle. And stop acting like I'm crazy. Ever since she got here, Jasmine has been keeping us afloat. I'm not sure anymore."

"Sure about what?" Jaymee asked with a hint of acrimony.

"This!" Ricky replied, turning away from her.

"Ricky, you do this all the time. Quit thinking small."

Ricky huffed. "Me, thinking small? Now, that's funny."

"We have to focus on the future," Teddy said. "What's done is done. We all know Jasmine has many weaknesses that can destroy this company's reputation. What I propose to you all is a tri-leadership."

"What do you mean?" Jaymee wanted him to be clearer.

"All three of us run the company as one. We are the brain trust." Teddy smiled at the both of them. "Our knowledge base will make business a lot better, not just keep it afloat."

Ricky grunted in agreement. "Now, that's an idea I can flow with. Equal power between the three of us."

Jasmine came out of her office ready to go home. She looked over at Ricky's office down the hallway and heard the voices.

"Another top-secret meeting about me," she said dismissively as she closed her door.

Jasmine went to the elevator, carrying a box under her arm. When she reached the garage, it was cold and desolate. The box felt like it weighed a ton as she struggled to walk to her car. From out of nowhere a clean-cut white man, dressed in a suit, approached from behind. She felt his presence and increased her speed. He ran to keep up with her. With the box slowing her down, she dropped it and dug deep into her purse. The man slowed up as well. She turned to face him. He reached in his back pocket. She pulled out a gun. The man jumped back and fell on his butt in fear.

"What do you want?" she yelled. Memories of the house break-in came back. The last thing she wanted to do was to be in that situation again.

He was too scared to move or speak.

"I'll shoot if you don't tell me why you're following me in this garage. How did you get in here in the first place?" she asked as she looked around to see if he was alone.

He kept his eyes on her gun. "Can I..." He gestured to her so he could pull out whatever it was in his back pocket.

"Slowly," she said, keeping an eye on his movement as well.

He pulled out an envelope.

"What's that?" she asked.

He couldn't take his eye off the gun. He sweated as he read. "I hear by serve you to appear in court in the case involving the Gloria Dean Company versus Dee Winters."

He stretched out his arm to hand the summons to her. Jasmine snatched it. The man got up and ran off in the direction he came.

She glanced over the summons. After she finished, Jasmine crumbled it up and stuffed it in her purse.

"The nerve of that bitch, fuckin' on the job and still wanting to get paid." Jasmine laughed. "America is definitely the land of opportunity."

She realized that the gun was still in her hand. Before putting it back in her purse, she took another glance around to make sure no one else was there. She picked up her box, then continued her struggle to her car.

CHAPTER **ELEVEN**

n his attorney's office, Teddy sat back with his feet up on the desk, popping peanuts in his mouth. He was in an unusually good mood today. He had a glow about him that read, *I have a plan, and it's working.*

When his attorney, David Overmeirer, walked in, he was surprised to see the smile on Teddy's face. Teddy was always grumpy and demanding when they had meetings.

"I see that stick up your ass has disappeared," David said, turning up the corner of his lips at his own joke.

"I'm on fire. I tell you, on fire."

"So, what is the big news that you have for me?" David glanced over at him.

Teddy smirked. "I found a loophole in those bylaws. If anyone had cared to read more, they would have seen that it states that if Gloria is incapacitated for more than one hundred and twenty days, the will would revert to her basically being dead and the leadership of the company would go to the board to decide. After a leader is chosen, then I make my move. Gloria called it her Death Clause."

"What makes you think that the board will side with you? We've gone this route before and came up empty."

"Each child under this Death Clause gets twenty percent. Ricky, Jaymee, and I would control seventy percent after the vote. No one to stop me from there." Teddy smiled.

The lawyer seemed skeptical. "You know where I stand. Death to the queen at all costs, but this seems far-fetched."

"Believe me, at one hundred and twenty days, Ricky, Jaymee and I will become key players in gaining control of this company. I got the numbers."

"Interesting."

"I got those two fools in my back pocket." Teddy grinned.

"You still need someone else to join you," David replied. "The board vote still appear to be deadlocked."

"Always the pessimistic soul. How can the board go against me if I have the votes? The board votes are one person, one vote. I will have another board member on my side soon." Teddy winked at him.

"What are you talking about?" David asked. "Are you sure about all this?"

Teddy pointed to his desk. David looked down and picked up a document. He read the cover.

"The Triad. What the hell is that?" David flipped through a couple of pages. The more he read, the more excited he became.

"I call it my insurance plan. As you can read, I have formed a partnership with Ricky and Jaymee."

David stopped reading and looked up at him. He was stunned by something he had read. "They read this whole thing and agreed upon it?"

"Even had their attorneys look at it. Funny what attorneys cost these days." Teddy smiled.

"But it's only been sixty something days. That's a lot of time. What are you going to do if you are successful in gaining control?"

Teddy was hugely pleased as he replied, "Sell her company to the highest bidder. Then I hope she comes out of her coma. It will make her want to kill herself."

"The company is only a third of her worth. It won't hurt."

"Not financially, but psychologically she will feel my wrath. This company is the heart and soul of her dynasty. Without it, she's like a white guy in the NBA—just average."

"And with it, she's like the mob boss David Stern." David laughed.

"Now you're getting it."

"Teddy, I'm sure you've told me before, but why do you carry such a vendetta against her? She has made you very rich."

"I made her very wealthy too, don't forget."

David nodded in agreement, though they both knew Teddy was wrong. His father's investment team had helped take Gloria's empire to an almost invincible level. When his father came aboard, the only entity was the fashion business. His advisors showed her how to diversify into different markets to gain money from multiple streams.

"What about Richard and Jackie? You need one of them to turn in order to swing things in your favor."

Teddy winked. "I got a plan for them too."

***

In the Intensive Care Unit, Jasmine held her mother's hand and lowered her head to pray. On a chair next to Gloria's bed slept Jackie. He had come to the hospital the day before and only left to take a shower.

"God, please help my mother through these trying times. She has so much more life in her. I would rather you take me than her…"

Little did Jasmine know that behind her stood Jaymee. It was news to her that Jasmine felt that way about their mother. For her to make such an offer was a huge step. Every ill thought she had about her sister was now being questioned in her mind. Jaymee tried to step back out of the room, but she brushed up against the wall, causing a slight rustle.

Jasmine opened her eyes at the sound. At first she thought it was just the nurse, until she heard a voice.

"I'm sorry," Jaymee said. "I didn't think anyone would be here."

The sisters exchanged a significant look of regret. "Don't be sorry. I'm just praying that she gets back on her feet. Then I can get out of you guys' way."

Jaymee saw Jackie sleeping, and acted as if someone had thrown a stink bomb in the room. "What is he doing here?" she demanded. "I want him out!"

Jackie stirred but kept his eyes closed. He didn't move an inch. Jackie wanted to see what might be said about him.

"He's family," Jasmine said, looking at her like she had lost her last bit of sense.

"I think he had something to do with Momma being in here."

"Jackie? Are you kidding me? You want to have this discussion with him sleeping in the same room?"

"He's supposed to have Momma's back! If he was doing his fuckin' job, then we wouldn't be here right now. He ain't a Dean!"

"He's probably more Dean than all of us. Don't judge him."

Jaymee gave up on the Jackie-bashing and walked to the other side of the bed. She quickly grabbed Gloria's other hand. She didn't want to be outdone by her sister.

"I always thought you hated her," she said, still trying to figure out Jasmine's angle.

Jasmine smiled at her ignorance. "I never hated her. We did have our days, but I never stopped loving her. Just because I left doesn't mean that I never wanted to see her again. I felt we needed some space between us. That's all."

"I guess that's why she left you in charge." Jaymee gritted her teeth. Just saying the words irked her.

Jasmine gave her a funny glare and shook her head. "Even during a time like this, you can't let this feud go. Ever since we were kids, you always had to one-up me. Instead of learning from an older sister, you opted to tear me down whenever you could." Jasmine wasn't angry, just sad. "In the final analysis, I think that was the determining factor in Momma's putting me in control. She knew you wouldn't have even tried to bring the family together."

Jaymee didn't have time to deal with her sister's pat analysis of all the wrongs she thought had ever been done to her.

"So, did you go out with Maxwell?" she asked suspiciously.

"Who?" Jasmine asked, playing dumb.

***

In the parlor room at the Gloria Dean mansion, Jasmine was in high gear as she tried on different outfits. She showed the flair that made her once the biggest supermodel in the world. Slouched down on a nearby chair was her longtime girlfriend Cleo, who watched in agony. Though she was modeling the outfits like a pro, the clothes were outdated. Most of these clothes were from the last time she lived in the house five years ago. Nothing seemed to capture the essence of who she was, at least according to Cleo. But when she came out in a bright orange dress, her friend had seen enough.

"Are those your prison work clothes?" Cleo asked. She tried to keep a serious face. "Where are the cameras?"

"What? You don't like this?" Jasmine knew it was ugly, but she wanted to exhaust all options in her closet first.

Jasmine had a reason for inviting her friend over. Cleo, a model herself, was a social butterfly. She knew what was in before it became in. An amazing beauty, she was Black and Filipino with a rock-solid body. Her cheekbones were simply to die for. Every designer wanted to work with her. And almost every guy wanted to sleep with her. In the industry, she was known as the superdiva for her extravagant spending sprees and the many male suitors she kept.

"Hell, nawl." She giggled. "Take that off and burn it! Burn all of your clothes, I'd say. Just start from scratch."

"Cleo, this is serious. I need something to wear."

Cleo huffed. "He's just a man." That was easy for her to say since she wore a two-piece outfit designed only for her personally by Sean Combs, the owner of Sean John.

Jasmine looked at her sideways. "What does that mean?"

"All he cares about is how the booty works. I know you've heard about him." Cleo rolled her eyes.

Jasmine brushed off the remark. She wanted to give him a chance at least. "Those are just rumors. I'll judge him for myself, thank you. He seemed nice over the phone."

"Oprah don't lie. You can trust her. If she calls you untrustworthy, then you are."

"Women cannot live on Oprah alone. You act like she's God."

"She might as well be." Cleo smiled. "She needs to come back."

"What about that Frey guy?" Jasmine asked, disputing what she was trying to say.

"That was different. Oprah was hoodwinked. I know."

"The media painted me the same way." Jasmine slipped off the orange dress. "It's all about their precious headlines."

"What? They lied on you?" she asked with a slight grin. "About what?"

"Yeah," Jasmine sneered.

Cleo sat back in her seat. "The media didn't lie on you. You were dating a drug addict and your mother did make a big announcement that she fired you."

"Forget you, bitch," she said, laughing. "You're lucky we're tight like that. And I did quit!"

Jasmine put the dress back on the hanger and took it back in the closet.

"You still love me," Cleo yelled.

"I don't know why. Maybe I need a criticizing bitch in my life."

"No, it's because I'm the only one you can trust. I keep it real."

She came out of the closet. "Sho'nuff can't trust my family except for my dad and Jackie. You know, those assholes are having meetings at night about taking over the company from me." The thought of the secret meetings brought a frown to her face. "They could at least wait until Momma died or something. I don't want to be the one at the top."

"Are you really surprised?" Cleo raised a brow at her.

She sighed. "I guess not. I just wish things were different. We could get so much more accomplished around the company if they just worked."

"That Teddy is something else. I wouldn't trust him for anything in this world. He would definitely sell his mother to snag a coin." Cleo acted like she was sticking her finger in her mouth to vomit.

"My mother always thought he killed his father."

"Wouldn't surprise me at all. I bet Ricky and Jaymee are falling for whatever scheme he's planning."

Jasmine scratched her head. The influence that Teddy had on her sister and brother was tremendous. She didn't see any way to battle that. Everything she did was by the book. And Teddy never read that book. All he knew was how to be deceitful. The subject started to annoy her.

"So what now? I have nothing else to show you," she said.

All along Jasmine had an eye on Cleo's outfit. The relaxed, elegant style of the design was good for chillin' with friends at home or out on the town. The top was made from some rare silk found in China. It had one strap on the left shoulder and the length hung down a little past her waistline. The Jay-Z Blue stood out mainly because it complemented her eyes and the short, revealing skirt she wore. Together, it all said sex appeal.

Cleo saw Jasmine gearing up to ask her about the clothes on her back. Yeah, they were best friends, but there was no way she was going to have her girl looking like her. That was a cardinal no-no rule in her book. Cleo got up and grabbed her purse. "What you need is a miracle and I know where it's at. Come on."

Cleo headed toward the front door while Jasmine scrambled to get her clothes back on.

"Where are we going?" Jasmine asked.

Cleo smirked. "Just bring your ass with me!"

***

At one of the most exclusive boutiques on Madison Avenue, Jasmine and Cleo had the run of the store. Since the owner shut down the place for them, they thought they would easily find something to wear. Unlike at home, all the clothes looked fantastic. The choices were plentiful and picking one seemed to be impossible.

The owner brought out fabulous dress after fabulous dress, showcasing that no store had a better collection. The owner's assistant brought out cocktails and small sandwiches for them to snack on as well. It took over an hour, but when Jasmine saw an appealing and revealing outfit in the owner's hands, she snatched it. It was a dress from Max Azria, the competition.

"That's it," she said.

The grin on Cleo's face showed that she was also impressed.

"I'm jealous. He better appreciate you," Cleo said.

"You like it?" the owner said with a smile.

Jasmine couldn't control herself. She was so excited about the outfit. The past couple of years had been hard on her. Dealing with Tommy's drug problems and growing her own business from scratch had taken its toll on her social life. She never shopped or even got out. Fearing failure she continued non-stop. It had been nearly two years since she had bought something new.

"I'm taking them all," she said cheerfully.

The owner smiled and grabbed the other clothes that lay around them. She then strutted toward the back.

Jasmine put the clothes up against her body. She turned around and slightly glanced at her butt.

Cleo saw her and laughed. "You ain't no J.Lo. But your booty will do."

They laughed.

"I don't know why we are still friends." Jasmine walked closer to the mirror. She wanted to make sure the color scheme matched her skin tone. "I feel like my life is getting back to normal."

"Good," Cleo responded enthusiastically. "So, I hope that means you're going to stay. New York is your only true home. Like it or not, you are one of those crazy Deans."

Jasmine laughed. "For you, anything is possible." She blew Cleo a kiss.

"You know I'm a freak." Cleo winked at her.

"Dick me and lick me is my policy." Jasmine smirked.

Cleo fanned herself with her hand. "You makin' me hot. So, when are you and this Maxwell going out to dinner anyway?"

She glanced at herself in the mirror again. A little smile appeared on her face. Jasmine didn't mean to show that much excitement for the date, but her emotions and hormones couldn't hide it. This was the first real date she'd had in years.

"Friday night," she said as her eyes sparkled.

A thought must have crossed Cleo's mind, because she bit her lip, not wanting to spoil the moment.

Jasmine saw the look on Cleo's face. "Spit it out," she demanded.

"Well, the dress you bought is Max Azria and the others are..."

"I know. Am I supposed to be that closed off that I can't appreciate the work of the competition?"

"I guess not." Cleo shrugged her shoulders.

Jasmine smiled. The truth was that if her mother was around, she would have scolded her severely. It was Gloria's strict policy that when they went out of the house, they better be wearing Gloria Dean on their backs. She had always either designed or made her children's clothes from day one. It was a policy Jasmine had followed when she worked for her mother. It was also a tradition that she took with her in starting her Jazzie brand.

"I'll take out the tags. It'll be our secret." She winked at Cleo. "Plus, I look too good to pass this up."

"Looks like you're getting your mojo back." Cleo smiled.

"I'm just trying to compete with you modern-day hoes." Jasmine snickered.

Cleo looked at her like that was never going to happen. "I hope you got your A game."

CHAPTER **TWELVE**

The next morning seemed like heaven for Jasmine. Her mind was consumed with thoughts of her upcoming date with Maxwell, and how stunning she was going to look. The dress lay next to her while she slept. Throughout the night, she would wake up and admire it. She imagined him slipping the dress off her, his big strong hands caressing her body sensually, arousing every fiber of her being. Based on Maxwell's reputation, he was versed in sexing women down. Rumor had it that he was well hung and had many women strung out wanting more. But Maxwell was the kind of guy who hated needy women. So, when the strong became the weak, he became the ghost.

Hearing the birds chirp, smelling the fresh morning dew, kicked her day off right. She was filled with so much optimism that nothing could get in her way of enjoying this day. Only positive thoughts were in her head, and that's the way she intended it to stay.

After finishing a hearty breakfast, she strolled out of the front door, whistling. She basked in the glorious sunshine that was shining down on her and jumped in her mother's antique 1956 Rolls-Royce. Her facial expression was upbeat as she neared the security gate. Yet then her mood plummeted like an anchor. She took a double take to be sure she was seeing correctly. What she saw was a homeless-looking man standing outside the gate, resting against a pole. The gate opened and the man stood up. She fretted as she drove out the gate. Her first thought was to run him over, but instead she stopped. The man swaggered to her window with an air of confidence that everything was in his control.

Jasmine couldn't face him. "Tommy, what do you want?" she asked, knowing that it was about money.

Tommy laughed out loud. He reeked of booze and musk. His ratty clothes were hard on the eyes.

Tommy was a forty-year-old Russian who stood five foot six. He weighed about a hundred fifty pounds. At one time, he was one of the most famous photographers in the world, but he got caught up with the wrong people and drugs took over his life. If he cared to clean himself up he would be a handsome man. But Tommy was now hooked forever. No rehab could cure his thirst for chasing the ultimate high.

"Babe, you left me. I came back to sleep one night, and you were gone."

"I've moved on!"

"Literally," Tommy said angrily.

She took a deep breath. Jasmine knew he must have seen her on TV at the fashion show. That was the only way he would have been able to find her. She had kicked Tommy out of her home in Baltimore over a year ago and moved to a new place so that he wouldn't be able to find her.

"What was there left for us to talk about? You left me to die." She glared at him.

He moved closer to her car window. "Whatever happened to 'until death do us part'? Unless you forgot, you are still my wife." He smiled.

The frown that graced her angelic face showed signs of a woman broken. She had tried her best to rid herself of him. Tommy was a part of her past that she desperately wanted to forget. Her grip on the steering wheel tightened. She wished that the steering wheel was his neck. Jasmine was willing to do whatever it took to get him out of her life. She just wanted it to be a permanent solution.

"What do you want?" she growled. "I have nothing to give you."

He took a look at the mansion and stepped back from the car to admire it as well. He huffed at her, thinking that she was messing with his intelligence.

"What about a piece of the good life?" He smiled. "Plus, Tucker's money."

"I paid Tucker off!"

"What about me?" Tommy asked.

"I'm for real. I really have nothing," she said, trying to convince him.

He suddenly reached inside the car and grabbed her by the collar. She pulled away and stuck her hand in her purse.

He backed off a little. "That's hard to believe. No money. Come on, Jazzy. Do I have *stupid* written on my forehead? You owe me. I know dear Mom won't mind."

In reply, she put her foot on the gas and roared off down the street. He kicked his foot up in the air, pissed that she had left him empty-handed.

***

Jasmine was feeling intense and irritated when she finished the presentation of the spring clothing line to the department heads. To add to her pressure, Ricky and Jaymee had finally attended a meeting. And with Tommy resurfacing, her whole life seemed terrible. She knew paying him off was the only option she had. Her focus for most of the day had been to figure out a way to get rid of him forever. Tommy wasn't the type to spend the money cautiously. He would definitely return for more.

When she went to cut off the projector, she was met by total silence. It angered her that no one had commented during the presentation. *What else do they want?* she asked herself.

"Are there any questions?" Jasmine asked, eyeing her siblings.

Everyone looked to the other person to respond. Jaymee smacked her lips and rolled her eyes. Her dislike for Jasmine never seemed more obvious. Her feud with Jaymee didn't bother her that much, but when it got in the way of how she ran the business, that crossed the line. She couldn't risk the staff losing confidence in her leadership.

A devilish look crossed her face, and Jaymee raised her arm in the air. At that moment, the tension elevated to a much higher level. Everyone figured Jaymee was up to no good. This was the face-off everyone had thought would eventually occur. The only question unanswered was how would Jasmine handle it.

"Oh, I have a question." Jaymee smiled.

Jasmine didn't know where it was headed, but nodded for her to proceed. She braced herself, expecting the worse from her sister. By the snickering smile on Jaymee's face, she knew a sucker punch was coming soon.

"How come this is the first time I'm seeing these designs? Unless I'm wrong, I still work here." She chuckled thinly. "You can't run this company all by yourself."

Jasmine dismissed Jaymee's accusation in short order. "If you would like to discuss this later, we can talk in my office."

Jaymee glanced around the room at everyone else, but silence prevailed. Nobody wanted a part in her feud with Jasmine. Her brother nudged her on the leg under the table to stop. Yet instead of tabling the discussion, she continued to call into question her sister's leadership.

"No," Jaymee said to Ricky. "We need to get this madness out in the air right now, right here. I want to know why you're keeping information about the new designs from us. Are you running a dictatorship around here? You're clearly not Gloria Dean!"

Ricky dropped his head in shame. He was always willing to back Jaymee, but this was clearly way over the limit for him.

Jasmine did not take up the sword, however. She deferred to Karen, her assistant, to respond. Karen couldn't believe what Jaymee had just blabbered out.

"I gave all the submitted designs from the design team to you, Ricky, and Mr. Hicks to review two weeks ago, requesting input." Karen was pissed off that Jaymee tried to make it look like she wasn't doing her job. The normally timid Karen was steamed. "And I never heard anything back from any of you. I even got e-mail confirmation that you viewed the e-mail."

Jaymee fanned Karen's heat off with her hand. She kept her eyes focused on Jasmine.

"I don't care what she did. I want to know what you did," Jaymee said. "If we're a team, then I would love for us to be that way."

The charade was growing tiresome to Jasmine. She put both fists on the table and looked directly in Jaymee's eyes. "As my assistant, Karen sent you the designs. If you don't bother looking in your in-box and don't come to important meetings, then maybe this isn't the place for you."

Ricky leaned over and whispered to Jaymee, "Give it up. You are looking stupid."

Jasmine gave her ample time to reply. Seeing Jaymee had finally shut up, she proceeded to talk to the group again. It felt great to win the face-off. She would have preferred to do it in private, but being able to show her leadership abilities wasn't so bad either.

"If there are no more questions, this meeting is adjourned."

The department heads bolted out of the conference room. Ricky did likewise. Jaymee wasn't as lucky. Jasmine made a point of beating her to the door. She slammed it shut before Jaymee could escape.

"What do you think you're doing?" Jaymee asked, trembling a bit in fear.

Jasmine raised her fist, and Jaymee quickly backed up. "Don't hit me," she whimpered.

Jasmine lowered her fist and pointed her finger instead. She knew what a coward Jaymee was underneath. Her reaction was the same as when they were growing up. Jasmine tried to be a good big sister, but Jaymee was always jealous.

"Don't you ever try that ghetto shit again," Jasmine said evenly. "This is a billion-dollar business and you are acting like a damn kid. You want to clear the air with me? Then do it now. Ain't nothing but air and opportunity between us. Please take the opportunity."

"This is my company," Jaymee cried. "It's not fair."

Jasmine realized, though she should have known, that her sister had some deep-seated delusions. She felt it was only right to set her straight.

"Until it says Jaymee Dean on the sign outside, this is Momma's company. And as long as I am here, you will respect her decision. I love you, but you and Ricky's shit is getting very old, very fast." She paused for a second and added a long-overdue warning. "Don't get on my bad side."

Jasmine opened the door, and her sister scampered out. *When will she learn?* Jasmine thought.

When Jasmine returned to her office, she was astonished to see Ricky standing by the window, admiring her view of the city. She entered cautiously, wondering what he could want. "What are you doing?"

"Momma wouldn't want us to be fighting like this," he said, continuing to look outside. "This is a time when we should be strong as a family."

His sincerity caught her by surprise. She didn't know if it was for real or not. Instead of cutting him off and banishing him from her office, though, she decided to see where the conversation was headed. If there was anyone who could see her side of things, it was her brother.

"So, what brought about this change of heart? I thought I was the devil around here."

"Nawl, the devil wears Prada." He grinned lamely. "Look, the first thing I want to say is, I'm sorry about the lawsuit. I never thought Dee would take it that far."

Jasmine wanted to say something sarcastic. She knew he was old enough to know better than to screw a model that was working for them, but she held her tongue.

"If you want me to testify, I will. Anything for the company." He stretched his back.

She was still trying to get a read on this sudden change. In her heart, she wanted to trust him, but the thought of all the private meetings, of them plotting her downfall, wouldn't disappear just because he took the initiative to talk to her.

"I hope you mean that."

He turned to face her, then flashed his charm. "I'm not Jaymee. I know it's not easy being the oldest child in this dysfunctional family. I remember you did a lot for us."

Whether he was sincere or not didn't matter at this point. It was good to hear that he had remembered all she had done for him. It was like seeing your child grown up. She sighed and approached him with open arms.

"Where has my little brother gone?"

They embraced.

"I grew up, that's all. I'm still the same."

She pulled away slightly. "You know that I'm not here to run you guys off. I'm here to protect the company. Momma had enough faith to put me in this position, and I'm not going to fail her."

He exhaled slowly. "It's just hard for Jaymee. She's been playing second fiddle to you her whole life. This was supposed to have been her golden opportunity to run the company, and now she's dying inside."

The phrase *tough cookie* was the first thing that came to her mind.

"You know, once Momma gets better, I'm gone. I don't want to get in her way." Jasmine put a hand on his shoulder. "How do you feel about me being here?" she asked.

"No sugar on it?" he said with a snicker.

"Give me the fat-free version." She laughed.

"Okay. It hurts, but..."

Ricky stopped talking as Teddy walked in the office. The brother-sister moment disappeared.

"You have a minute?" Teddy asked Jasmine.

"You do know about knocking?" She gave him a dirty look. Jasmine had been enjoying the sudden truce with Ricky.

Teddy would have left, but once he saw Ricky, he came right in.

"We're all family here, right? No secrets." Teddy gazed at him suspiciously, and Jasmine could guess the reason for his concern. He didn't know if Ricky had sold them out or not. He couldn't afford for him to trade sides now. Ricky was vital to the success of whatever conspiracy he was hatching.

Jasmine plopped down in her chair. "So what do you want...Uncle T?" she asked wearily. Whatever he had on her brother, she aimed to find out.

Teddy smiled. "Where's Jaymee at?"

Ricky peeked at his watch. "She went to get Brittany."

***

"Muthafucka, I said by five o'clock," Jaymee screamed at the top of her lungs.

She stood outside her brownstone, pointing her fist at the window of a maroon Mercedes-Benz CL 550 coupe.

After her long bout of cussing, the driver let down his window. He was a handsome brown-skinned man, wearing dark-rimmed Prada eyeglasses. Kenny Mayfield was Jaymee's off-and-on boyfriend. He was also the father of her daughter, Brittany. Sitting behind Kenny in the car was their eight-year-old daughter. She sat quietly while Jaymee finished her tirade. Surprisingly, the girl resembled Jasmine.

Kenny stared at Jaymee like she had lost her mind. It was apparent this scene was a recurring one.

"Get my child out of that car," She continued to talk at the top of her voice.

"It was five after five when I pulled up. Why you trippin'?"

"That's my five minutes," she snarled.

"Calm down. Damn. I'm not doing this in front of Brittany anymore." He was pissed off. Seeing her neighbors peeking through the curtains made his embarrassment all the worse.

Jaymee glanced in the backseat and saw her daughter's stricken face. She hated that Brittany was placed in the middle of their fights. She couldn't seem to control her anger. Though Kenny was steaming mad, he knew how to confront it.

"Brittany, run into the house. I have to talk to your mother...okay?" he said calmly.

She got out, kissed her dad on the cheek, and slowly dragged herself into the house, her head hanging. Once she went inside, he stepped out of the car and leaned against it. He towered over her.

"Jay, you can't keep doing that shit. We always said we wouldn't show her that bullshit. I don't like it."

"I'm sorry," she replied, full of regret for her actions.

"Sorry don't cut it. Why do you think we broke up?" he asked, hoping to jog her memory.

"I should be running that company."

"Damn!" Kenny slit his eyes at her. "I should be president of the United States, but I ain't bitchin' over it in front of my child. You got a great life. Who cares who runs it? You all have a level of comfort that most people will never see."

"You don't understand." She pouted.

"I never did. Where I'm from, we make lemonade with our lemons, not throw them at everybody."

She broke down crying, but he didn't want to comfort her. This routine was tiring for him. Nothing had changed with her. He wanted them to be a family again, but that issue was up to Jaymee. She needed to let go of the business in order for that to happen. Hesitantly, he went and held her.

"This feels so good," she said. "I've fucked up so much with us. I don't know why you still care."

"The important thing is that you don't mess it up with your daughter," he said, gazing into her eyes.

"Somebody should have told my mother that."

He started to say something, then realized it would only lead to more discussion of her work. The subject he hated to hear about most. It had destroyed their relationship and was on track to destroy Brittany's childhood as well.

"When she gets better, just sit down and talk to her," he said.

"About how she prefers Jasmine over me?" she said bitterly. "I don't want to be around for that conversation. I was betrayed. I gave my all to her, and she just kicked me in the teeth. She told me that she was grooming me for the future." Her sniffles had come to an end by now, and she fetched a tissue out of her purse. "But I'm okay. She and her precious Jasmine have a big surprise coming."

Kenny saw the evil in her eyes. It was another story that he didn't want to be part of.

"What are you planning on doing?"

"Nothing," she said with a tight smile.

"You can't blame your sister for taking over. Your mother made that decision."

She kissed him on the cheek. "Good night, Kenny," she said, sauntering off toward her house.

Kenny couldn't help but wonder what evil plan that she was going to unleash. He wished he could say something to stop her from going through with it. Yet he knew that once she set her mind on something, stopping her was almost impossible.

CHAPTER **THIRTEEN**

After a long day at work, Jasmine dragged herself to her car. Her feet hurt and she had a migraine that felt like someone was physically squeezing her head. The parking garage was almost empty. As she made her way over to her car, she saw Tommy leaning up against the Rolls-Royce.

He smiled as she approached. "It's payday," he said, rubbing the hood of the car. "I should buy one of these."

She instantly dug into her purse. Her hand gripped something, but it remained inside.

Tommy laughed. "You gonna shoot me."

She actually wasn't sure what her next move would be. His drug-lined face gave her the creeps. Jasmine wasn't a killer, but the thought had crossed her mind a few times. Tommy was that typical bad guy who her mother and father hated. But out of spite for her mother, she pursued the relationship. After love came marriage, and then she discovered Tommy's addiction. Thinking he would change, she stuck it out and tried to help him beat the disease. Now, having left that part of her life, she desperately wanted to do the same to him. The last thing she wanted was to have him continue to come in and out of her life at will.

"I know you didn't think I was going to go quietly."

Across the way, in his dark-tinted Benz, Teddy watched, unnoticed by them.

"You never do," she said with regret.

Since Tommy had reappeared, she had hardly got any sleep. It was pure torture knowing that he was creeping around. She grabbed an envelope inside her purse and tossed it over to him.

He snatched it out of the air like a dog catching a Frisbee. Tommy quickly glanced inside of it. A huge smile graced his face.

"That's my girl," he said, still focusing on the money inside the envelope.

"Just leave me alone," she begged. "I paid Tucker everything. I'm through with you."

He strolled over to her. She clutched hold of her gun in the purse again, but didn't pull it out for him to see. Tommy stopped dead in his tracks.

From his car, Teddy saw that he was counting money. That piqued his interest even more. *What is she hiding?*

"This will do," Tommy said.

"I don't want to see you ever again. I swear, Tommy, I'll kill you." Her frustration showed on her face. She hoped this was really the end.

He glared at her. "Is that a threat, my lovely wife?"

She was not going to stand for being challenged. "The divorce papers will be sent to you next week. Sign them and I'll send you the rest."

"Where did the love go?" he asked jokingly.

She didn't respond as she opened her car door. At one time, she loved him so much that she gave up her family to be with him. Now she hated him so much that it gave her ulcers when he was around.

With his mission accomplished, Tommy strolled off with the money in his hand.

***

On a brisk Friday evening, at Bouley, Jasmine came in sweating slightly. She had run up Greenwich Street, past Washington Market Park, in order to not be too late. With Maxwell in sight, she flicked her hair with her hands. She hoped that would do the trick. His eyes lit up as he gazed at her exquisite beauty heading toward him. Jasmine reached his table and stood at her chair.

"Finally!" He smiled.

Her eyes sparkled. "I hope you're not mad at me. I'm not one of those women who have to be fashionably late."

A bead of sweat rolled down her cheek, and she grabbed the napkin off the table to wipe it off.

He laughed. "They do have valet service. You ran didn't you?"

"It was faster to park myself." Her eyes drifted down toward her chair.

"Well, it's nice to see you again." He laughed again.

"What's so funny?" she asked.

"Please, take a seat," he insisted.

Jasmine didn't move one inch. She wasn't a prima donna or anything like that, but her mother had instilled in them that a man should treat you like a woman at all times.

Maxwell looked stumped, not knowing what she expected him to do. She imagined that he was so successful, most women catered to him. Not until the waiter came up to pull out her chair that he finally got it.

"Oh, I'm sorry. I don't know where my head is at." He quickly rose to his feet to pull out the chair for her.

"You do realize you got the number one pick."

As she sat down, she kept her eye on him. His strong masculine physique made her melt. Maxwell did have a body like LL Cool J, but it was his eyes that captivated her heart. She hadn't been with a man for a long while. She had had about one good year together with Tommy, then it went downhill. What she saw in Maxwell was a fresh start. He didn't know, but she'd had thoroughly checked him out by a police friend to make sure he wasn't involved in drugs or any other criminal activity, like his music suggested.

He smiled at her. "Looks like a championship year."

"I have to keep an eye on you…Kobe." She grinned.

"Take a picture. Better yet, let me take your picture. You look so beautiful, Shaq."

She raised an eyebrow. "You know how they ended."

He winked at her. "I'm talking about the championship years."

They laughed and gazed into each other's eyes. Both of them studied the other's moves, liking what they saw in each other.

"So, who is Maxwell Kennedy?"

Maxwell smiled. "I'm the rose the concrete couldn't hold."

"Oh, really." She laughed. "So, what are you looking for?"

"You," he said, smiling into her eyes.

***

Around eleven-thirty that night, Jasmine headed home on cloud nine. Her evening with Maxwell had been splendid. He was the perfect gentleman. She felt like a schoolgirl, driving home with a stupid grin stuck on her face. Though it was only lust, she thought a love connection was possible and sex was imminent.

As she turned down the lonely street to the mansion, her cell phone rang. The call ended her passionate thoughts. Seeing a familiar name on the caller ID, she rushed to answer it.

"Girl, he sang to me at dinner," she said full of excitement.

It was Cleo on the other line. "So, I take it things went well."

"I melted…I don't care what the media says about him."

"You didn't sleep with him?" Cleo asked, like a mother would ask her teenage daughter.

"No, of course not."

"Good!"

I should have, Jasmine said to herself.

She thought back to their good-night kiss at her car. He grabbed her seductively by the waist and kissed her with his luscious full lips. Her body tingled all over. She wanted more, but knew she couldn't put out on the first date. That in her book was a definite no-no.

"So, is the wedding scheduled yet?" Cleo asked jokingly.

"I'm not going to lie, I want him. Not just sexually, but that boy's body is tight. I hugged him and I thought I..." She laughed.

"Take it slow, freak," Cleo said, being serious.

"I will for you," she said to appease her friend.

In reality, Jasmine had to appease her hormones first. If the opportunity presented itself, she had already determined that she was going to sleep with him. It was like his body was calling her and she had to pick up the phone.

"When are you two going out again?" Cleo asked.

"We're going to a celebrity mixer at the Plaza next Friday."

Cleo got excited herself. "That's great. I'm going there also. It'll be like old times."

"I hope not." Jasmine rolled her eyes. She glanced at the street sign and realized her house was only a couple of blocks away. "Hey girl, I'll call you tomorrow. I'm going to give him a call while I'm thinking about him. Bye."

"Sprung," Cleo said as she hung up.

Jasmine started searching through her cell phone for his number. Right when she found it, a patrol car flew past her. She glanced down the street and saw a multitude of people, lights, and police officers near the mansion. She sighed in disbelief. Her blissful glow disappeared the closer she got. With only her staying there, she thought it must have been a break-in.

"What's going on?" she asked herself, astonished by the bright lights.

A police officer flagged her over. "You can't come in here," he said, peeking inside her vehicle. "You have to turn around and go home."

"I live there." She pointed at the mansion. "That is my home."

"Please hold up," he instructed her.

Jasmine braced herself for the worst. By the officer's seriousness, she knew it was more than a break-in. She jumped out of the car, her eyes fixed on the windows of the house. She got a glimpse of several officers talking in the kitchen.

"What happened?" she asked, praying that no one was dead.

The officer saw the deep concern on her face. "I take it you're Mrs. Dean?"

"It's my mother's house. I'm Jasmine," she said, trembling. "What happened?"

"There's been a homicide. Come with me...please?" he asked.

She panicked, thinking one of her siblings had been killed. Though they were at odds, the office situation didn't change her love for them. To her recollection, only she, Jaymee, Jackie, and Ricky had keys. Her heart began to race. Everything became blurred. She couldn't take the pressure anymore, so she stopped walking. Her legs felt like a ton of bricks.

"No, no. Tell me who it is?" she demanded.

People in the street stared at them, gossiping amongst themselves. The Dean family had been a mystery to those in the neighborhood. To protect her privacy, Gloria made a point not to socialize with the neighbors, no matter who they were. In her neighborhood were the elite of New York City. But she didn't care. Gloria called her neighbors pooparazzi—people just waiting to drop shit on her name.

The officer did his best to maintain control of the situation. "Believe me, we're trying to figure that out right now as well. I hate to ask you to do this, but someone needs to identify the body. All we know is that it's a male. We saw no forced entry. Was anyone here this evening?"

"I gave everyone the night off," she said softly. "I'm the only one living here right now."

"An unidentified person called the murder in as a disturbance."

In her mind, it could only be Ricky. Jackie was too careful and cunning for anyone to catch him by surprise. Jasmine instantly thought about how her mother would take the news of her baby being dead when she came out of the coma. The thought *I failed miserably* crossed her mind.

"Do you want to wait? We can do this at the morgue downtown." The officer looked like this was the part of the job he hated.

The thought of going to the morgue was too intimidating for Jasmine. Imagining her brother lying in a cold steel file cabinet made her skin crawl. She mustered up some hidden strength she didn't think she had.

"No, I'm ready."

They walked up the circular driveway, passing TV crews, policemen, and the nosy neighbors. Her head dropped when she saw the yellow caution tape near the front door. Unexpectedly, Jasmine's cell phone rang. It was Maxwell calling. She gazed at the screen with longing for a brief second, then turned it off.

At the door, she took a deep breath. It was almost like moving in slow motion. As she entered the house, her eyes roved in every direction, trying to figure out what had happened. The policeman guided her to the kitchen. She noticed that there had been a struggle by all the broken items on the floor. She winced and became ill as she spied a big puddle of blood on the floor. They walked around the long kitchen island. She saw some work boots pointing up toward the ceiling. By the size of them, they surely belonged to a man. She started having some hope that it might not be Ricky. He only wore Air Jordans or Italian-made shoes.

The officer saw the man's face first. "I'll be right here with you," he said softly.

He grabbed her by the hand and they went to the other side of the caution tape, where some policemen blocked the person's face from her. The officer with Jasmine nodded at them and the men stepped out of the way.

Jasmine closed her eyes and prayed. They stepped close enough for her to fully see the face. Jasmine was shocked when she opened her eyes and saw that it was Tommy. A part of her was relieved, knowing he wouldn't bother her anymore. Yet she stared at his sliced throat, mortified by the blood.

"Do you know him?" the officer asked.

She was so revolted, she took a moment to clear her throat. Even though they despised one another, she was once in love with him. Her heart ached as she turned and clutched the officer's chest.

"That's my ex-husband. I mean, my husband. His name is Tommy Cannon."

Under the officer's arm, Jasmine noticed a cuff link on the floor under the sink. Her eyes grew big, thinking how she could retrieve it without the police noticing. She headed over to the sink and forced herself to dry retch. Jasmine pretended to drop her purse and bent down to grab it. Right when she leaned over, though, another officer beat her to it. She did get a better look at the cuff link and saw the initials RD engraved on them.

"Are you going to be okay?" the officer asked.

"I'm okay," she replied, half thinking that Ricky had killed Tommy.

"We need to take you down to the station to answer a few questions for the detectives. Is that okay with you?"

Jasmine nodded. A crime technician reached down and covered the body. The officer followed her out the door.

***

In his pajamas, with his back against the headboard, Ralph Perkins, Gloria's attorney, went through some of the Gloria Dean Company documents. He reached a certain part and stopped. His frown grew every time he reread the section that bothered him. He reached over to his nightstand and grabbed his Franklin Covey day planner. He quickly flipped to the date that Gloria went to the hospital, and then to the present date. He started counting on his fingers.

"This is a catastrophe," he said with a bug-eyed look.

He leaned over and grabbed the phone. Before he finished dialing Jasmine's number, his phone rang. He answered it.

"Hello."

"Mr. Perkins, this is Jaymee Dean."

Ralph glanced down at his watch. It was after one in the morning. It was crazy enough that he was going to call Jasmine, but that call was necessary. He represented her interest in the company. For Jaymee to call him, it must have been serious—especially since she never liked him, mainly due to his influence on her mother.

"Is everything all right?"

"Jasmine is in jail or something like that," she replied, sounding frazzled. "I didn't know what else to do besides call you."

Ralph was already clambering out of bed. "Which precinct did they take her to?"

"The one on Park Avenue South." She ruffled through some papers. "Two twenty-five Park Avenue South. I'm going down there to get her."

"What happened?" Ralph asked.

"Tommy, her husband, was murdered."

"What? Doesn't he live in D.C. or something like that?" Ralph asked. He was confused by the way Jaymee was talking.

"I guess he came back and someone killed him in the mansion."

Ralph was alarmed by what she said. "Who did it? Not Jasmine, right?"

"Nobody knows," she said.

"Jaymee, if you make it to the police station before I do, make sure Jasmine doesn't say anything to them until I get there. Okay?"

"Sure," she said as they hung up.

CHAPTER **FOURTEEN**

New York City's wee hours of the night invited crime without limits. This was the time when seemingly normal people turned into wolves. The jail cells at the precinct house were filled up. Down a long corridor, a short distance away from the madness at the booking entrance, was the interrogating room. In the small room with two chairs and a table, lead detective Jake Lennar faced a mournful Jasmine. Another detective, Anthony LoForte, stood off in the corner just staring at her. Every couple of minutes, he would pace across the room to further intimidate her.

They all looked exhausted. Jasmine had told them the same story over and over for the past forty-five minutes. Jake kept trying to shake her story, and his partner acted like he couldn't care less. She knew what Lennar thought. She was a spoiled rich kid, and since she was black, that only made it worse. No matter what she said, in his mind, the case was closed. She had motive and she had opportunity.

After Jasmine had finished telling the story for the seventh time, they sat in silence for a couple of minutes. The detectives continued to stare at her. The temperature in the room gave her goose bumps. She rubbed her arms to stay warm. Tired of the silence and cold atmosphere, she stood up to leave. The detective in the corner put his hand on the door to block her path.

"Sit down, Ms. Dean," he said in a calm tone. "Unless you have something to hide."

She threw up her hands in exasperation "This is bullshit. I told you all I know! You can't hold me. I know my rights."

Lennar leaned back in his chair. She was right; he didn't have anything on her. But since she hadn't asked for an attorney, they were going to keep the pressure on until she gave them a confession.

"Murder solved," he said sarcastically, glancing at Anthony. "Sit your ass down," Lennar yelled. "I can make your life a living hell."

"You act like I killed him. I told you I was at dinner with Maxwell Kennedy."

"Now, how does a married woman go out to dinner with a known gang member? What husband wouldn't get mad?" He winked at his partner. "He caught you probably in bed with this Maxwell guy. A fight ensued. Maxwell shoots him. Then you and Maxwell stage the crime scene and leave for dinner. You come back and play the innocent victim." Jake got up in her face. "I know your type. You think money can buy you anything!"

Jasmine rolled her eyes. "Really! It's amazing how ignorant the police can be at times. Even I know rap music is about the streets, but that doesn't mean that the artist came from those streets. It's just music. Elton John and Luther Vandross sang about making love to women, but they're gay," she said cynically. "By the way, I hope you're not the brains around here. Tommy was killed with a knife, not a gun."

Her comment fired them both up. Pointing out their ignorance only aggravated the situation. Then the door burst open. Ralph stepped inside fuming.

"What are you doing with my client?" he said in a frosty voice.

Jasmine stood against the wall, eyeballing the two of them. The detectives looked afraid. Ralph walked over to Jasmine.

"Are you all right?" he asked, keeping an eye on the men.

"I'm fine. I just want to get out of here," she whispered.

"We're leaving now—unless the detectives have evidence that would implicate my client?" He glared at them. "I will be talking to your lieutenant."

The detectives didn't say a word. Ralph saw the pain in Jasmine's face. He consoled her by placing his arm around her. He then ushered her out the door.

When they got to the lobby of the police station, Jaymee appeared out of nowhere. Jasmine shook her head briefly to make sure she wasn't delusional. What amazed her most were the tears Jaymee had in her eyes. She cared to come down to the station at this late hour.

Jaymee hugged her. "Are you all right?"

Jasmine took a deep breath to process all the strange things that had happened to her that night. She didn't know how to read her sister.

"I don't know," Jasmine said, tearing up.

"I'm sorry about Tommy. I know you did love him at one time," Jaymee said sincerely.

Jasmine nodded in acknowledgment but didn't respond. Being able to trust her sister was too bizarre. Jaymee had been nothing short of Satan since she returned. Accepting this new person would take more than a moment to absorb.

"I have a couple of spare bedrooms at the house you can sleep in if you like," Ralph offered. "You can't go back to the mansion!"

Jaymee stepped in. "No, my sister will stay with me. I won't have it any other way."

Jasmine didn't care where she stayed as long as she could get some sleep. The whole night had been overwhelming. With the murder and now Jaymee's kindness, the memories of her fabulous date with Maxwell seemed ages ago.

Jasmine gave Ralph a surprised look. He knew exactly what she meant by her expression. It was peculiar to him as well. Seeing a possible opportunity to patch up their dislikes gave her hope that Jaymee had finally seen the light. Jasmine felt open to seeing where the opening might lead her.

"Ralph, thanks for the offer, but I'm going to stay with Jaymee for the night," Jasmine said.

"You can stay as long as you like," Jaymee said as she tightly gripped Jasmine's hand.

Jasmine didn't respond to her comment. She hugged Ralph and they started to walk off.

"Wait, Jasmine," Ralph hollered after her. "Tomorrow, we need to talk. I'll call you."

"About what?" she asked.

Just then Jasmine noticed her sister's eyes light up like a firecracker. She wanted to learn the information now, but this newfound buddy-hood with Jaymee made her leery. In the back of her mind, she figured it was a part of a bigger scheme to wrestle the company from her hands. Jaymee's angle was the puzzling part.

"Get some sleep," Jasmine said lightly. "I'll call you in the afternoon." She glanced at Jaymee, who looked disappointed. Good, Jasmine thought. So it will just remain our secret.

CHAPTER **FIFTEEN**

I t was dreary; the clouds hugged each other, forming light showers throughout the day. Even though the weather was forbidding, Tommy's funeral was beautiful. Jasmine went all out in, making the best possible arrangements. Since they were still married at the time of his death, she felt a respectful ceremony was expected of her. A quarter of the attendees at the ceremony were family and friends of hers, and the rest were reporters hoping to find a story. Jasmine wore a black dress and a veil that covered her face. The eyes of everyone there were upon her. By now the news of their estranged relationship was out. Inquiring minds wanted to know how she really felt and to figure out if she could have murdered him. Though the police had no evidence, Jasmine remained their prime suspect.

Jasmine got up to deliver the eulogy. She stumbled as she passed by the casket, though, and Ricky helped her to the podium. In her mind flashed images of Tommy's bloody, unmoving body lying on the kitchen floor. It was still a mystery to her why someone killed him in the mansion. She glanced at the few people in attendance as the flashbulbs from the cameras hit her eyes like waves of fireworks.

"We all must eventually die," Jasmine said, shocking everyone. "What I mean is, God has a plan for us all to come home at different times. I wished that Tommy's could have been later and more peaceful." She sighed. "When I met Tommy…" A smile came to her face. She thought of the happy times when she first met him. "He literally swept me off my feet. I thought the world of him. He could do no wrong in my eyes. Even though he was not perfect by any means, I loved him as a friend, lover, and husband. Like all of us, he had some qualities you would love and some you just hated. He could be gentle and caring when he wanted to be."

She reached under her veil and dabbed her eyes with her handkerchief. Far off, near another cemetery plot, she saw the lead detective staring at her. For a brief moment she blanked out. People looked around, wondering what was going on. When she looked again, Jake was gone.

"Oh, I hope and pray that God finds a place for Tommy in heaven to rest eternally," she said, ending her speech abruptly.

She sat down. For the rest of the service, she constantly looked over her shoulders, at the location where the detective had stood.

Teddy saw how she kept looking back, and when he noticed the unmarked police car driving off, a smile came to his face. Jasmine potentially facing murder charges could lead to him running the company by default.

After the ceremony ended, Jasmine hurried into the limousine by herself as the flashbulbs went off. Settling in her seat, she began to cry under her veil. This had been the first time she'd had time alone to reflect on Tommy's death. Before the limo took off, Ralph jumped in.

"We need to talk, now," he said.

Jasmine's face took on a disgusted expression. She knew what it was about, and she just didn't want to talk about it. He saw her resistance.

"Jasmine, I understand that this isn't a great time, but…"

She removed her veil. Mascara had run all over her face. "What is it?" she asked, raising her voice. "I can't deal with anything else right now. I need some space."

"I think Teddy is planning something."

Jasmine was perplexed. "The board won't stand by and let him take control of the company. He doesn't have enough controlling interest. He only has thirty percent. He needs a lot more than that to boot me out."

"But if your mother doesn't come out of her coma in the next six weeks, it may be cause for concern. Are you sure that Ricky and Jaymee will back you?"

Jasmine thought hard about his question. She knew her brother and sister wanted to head the company, but the idea of them letting Teddy take control was, to her mind, out of the realm of possibility. She figured that if it came down to a vote, they would always want to keep a Dean at the head. Plus, since Tommy's murder, she and her siblings had been friendlier toward one another. They talked about keeping the family together and protecting the Dean legacy, giving her no clues that they wanted anything else but family unity.

She confidently told Ralph, "I'm sure they will side with me. He should lose six to one. Ricky, Jaymee, and Jackie all hold ten percent each and with you and my father holding five percent each, I think I'm looking pretty good." She saw Ralph's doubt, and she added, "Even if he got Ricky and Jaymee to turn, it would be a deadlock and things would stay as is."

Ralph chuckled. A deadlock meant the status quo. Teddy didn't have enough votes to make a serious move to run the company. He had been so wrapped up in how Ricky and Jaymee would vote, he forgot that Richard and Jackie had a deeply rooted hatred for Teddy. Now that Ralph thought about that angle, it gave him the confidence not to worry.

"I see your point exactly. You're right, but I still want your mother back," he said.

Jasmine exhaled. "I pray she comes back too. You think I like this? Hell, I hate the way she set up this board-voting b-s."

Ralph shook his head, understanding her point. "I know, but when she told me about the Death Clause, I was against it. We never thought this day would come this fast or this way."

"I just don't know how much fight I got left," Jasmine said.

Jasmine turned to face the window while the car drove out of the cemetery. The enormous pressure saddened her. Thinking about Tommy and her mother's fate weighed heavily on her heart.

Ralph moved closer and placed her head on his shoulder.

"I know this is a huge load for anyone to carry. But you're not alone in this. I'm here for you every step of the way," he said caringly.

All she could do was cry silently. With the pressures mounting, quitting seemed like the best solution to stop the walls from closing in on her.

***

A few days later, at the police precinct, Jake had several old-fashioned magazines stacked up on his desk. Most of the covers were graced by Jasmine. He sat at his desk, reading about Jasmine in the newspaper. The headline read: Husband of Former Catwalk Queen Murdered.

When his partner, Anthony, sat down at the desk across from him, Jake looked at him.

"That Dean family is very interesting," Jake said. "A lot of skeletons!"

He got Anthony's full attention with his comment.

"Jake, Captain said leave them alone."

"Can't I read about the people in high society?" Jake grinned.

"Yeah, but you don't read," Anthony mocked. "Leave them alone."

Jake put his paper down. He leaned forward. "Something is not right. I'm gonna keep my eye on her." He pointed at her picture in the newspaper.

Anthony slit his eyes at him. "Don't start something you can't finish."

Jake threw his hands up in the air. "I'm innocent." He laughed as he closely focused on Jasmine's face.

***

Teddy slowly walked into his home, a gorgeous mansion across the bridge over toward Newark. It was his rest haven away from the hustle of the city. He still had an apartment at the Trump, where he stayed most of the time. His home was somewhat of a hideout for him. Only a few knew of it. As he turned on the lights in the kitchen, he was immediately punched in the jaw. He fell hard to the ground. When he regained consciousness, he saw Jackie seated at his table, looking down at him.

"What was that for?" Teddy asked, scared for his life. He knew of the dirt that Jackie had done for Gloria. It was always said that if Jackie visits you, then it's not good.

Jackie just stared at him.

"I didn't do anything," Teddy said to get a response out of him.

Jackie pulled out a pack of gum and put a stick in his mouth. Standing up, he walked over to Teddy, who still was frozen on the floor.

Teddy saw the nickel-plated .38 in Jackie's shoulder holster. He figured that he was coming to kill him.

"Jackie, how's your cousin?"

Jackie stood looking down at him. "If I find out you had something to do with my cousin being in the hospital, I swear you're a dead man. I am going to love torturing you, like pulling the legs off of a spider. I don't like you...never have. So believe me, it would be a joy to see you scream."

Teddy almost broke down crying with guilt. Knowing that Jackie was not joking about the torturing, he knew any signs of an admission would lead to his own demise. His innocent man act was definitely an

Oscar worthy performance.

"I promise you, I don't know anything. I love Gloria like the rest of you."

"Just remember what I said. Like a spider." Jackie stepped over Teddy and walked out the door that Teddy had come in from.

Teddy continued to sit. He didn't know what to think about Jackie's visit. But by Jackie's drawn face, he did know that the next visit wouldn't end the same way.

"Jackie has to go." Teddy mustered up a smile.

***

Gloria's condition hadn't changed one bit. Jasmine was sitting across from her reading the *Da Vinci Code*. A chill went through her body every time she glanced at her mother. Seeing the tubes going in and out of her body, and monitors ticking and beeping, was very disturbing to her. She tried to focus on her mother's face instead of her surroundings, but couldn't.

Her cell phone rang and she jumped, thinking it was one of her mother's machines going off. She realized it was her phone and answered it.

"What's going on, Jaymee?" she asked in a panic.

"Is everything okay?" Jaymee replied.

Jasmine had to think for a moment about what she meant. "Yeah, I just got a lot on my mind."

"What time are you coming home?" Jaymee asked in a caring fashion.

Since the death of Tommy, Jaymee had been her biggest supporter. Not only did she provide comfort at home, she championed Jasmine's decisions at the office as well. Jasmine wasn't quite sold on this new Jaymee, even if she was being the sweetest person around. Jasmine did enjoy the sisterly moments they were sharing. With the grass high, she still was aware of the snake in the grass that Jaymee could be at a moment's notice. But for now, she played along with the game.

"Right now I'm at the hospital with Momma."

Jaymee hesitated before responding. Jasmine was aware that during the past couple of weeks, she had cut down on seeing her mother because it sickened her. Gloria was always strong and vivacious. With her being reduced to a shell of herself, it was hard to even look at her. No life, no drama—this was not the mother she knew and feared.

"Are you still there?" Jasmine asked, breaking the long pause.

"How is she?" Jaymee asked softly.

"Well, the doctor says her health is getting somewhat better because she's getting a lot of rest. The problem is that they won't really know until she wakes up." Jasmine grimaced at the thought that her mother wouldn't wake up. That possibility she kept in the back of her mind, but it crept forward from time to time.

"Kiss her for me," Jaymee said grimly.

"I'll be back at your place soon. I have to go to Momma's to get some clothes."

"I can meet you there if you want," Jaymee said.

Jasmine smiled. "Hey, I'm the big sister."

"I don't know if it's safe there."

Jasmine looked over at her mother, lying still. "I'll be okay. Nobody will be there. I'll be in and out. I'll call you when I'm on my way."

It had crossed her mind that maybe Tommy's killer was really after her. The only person who hated her enough to kill her was Teddy, though, and even with their long history, that seemed far-fetched.

"It's okay to be scared," Jaymee said.

"In and out. If I hear or see anything, I'll run straight out."

"Don't be like a white person and try to investigate," Jaymee snickered. "They always die."

"Is Ricky coming over?" Jasmine asked. "Or is he hanging out with Teddy?"

"Ricky is starting to see Teddy for who he is. I don't think they are tight anymore."

"I hope you're right. Teddy is a bad influence."

Jaymee smirked. "Ricky's probably somewhere freakin' some skank. Black, white, Spanish, or Asian, he got a different flavor for all occasions."

"Well, I'll see you when I get there," Jasmine said as she hung up the phone.

***

Flying high in Teddy's new Gulfstream G650, Teddy and Ricky were accompanied by beautiful half naked women, laughing and giggling as Teddy told jokes. Showing off was Teddy's specialty. And his new plane was definitely impressive. He had designed the interior of the plane. All of the chairs and sofas were of rich cream leather. The floors were covered by red silk carpets. He had illuminated soffit ceilings in the main area of the cabin and the master bedroom. Teddy had plasma TV's everywhere and a surround-sound system created by Beats by Dre. On the outside of the plane were the words "The Real Playboy" next to an abstract drawing of his face. Teddy wanted everyone to know he was wealthy and who the plane belonged to.

Ricky was like a kid around Teddy. His mother flaunted her wealth when the situation deemed necessary, but Teddy was like an old Wall Street white rapper who had to show his wealth all day, every day. In many ways he wanted to be just like Teddy, but he knew Teddy had an ugly side to him that his mother had warned him about.

Ricky nudged him. "Hey, when are we going back to New York?"

Teddy smiled. "I told you we were heading to Turks and Caicos for a day or two."

"You were serious?" Ricky asked, looking at his watch. "What about work?"

Teddy laughed. "You have nowhere to be. Plus, I need to talk to you."

"About what?"

Teddy got up. "Follow me. Ladies, we'll be right back. Business." He led Ricky to his master bedroom and sat in one of the recliners. Ricky sat in the other one.

"What's up?" Ricky asked, hoping to get straight to the point.

"How do you see your future?" Teddy was dead serious, and Ricky felt a little uncomfortable.

"Why?"

"I mean, do you see yourself ever getting your own label or brand off the ground? Even if your mother survives, do you see this happening for you?"

A lumped formed in Ricky's throat. He didn't know how to respond, even though he figured the answer was no. "Why are you asking me this?"

"You're talented. I don't want you wasting your time following behind your sisters and mother. Be your own man."

"I am my own man."

Teddy slanted his head at Ricky. "Do you really believe that?"

Ricky sensed a ploy. "Why are you bringing this shit up now?"

"I am offering an opportunity for you to achieve all your dreams."

"At what cost?" Ricky feared the cost was way higher than what he could afford.

"Randolph James has contacted me about the what-if's surrounding your mother's recovery."

"What what-if's are you talking about?"

"Let's face it, your mother might not make it. She's no better now than last week."

"Don't say that."

"I'm not being mean, it's just the truth. James wants to merge with you and me if your mother doesn't make it. They have promised me that you will be given the reins to run the company as you see fit."

Ricky was stunned by his statement. It seemed too good to be true.

"Why me?"

"Why do you think I wanted you to join me in running the company right after your mother's accident? Because you're brighter than Jaymee. No offense."

Ricky nodded in agreement. "So who do I need to talk to about this?"

"No one right now," Teddy said hastily. "You can't tell anyone about this discussion."

"Why not?"

"Think, Ricky. What happens if your mother makes it and this comes out? You would be in the doghouse forever."

Ricky sighed. "Yeah, you're right."

"Are you in?" Teddy smiled at him.

Ricky considered his other options fleetingly. Jasmine still treated him like a little kid. Jaymee was so greedy, there was no way he'd ever have any power if she was on top. As for Teddy . . . well, Ricky still was a Dean. "All right. I'm in."

Teddy stood up. "Now, that's what I like to hear. Let's go toast to the future. Our future."

CHAPTER **SIXTEEN**

At the mansion, a person clad in all black clothing and a ski mask broke the service entry lock on the gate and entered. Since the murder the house had been vacant, and an advanced security system was being installed next week. With the place being empty, the security guards overseeing the property were either fast asleep or goofing off. The person crept into the house unnoticed. When he got inside, he tore off the caution tape with glove-covered hands and clicked on a flashlight. The burglar then made his way up the staircase. By the way he moved through the house, it wasn't his first time there. He went to specific spots, tugging and pulling to see if he could find what he came for. When he reached Gloria's bedroom, he pulled a mirror off the wall. Behind the mirror was a safe. The masked person studied the numbers on the safe for a few moments, then quickly turned the dial: thirty-six right, twenty-one left, and fifty to the right. The lever gave way and the safe opened.

Shortly after the break-in, Jasmine drove up the street. It reminded her of the night Tommy died. Still not convinced that the wrong person had been murdered him, she felt it best that no one saw her enter the house. So, she decided to take the service entrance.

At the service gate, she noticed the lock lying on the grass. She immediately picked up her phone and dialed 911.

"Nine-one-one, what is your emergency?" the operator asked.

Jasmine whispered into the phone. "I need an officer at 1 Dean Way. There's a break-in happening right now."

She saw a flashlight silhouette bounce against the wall. Jasmine glanced at her watch. It was almost nine o'clock.

"Hurry," she said, ducking behind a tree.

"Stay outside until the police get there, ma'am."

"I can't let them get away." She hung up the phone.

Jasmine immediately grabbed her gun out of her purse and headed in the door. She wanted to put an end to all the drama once and for all. Once inside, she thought about how crazy it was for her to be inside the house. But looking at her gun gave her confidence that she would be okay. So, she went on. Her legs shook as she slowly crept through the house. Her forehead started sweating profusely. Yet she heard nothing and saw nothing. As she eased into the dark kitchen, her elbow hit a wineglass on the counter. It toppled and shattered on the floor.

Startled, Jasmine reached out to turn on a light. Her hand located the switch on the wall and flicked it on. The window over the sink was open. Quickly her gaze dropped to the counter. It had a knife stabbed into the cutting board. Under the knife was a note. She slowly edged over to it with her gun drawn, ready to shoot. Without picking up the knife, she read the note. The words made her weak in the knees. From the back of the house, she heard a noise. Her fear got the best of her. Jasmine dropped the gun and sprinted to the front. She flung open the door and ran right into Teddy's arms.

"What are you doing here?" she asked, astonished.

Tongue-tied, Teddy couldn't say a word. Jasmine pulled away from him and ran toward the flashing blue and red police lights pulling up to the gate. Teddy tried catching up to her, but the police officers apprehended him before he got close.

When she looked back, she saw a flashlight in his hand. "Arrest him," she yelled.

Teddy looked at her in disbelief. "What are you doing?"

Angry at the house being violated, she wouldn't even look at him.

"Don't talk to me," she said.

The police handcuffed him. As they escorted him to the patrol car, Jasmine cried in one of the officer' arms. In her mind, the mystery was solved. Teddy had murdered Tommy, case closed. She figured the target was supposed to have been her instead. But the part that made no sense was: what he was trying to find in the house?

***

At the same police station, Jasmine gave her statement about what happened. This time the interview was a lot more pleasant. On her way out of the station, she saw her two detectives at their desks. She rolled her eyes at them.

After leaving the station, instead of heading to Jaymee's, Jasmine went to Maxwell's penthouse on the Upper East Side. Once he opened the door, she fell into his arms. He couldn't believe how drained, tired, and fearful she appeared. The strong woman admired and respected for her strength was reduced to nothing.

"Is there anything I can do?" he asked with sincerity.

He led her into his deluxe media room. They sat down across from each other in two leather recliners. Maxwell's butler brought them some hot tea. Jasmine quickly grabbed it and sipped. She noticed his intent watching.

"I'm sorry for coming by so late. I just wanted some friendly company. I'll leave if you want." She surveyed the place to see if he might have guests.

"Are you crazy?" he said, kissing her on the lips. "I'm here for you."

"Thanks," she replied, hugging him again.

"Did you call your sister?" he asked.

She shook her head. "That's a long story."

He smiled. "I'm sorry about everything that has happened to you, but I'm glad you thought enough of me and came here."

"We were about to get a divorce." Her teeth ground together. She felt compelled to tell him the whole truth. Honesty, loyalty, and trust were the most important building blocks to a relationship in her book. They even outranked love. If this relationship with Maxwell had any chance of surviving, she wanted to give him full disclosure of her heart.

"Another long story? Don't feel pressured to talk," he said with a smile.

"It's actually a short one. Meet the bad guy. Marry the bad guy. Find out that the bad guy is bad and struggle to leave the bad guy. Then the bad guy never stops following you." She sipped her tea again. "And then someone kills him. It wasn't me, if you have any doubts."

Maxwell smiled. "I don't know. You do look dangerous."

Jasmine smiled back at him. His presence was comforting. "Good joke."

"Anyway, why was Teddy at your place? You don't think he's involved with the murder, do you?"

Her mind wanted to say yeah. The problem for her was that putting him in the equation didn't make sense. By now she'd had time to process what happened. Teddy had no reason to kill her husband. Plus, the police found nothing out of the ordinary.

"That's the question I want answered. He didn't know Tommy. Nothing right now makes sense."

"So, what does Jaymee and your brother think?"

Jasmine thought deeply about his question. "I don't know."

***

At the crack of dawn, Jasmine snuck into her sister's house. Coming in from the tennis court and swimming pool area, she expected Jaymee to not hear her. Once she got inside, though, Jaymee caught her going up the staircase.

"Where have you been?" Jaymee asked in a motherly way.

"Can we talk about it in the morning?" Jasmine asked. She looked weary and frustrated. Her night had been filled with thoughts of her own death.

Jaymee pointed to the clock on the wall. "It's already morning."

"You know what I mean. I had a crazy night. All I want to do is put this head on a pillow," Jasmine pleaded.

"Last night they arrested Teddy. We have to get him out," Jaymee said with urgency.

Jasmine rolled her eyes.

"What?" Jaymee wanted her to explain her facial expression.

"You know where they arrested him?" she asked.

Her sister was baffled. "Where?"

"At Momma's house."

"What was he doing there?"

"That's the million-dollar question. I racked my brain all last night trying to fit the pieces. There's just no connection with Tommy's death and what happened to Momma." Jasmine took off her shoes and walked into the living room. She lay down on the couch.

"How come you didn't tell me this last night?" Jaymee asked, worried.

"I was tired and didn't know what to think. I really thought he was trying to kill me. Hell, he probably was. I know he wants control of the company."

"Why would you think that?" she asked. Jaymee sat down on the carpeted floor.

"I found a note in the house that said, *Death to tyrants.* It was under a knife."

Jaymee stared at her. "Isn't that what John Wilkes Booth said before he shot Lincoln?"

Her sister's concerns were now legitimized. "Yeah. What Booth said was *Sic semper tyrannis*, which means something like that."

"That's crazy!"

"Scary and weird." Jasmine was convinced that Teddy wanted her out of the picture. "That note sounds like Teddy."

Jaymee was still giving Teddy the benefit of the doubt. "I just don't think he would try to kill you. I will admit that remark sounds like him, though. What happened?"

"I saw that note, then ran out of there. When I got outside, Teddy was there waiting. He couldn't even tell me why he was there." Jasmine shook her head, still confused by the developments. "He's up to something."

The sisters locked eyes for a second. Jasmine could tell that Jaymee was stuck between a rock and hard place. Their relationship was better, but she still wanted to run the company, so she had to be pro-Teddy.

When Jaymee's house phone rang, the silence was broken. She quickly answered it. Jasmine closed her eyes.

"Hello…yes, it's me…why?"

Without warning, Jaymee fainted dead away, sliding onto the floor. Jasmine rushed to her aid. She frantically picked up the phone.

"Hello…yes, she fainted…oh, no." Jasmine got woozy herself. "We'll be there in fifteen minutes."

She picked up Jaymee and dragged her over to the couch. She rushed to get some water. When she returned, she splashed Jaymee in the face. The water instantly helped her regain consciousness.

"Jasmine, I can't handle this alone."

"We're family," Jasmine said, trying to be strong for the both of them. They hugged one another. "So we'll face it together."

***

Later that afternoon, around Gloria's hospital bed, her kids stood around thinking this was the end. All of them had sorrowful faces as they stared upon her lifeless body. It was the worst of times and the best of times. As a family, they hadn't been on the same page for many years, but in this case they wanted their mother's life to be spared.

"I hate seeing Momma like this," Ricky said, taking a deep breath to avoid crying.

The doctor walked into the room. He went over to Gloria's side and checked her chart, then turned to the kids.

"There's no easy way around this. We need to operate. If we don't, she may die in the next couple of hours."

"What happened? You said she was doing better." Anger spread over Jasmine's face. "This is bullshit!"

The intense look on Jasmine's face scared the doctor a little. Jackie and Richard walked in. They stood back a little, trying to assess what was happening. Jasmine hugged them, while her siblings ignored their presence in the room. Ricky normally would have spoken to his father and Jackie, but due to his alliance with Jaymee, he had to play the "against them" role with her.

"I—I thought she was," the doctor stuttered. "We noticed that her heart was not pumping enough blood. Further analysis showed a huge blood clot near her heart's main vessel."

"Can she still die, even with the surgery?" Jackie asked, wincing.

"That's just what you want," Jaymee said. "It's your fault!"

Jackie gave her a frightening glare, warning her that her antics were wearing very thin with him.

Jasmine remarked harshly, "Jaymee, not now!"

The doctor responded at last. "Yes, but she will definitely die if we don't to the surgery."

All the children looked at one another.

"Can we get a second opinion?" Jaymee asked.

Richard eyeballed the doctor. "Is there time for it?"

"No. It's imperative that we operate now."

Everyone exchanged glances for a second time. Jaymee hugged her mother, then shoved her way past everyone to escape the room.

Jackie, Ricky, and Richard both deferred to Jasmine to have the final say. She rubbed her head. The decision seemed simple, but if her mother didn't survive, she knew the others would blame her. Still, it was a gamble she was willing to live with. Her mother was a fighter and would survive.

"I need a decision!" the doctor said.

She exhaled. "Operate."

Several hours later, the family sat quietly in the waiting area. No one even looked at one another. Their eyes were mainly fixed on the door leading to the operating room. When the automatic doors opened, everyone sighed in anticipation. The doctor stepped through and took off his operating mask and headgear. He saw their weary faces. He scratched his head as he got closer. This didn't seem like a good sign to them. Jaymee dropped to her knees to pray. Jackie grabbed her by the hand and prayed with her. Jasmine stood up and grabbed Ricky's hand. Richard started bawling. His tears astonished his kids. Their whole lives, they had never seen their father cry.

The doctor reached them. His jaws tightened as he looked at their pain.

"She made it," he said with a smile.

Ricky hugged the doctor briefly. But the biggest surprise was that Jaymee went and hugged her dad. His tears had made her see that he still cared for their mother.

"When can we see her?" Jasmine asked. "Is she still in a coma?"

Her question got the attention of everyone. They stood still waiting for the doctor's response.

The doctor didn't know what question to answer first. They both were difficult.

"Yes, she's still in a coma. And I don't know for how much longer, or if that will ever change. But for now she's alive and a full recovery is possible. Someone will come and get you when she is ready for visitors."

Delivering the news made the doctor looked drained. Though Gloria was alive, Jasmine guessed, he didn't expect her to make it. Before he showed his emotions, the doctor walked away.

CHAPTER **SEVENTEEN**

I n his office at home, Teddy was growing red in the face as he listened to the person on the other end of the phone. His mood worsened the more the conversation continued. The normally talkative Teddy did not interrupt once. Almost in tears, he turned his face toward the window. He saw the clouds swoop in and cover the sun like a lid closing a jar. He grimaced as she blew off some steam. Finally, Teddy had heard enough.

"The deal was five point five billion. If you're not interested anymore, then I'm sure someone will pay that amount!" Teddy said aggressively. "That even includes the property."

After his words left his lips, a dial tone was heard. He couldn't believe the person had hung up on him.

"Hello, hello," he said, still in disbelief.

Teddy slammed the phone down. He then picked it up, ripped it out of the wall, and threw it into the burning fireplace. Not talking to another soul fit right into his plans for the night.

A faint knock on the office door caught his attention. He straightened up his clothes.

"Yes. Come in," he said as he sat down in his chair.

A petite middle-aged Hispanic maid cautiously entered.

He gave the uniformed woman an evil glare for the interruption. "Amanda, what is it?"

His menacing look scared her. She noticed the fireplace and saw the phone burning. It made her choke on the gum she had been chewing. She stood speechless.

"You came in here for a reason, I presume," he growled. "My time is precious. What is it?"

Having swallowed her gum, she chewed on her lips nervously. "Yes, sir, you have a guest."

He peeked at his watch and sinisterly smiled. "My insurance policy is right on time," he said out loud.

"Excuse me, sir?" she asked, having no clue what he meant.

"By all means, let him in. Let's not keep him waiting."

"Okay, sir. Is there anything else you want me to do for you?" the maid asked while heading toward the door.

He pondered what would be happening next. "No. That will be all for the night. Go out and spend some time with your friends. I'll be fine."

"Thank you, sir," she replied as she quietly left the room.

From his desk drawer Teddy pulled out his best box of Cuban cigars. He smelled one of them and smiled. He walked to his bar by the fireplace and poured two glasses of twenty-year-old port. His hands full, he headed back to the desk with the glasses. He sat back down and lit a cigar.

The office door opened up, and Richard walked in. The first thing he noticed was the phone cord dangling out from the fireplace. An uneasy feeling gave his body a shiver.

"Is this a bad time?" Richard asked. "Should I have called first?"

Teddy smiled to ease away the awkwardness. "No. Never. Have a seat. Take a cigar. If I remember correctly, you used to love this port."

Richard glanced at Teddy and the glass of port on his desk. The fast-talking Teddy irritated him. The wine and the cigars made him weary. Richard knew he was up to no good. They hadn't had a civil conversation in years. The hatred they felt for one another went back to the day Gloria made Teddy a partner. Plus, Teddy was always making disrespectful remarks about Richard's failed business attempts and calling him a leech behind his back.

"What the fuck do you want, Teddy? It's not like we're close, so save the niceties."

Teddy acted like he was surprised by the rudeness. He sat there open-mouthed. Richard played it calm, but really he was on eggshells. Teddy was so clever and unpredictable, it was scary.

"I only came here because you said Gloria was in trouble financially," Richard said angrily. "Don't waste my time."

Instead Teddy took a long, lingering sip of his drink. "We go back many years. You remember the old days?"

Richard stood there, waiting for him to get to his point.

"Well, I do. I know things got ugly for us during the divorce. But I want to apologize for what I did then," Teddy said, pretending to be sincere.

Richard busted out laughing. "You never cease to amaze me. I must be getting punked. Where are the cameras?"

Richard huffed. The snow job was not working. Richard was a formidable opponent, and Teddy knew it. Being from the streets, Richard knew all of the games people played. He suspected that he was about to be a part of one himself. That was Teddy's style: to make everything grand before swatting you across the head with the hammer.

"Okay, let me cut to the chase," Teddy said with a raised brow.

"About time." Richard looked at his watch.

"Please take a seat," Teddy offered again.

Though he was hesitant, Richard obliged and sat down. He blatantly glanced at his watch again.

"I hear the violin playing, so what lyrics you got to tell me?"

"Your daughter is burying the company. We're all going down with her."

"That's funny. What I hear is that she's doing a good job under the circumstances."

Teddy made a skeptical face. "You have just as much to lose as I do."

"How do you figure?" he asked. Richard thought the comment was absurd. His ownership in the company was too small to make a difference. But the five percent did keep him living a rich life.

"Need I remind you that you have two other children to think about? You should also think of the people you deal with because you're nothing without the Gloria Dean seal of approval. Nothing! It's reality check time, Stedman Graham. I know you're broke." Teddy laughed at his own joke.

His words hit home for Richard. He was almost broke. Due to some bad investments he had leveraged nearly all that he owned. It was also true, to some degree, that he only survived based on his connection with the company. If Jasmine did bring it down, that would affect the other two kids as well. Yet he had a problem with Teddy giving him this information. Unbearable as it was, he knew there was more in store.

"I still don't see why you're talking to me. I'm nothing to the company." Richard shrugged his shoulders arrogantly.

"On the contrary, my friend, you hold the key to making everything a reality."

Richard was more puzzled than ever. His part in this bizarre situation was hard to figure out. He suspected that it had something to do with Teddy running the company. How he was going to achieve that seemed far-fetched to him.

"How?" Richard asked.

"Sales are down, and she's making costly errors. You know the business just as well as I do. To stay on top, you have to have the best products out. The designs are second-rate at best. You saw them. The design team is screaming for a change in leadership. She's green."

Teddy gave him a grim look. "Her fashion sense is dead."

Richard laughed. "You're not selling the company."

"Who said anything about selling it? I want to preserve the legacy."

"That's bullshit! Gloria told me all about the offers and how you have been trying to get her to take them. The nerve of you. That company has been in her family since the sixties. Have you any decency?"

"Money is my source of decency," Teddy shouted at him. "What's yours?"

"This meeting is over." Richard stood up to leave.

"Sit your broke-ass down!" Teddy pointed at him to sit like a house pet. "Here's how it is going to play out. Next week, there will be an emergency board meeting called, and you will vote in my favor." Teddy leaned back in his chair and puffed on his cigar.

Richard did all he could to not lose his cool. He hated people telling him what to do. He thought what Teddy said was ludicrous. *How was he going to make me vote for him?* he thought. The last thing he would do in this whole world was vote against Jasmine.

"You and what army is going to make that happen?" He balled up his fist. Ready to pound him into the ground, he started to walk over to Teddy.

"You remember a woman named Vanessa?" Teddy said smugly.

That stopped Richard short, and a look of fear appeared on his face. Teddy now had the upper hand. Richard looked lost and frail.

"That was between you and I," Richard said somberly. "What do you want from me?"

"So, you do remember her?" Teddy smiled. "Now maybe we can have an intelligent conversation."

"I didn't kill her," Richard cried. "You know that."

The intimidating man that had stood before Teddy had been degraded to a weak bum with no ground to stand on.

"That's not what the police think." Teddy shook his head. "I told you that fetish with the hooker would bring you down one day."

"She wasn't a hooker. She was a model. And I didn't kill her."

"A model, a stripper, a hooker—same thing. Let's not battle over semantics. It's really beneath us, wouldn't you say?" Teddy chuckled.

"What do you want from me?" Richard asked, almost begging. "I have nothing."

Teddy rolled his eyes. "Did you totally miss what I said before? You will vote for me at the board meeting."

"How do I know that you're not bluffing?"

Teddy reached inside his desk drawer. He pulled out a file and flung it across the desk.

"Read it," he demanded.

Richard grabbed the file and his eyes opened wide. It depressed him, seeing the pictures of the woman battered, her throat cut from ear to ear. As Richard read on, he knew that if Teddy went to the police with this evidence, it wouldn't matter what he said. The only thing that would matter was the bloody shirt and weak alibi that he had. Teddy smiled, knowing he had Richard cornered.

"So what are you going to do with this?" Richard asked.

"Hopefully nothing," Teddy replied smoothly. "This is what's best for the company. Everybody makes a killing."

"I'm only one vote," Richard said, still confused about what Teddy was doing.

"Let me worry about the details." He winked at Richard.

"Ricky and Jaymee won't agree to sell the company. You might have me, but they don't care. They may not like Jasmine, but they understand family."

"You just do as you're told!"

"Jackie will kill you."

"This is a mandate, not a proposal."

"What are you planning, you bastard? If you hurt one person in my family, I swear I'll kill you."

Teddy looked at his watch. "You can leave now." He grabbed the newspaper on his desk and opened it up like Richard wasn't even in the room.

Richard saw that the conversation was over, so he despondently dragged himself to the door. All the way out, he couldn't help wondering what Teddy had up his sleeve.

***

Late on a Friday evening at the Gloria Dean Company, Ricky sat talking to Richard. From the moment that Richard walked in, Ricky felt he had a hidden agenda. His father's odd behavior didn't help the situation either. Ricky didn't know if his dad was nervous or what, but he was constantly fidgeting. For the first half hour, they chitchatted about how his office was set up. Though the advice seemed good, he knew that his father didn't come to give ideas about that. He could tell some important issue was troubling Richard.

"So, Pops, I take it you want to talk about something."

"You got me," Richard said, putting his hands up in the air, surrendering.

"So what's going on?"

"Are you happy with Jasmine running the company?"

The question threw Ricky for a loop. Richard had been up to now her biggest supporter. For him to cast doubt was strange. Ricky couldn't figure out where his reason for questioning her leadership had come from. He knew for sure it wasn't Richard's doing. Jasmine was his heart and everybody knew he was willing to walk through fire for her.

"You sound like Teddy asking that question," Ricky said.

Richard forced a laugh. "Now, that's a slap in the face," he said.

Ricky, as planned, bought the act. "I'm sorry," he said. "This is between you and me?"

Richard leaned forward in his chair. "Of course. I just want to know if she's the right one for the job."

"Well, I know what Momma wants, but she's taking a long time to get back up to speed. This isn't a reality TV show. This is real business, not *The Apprentice*." He chuckled.

Richard nodded in agreement. "Does your sister feel the same way?"

Ricky laughed again. "Please. What do you think? She's looking for another job as we speak, but don't tell Jasmine."

"I thought you guys had been getting along pretty well lately," Richard remarked, wondering what changed.

"We have. I got all the respect for Jasmine in the whole world, but I have my own opinions. The only thing that matters here is that a Dean runs the company while Momma is in her coma."

"So what about Teddy running it?" he asked Ricky.

Ricky narrowed his eyes at him. Just the thought was absurd. He compared his father's question to Osama Bin Laden running the world. "He can help us run the company, but that's all. The bottom line here is that we need to hold it down until Momma gets back. That's all."

He could tell his words comforted Richard, because his father all of a sudden changed the subject.

"I guess things are crazy around here with the new campaign about to launch. What is Teddy doing?" Richard asked with a raised brow.

"Sitting around acting like it's Sunday afternoon. Now, he's a real waste. Momma should have gotten rid of him a long time ago." Ricky shook his head with one eye on his father. He knew that was what Richard wanted to hear.

His father relaxed some more. "You remember those summers in Aspen?"

"Yeah, we seemed like a real family back then." Ricky smiled as he reflected back to those times.

"I'm thinking about us all going there when your mother gets better. I think we all need a break. It'll also give us time to become close again."

"I feel that." Ricky thought it was a wonderful idea. He yearned to have a closer relationship with them all since he was the youngest. But most of all, he wanted a better relationship with his father. It always hurt that Richard had a stronger bond with Jasmine. He felt, since he was the only son, they were supposed to be tight.

"I hope your sisters share the same enthusiasm."

"I'm there. I'm sure Jasmine will be cool with it. Jaymee's got some things she has to work through. You'll have to talk to her yourself." He put his hands up in the air. "I'm not touching her with that subject."

"I will definitely do that. I think it's time we rebuild this family," Richard said with a nervous smile on his face.

Richard put his fist out for his son to give him a pound, and he did. They both nodded at each other, optimistic about the future of the family.

CHAPTER **EIGHTEEN**

At half past midnight Teddy parked his car in front of an abandoned warehouse near the East River. He glanced out at the seven other cars parked there with a grimace. As uninviting as the docks in Brooklyn appeared, they remained a hotbed for illegal activity during the late hours of the night. Teddy was unsure of what was coming next. When his feet hit the gravel, his body tensed up. He moved at a turtle's pace until he entered the building. Peeking inside, he saw that it was dark, shabby, and dreary. With the only source of light coming from the moon and streetlights, it was a strain to see anything clearly.

Within a few steps, Teddy stopped dead in his tracks when he saw two guys far off in the corner smoking cigars. Once he realized who they were, he strolled over to them. As he passed each wide cement pillar, he noticed silhouettes of men stationed with guns already drawn. He counted ten in all. Teddy acted unbothered by the menace, even though he was ready to piss in his pants.

"John," he said, smiling as he approached the two cigar smokers.

"I don't know what you're smiling about," John said as he removed the cigar from his mouth. "The deal is still not done."

John Lincoln was a tall, fit white man in his mid-forties. To all who knew him, he was a pompous asshole. His family at one time did have millions, but now he was just one of the working-class rich people trying to reclaim their empire. He spoke with a bit of a British accent and thought he was better than everyone. He almost always wore a houndstooth jacket and a derby to boot. Yet he was from Connecticut and only had been to England a few times. The act did work in many affluent circles. Many people trusted his word based on how he talked and dressed. Teddy was one of them.

"Tomorrow is a whole new day," Teddy announced. "I will be the new CEO and my first order of business is to sell the company to the highest bidder."

John rose to his feet. "So, you're trying to cut me out?"

"Don't be moronic. We have a deal. Rest assured, we will all get our deserved cuts." Teddy rolled his eyes. "For someone so wealthy, you are very barbaric in your thinking. Look around—could I really double-cross you?"

"I have little patience for your American ways. If you decide to screw me, then you will definitely get screwed."

"What are you going to do? Sew my ass to my face?" Teddy chuckled.

"That would keep you from talking so much," John said scornfully as his bodyguard gripped his gun.

"Just remember, I want my half a billion dollars wired the minute you are officially the new majority owner, and I will then take my place as the minority owner with options."

"Very minority. Like a white man in Nigeria," John said, low enough not to be heard by Teddy. "Don't forget about Jaymee Dean."

"What?" Teddy had forgotten about the inclusion of Jaymee in the deal. He didn't think she was that important.

"Hold on, Teddy, the deal doesn't happen without her." John coughed uneasily. "I thought you handled that end already."

Teddy saw his nervous energy. "Why her?"

"That is no concern of yours. Just make sure you tell her. Your life might depend on it."

The darkness hid the beads of sweat popping up on Teddy's face as he walked away. In his present circumstances someone could definitely shoot him in the back of the head.

"Once the deal is done, I want him erased," John said quietly to his bodyguard.

***

Sex was in the air as the night sky swallowed the sun. In Maxwell's mind the sweet aroma from Jasmine's perfume made her more desirable than ever. Tonight, he felt the mood was ripe to make his move. Since the day he met Jasmine, he had dreamed of sleeping with her so he could brag to his friends. On this date at his penthouse, he had made a great dinner, served the best red wine that France had to offer, and catered to her every desire. There was no way she was leaving his place without him knowing how the booty worked.

Little did he know, that was right in line with her thoughts. Through their time together, she had grown horny every time, imaging her hands caressing his naked butt and her lips licking the nipples on his chest. Jasmine was so prepared for this night that she bought a three-pack of Magnum condoms just in case he didn't have any. From glances at his crotch, she figured they should fit.

After dinner, they headed toward his couch in front of the fireplace. Jasmine took it upon herself and led him to his bedroom instead. Her move shocked him. His excitement showed in his pants as the front bulged out. Jasmine thought, *Yeah, we'll fit!* When they got to his bedroom door, she stopped and kissed him on the lips. She held him for a moment. It was her way of making sure she really wanted to go through with it. That wasn't a problem, because the kiss heightened her desire for him. Jasmine wanted him now more than ever. He stared at her like a little boy falling in love for the first time. Maxwell had plenty of women come in and out of his life; some of the women were famous and some just groupies. Jasmine was the woman that he dreamed about when he was growing up. In fact, before he made it, becoming famous, he'd hung a magazine pullout of her on the basement wall at his mother's house.

"Is everything okay?" she asked, noticing his daze.

He was unresponsive. It was like a marathon with only ten feet to the finish line. All he had to do was enter his bedroom, and it was on. This was the one accolade that he never thought would be achieved. Now that it was ripe for his taking, he was lost. Mainly, Maxwell knew making love to Jasmine would be different than the rest. For the first time in his life, he was worried about his heart being broken.

Jasmine thought his panic was cute, but she also wanted to hear from his heart his true intentions. "How do you feel about me?" she asked with a smile that would light up the room.

Maxwell came out of his daze. "You know that answer."

"I want to hear it from those lips. Those luscious lips," she said seductively.

Maxwell's dimples smiled at her. "Okay."

She looked at him straight in the face.

He didn't flinch. Maxwell licked his lips. Words were his mastery and his calling card in the hip-hop world. "I like looking in your eyes. There's something special about them. Something romantic, but mysterious...almost erotic, definitely sensual. They say so much with every twinkle. I see pain meeting joy as you rise from the ashes of the dark side. You have been covered with grief. In the past you've faced many a tragedy, but today I see an amazing, strong beauty. You are that rose that grew in the concrete jungle. You are the love that men rumble for. But like a great explorer, I'm trying to capture the forbidden, which is your bleeding heart of love. Now, can we get this party started?" He laughed.

"Do you have any whipped cream in the refrigerator?" Jasmine asked. She gave him a sexy romantic look that melted his heart. It was the perfect icebreaker.

They burst out laughing. Maxwell had read her all wrong. He pegged her to be somewhat of a prude. She was so high up on his pedestal of women that he imagined that she was the kind of woman that only had sex missionary style. She, being a freak like himself, took things up a notch. He felt the sex menu was now expanded.

He licked his lips. "I think I can get that."

"Hurry back. I'll be waiting," she said, grabbing his butt briefly before he left.

He flew to the kitchen. Maxwell was so anxious to get it on, he threw items from the refrigerator on the floor to get to the whipped cream. He held the can up like he had just won a Grammy. As the refrigerator door was closing, he saw some strawberries and his imagination took off to the heavens.

Jasmine went inside his bedroom and got undressed. Her body was like a statue in a museum. The curves were beautiful and sensual. Her C-cup breasts and soft, round butt filled the hourglass body nicely.

At first she thought she was going to keep her panties on, but sensed that they would be coming off soon anyway, so she threw them with the rest of her clothes. She got under the covers stark naked. She surveyed the room and saw a stereo on the wall. Jasmine jumped out of bed and went over to scan his collection of CDs. Once she saw the greatest hits by Luther Vandross, she threw it in and pushed play. Hearing Maxwell's footsteps, she quickly returned to the bed.

He came into the room with a tray carrying a bottle of wine, a couple of glasses, a bowl of strawberries, and the can of whipped cream she had requested.

She giggled at the sight of the strawberries. "I see you're a real dessert freak," she said.

"I like strawberries and cream on my pie. I don't know how you do it in your family." He laughed.

"So I'm your pie?" she asked. The way he looked at her was

breathtaking. She wiped her forehead. "You're making me hot already."

She pulled back the covers, unveiling her nude body. Maxwell was ready to bust out of his pants, staring at her shape. He grinned, but before he could totally enjoy it, she covered herself up again. Jasmine winked at him.

"Do you deserve this?" she asked playfully.

"You're cold-blooded," he said, shaking his head. Maxwell couldn't believe how perfect her body looked. His mouth watered, desiring to suck on her perky breasts and anything else she had to offer. He licked his lips.

"Just doing a little advertising." She smiled.

Maxwell put the tray down at the foot of the bed. He started getting undressed himself. It took a whole lot of restraint to not go straight for the gusto. For her benefit, he decided on foreplay even though that wasn't his normal plan of attack. Maxwell was a "do her up against the wall or from the back" kind of guy.

As Jasmine grabbed the bowl of strawberries from the tray, she took a glimpse at his well-sculptured body and exhaled. When he removed his underwear, she felt faint. He was exactly what she had wanted to end her sexual drought. Seeing his package made her want him inside her now, no waiting or foreplay needed. Jasmine was desperate for sex.

Maxwell finished undressing and strolled over to her. He sprang up higher the closer he got. Her attention was focused solely on his love muscle. He got in bed next to her, took the bowl of strawberries from her, and put it on the end table.

"Are you ready?" he asked with a grin.

"Bring it."

"First, I'm gonna need you to sign the love contract," he said, winking at her.

She smirked. "Okay, Chappelle."

Maxwell flipped the covers back and proceeded to spray her with whipped cream from her navel to her knees. The coldness sent a chill through her body that exhilarated her. He laughed at her shivering. He kissed her on the lips, then slowly made his way down her body sucking up all the cream on his way to her treasure. She quivered in excitement.

Jasmine grabbed his muscle and massaged it. *Mr. Big Stuff,* she thought. *At least I got the right condoms.*

He reached his destination and went to work. She climaxed three times in the first three minutes. The experience blew her mind. Jasmine couldn't believe how well he connected with her body. She trembled with the anticipation of how good it was going to feel once he entered her. Her vagina began to pulsate like a vibrator.

Yet as he put his final touches on his job down south, his phone rang. They acted like they didn't hear anything.

"I want to taste you. Pass that whipped cream, naughty boy," she said, blowing a kiss at him.

The person calling hung up and called right back. The ringing repeated over and over, but they still ignored it. It was going to take more than that to destroy this night. Jasmine wanted to release herself from the sexual tension that weighed on her shoulders.

She sprayed his mid-section and started making her way down on him slowly when her cell phone rang. Her lips stopped at his navel. Now her phone rang and rang to the point of irritation. He winced and took a deep breath to control himself. Maxwell was ready to explode.

"Don't stop now," he begged.

"I'm sorry. It might be an emergency. I better get it. Sorry." Jasmine got up and sashayed naked to the living room where she had left her phone.

Maxwell couldn't believe his predicament. He stared down at himself and shook his head. His hand gripped his private part. Maxwell's attention was immediately drawn over to the mirror. Seeing himself in the mirror made him laugh. With whipped cream still around his lips, he looked like a naked clown.

"This is a first." He laughed.

Jasmine came back in the room with a frown on her face. By her expression he knew that their romantic evening was in jeopardy. He sat on the side of the bed. "What is it?"

"Don't hate me, but that was the hospital. They said my mother called out my father's name."

"She's awake?" he asked, surprised.

"No. She's still in a coma. I have to go talk to her doctor. They think it's a good sign. With tomorrow's board meeting, that would put an end to all this crazy takeover business." She had a concerned look on her face.

"You don't have anything to worry about. Do you?"

"No. I just have to fight off another one of Teddy's tactics to make me look bad."

She put her clothes back on while he stood there thinking about what could have been. In the back of his mind he had hoped that she would at least give him some head. Once Jasmine got dressed, she went over to him and kissed him softly on the lips. As sensual as the kiss was, it was also demoralizing. It was the final sign that said their night was over.

"Bye, baby," she said endearingly. She then grabbed his penis. "Definitely next time. Ooo, I hate I have to go. Rain check?"

"I'll be at the bank soon." Maxwell looked like a broken-hearted puppy dog.

She glanced at his body once more. "I hope you are." She smiled. "Next time, no foreplay... Well, maybe a little." Jasmine winked at him.

"That's cool." He winked back at her.

"Bye, love." She blew him a kiss as she rushed out the door.

***

Around midnight that same night, Richard secured his house by checking the windows and doors. He went over to the alarm box near the kitchen and began to push in his code. Before he could finish, he heard a knock on his back door. He glanced at his watch. *Who could it be at this hour?* he wondered. He slid over to the window and looked out. Once he saw Teddy's sparkling smile, a feeling of disgust came over him. Teddy was the last person he had wanted to see. It crossed his mind not to answer the door, but the knocks seemed to get harder, louder, and longer. After much mental debate, he opened it.

"Do you know what time it is?" he said sternly.

Teddy ignored him and pushed his way inside.

"I'm thirsty," Teddy said as he headed over to the refrigerator. "What do you have?"

"Why are you here?" Richard asked with contempt.

Teddy opened the refrigerator and grabbed a beer. He took a sip, then savored the taste as it went down his throat. "I had to come by to make sure that you wouldn't go cowboy on me in the meeting tomorrow."

"What you talking about?"

"I don't need you messing things up by trying to be a hero. That's what I mean. Play your role, and you'll remain a free man. If you don't, by Monday morning you'll be sitting in lockup waiting to be processed."

Richard didn't appreciate the threats. It was one thing to be cornered, but for Teddy to gloat in his face added insult to injury.

"You can get the hell out of here," he demanded.

Teddy rolled his eyes. "Remember the score. You have no points. No edge. No fuckin' reason to be thinking for yourself!"

Teddy took another sip. He threw a file folder across the table.

"That's your copy," he said with a smile. "Just a little reminder."

"You're gonna burn in hell, Teddy," Richard said with enmity. He spied a knife on the sink, right within his grasp. He grabbed it. Killing Teddy seemed like a great idea.

Teddy laughed. "Yeah, right, you're gonna stab me in your own home. Please. Richard, you couldn't be in prison thirty seconds before crying for mommy. Put the knife away."

Teddy sauntered out the door. Enraged by his visit, Richard snatched the file folder up from the table and hurled it up against the wall.

***

It was way past visiting hours at the hospital, but since the Dean family had invested a ton of money in the hospital, they were able to go and come as they please. With Gloria's care having been extended, she was in her own room, which looked like a hotel penthouse suite. She had comfortable couches, chairs, and a large flat-screen TV in her room.

Jasmine rested in a chair that let out into a bed. The woulda, coulda, shoulda night with Maxwell was now fading from her memory. Her hormones were still raging, but tomorrow's board meeting loomed foremost in her thoughts. She couldn't help but think that Teddy had something up his sleeve that she hadn't considered yet. Jasmine just couldn't imagine what it could be. Outside of a vote, which she was sure she would win, he had no chance of gaining control of the company. She still prayed that when the morning came, her mother would be awake. The doctor had said that the outburst that she had was a good sign that she might come out of her coma soon.

When that would be was still a big question unanswered.

CHAPTER **NINETEEN**

All through the day the tension built as the six o'clock board meeting approached. Ricky and Jaymee had avoided interaction with Jasmine by keeping their office doors closed. Teddy didn't even bother coming into work. Jasmine noticed how everyone avoided her. It crossed her mind that her siblings might join forces with Teddy. The thought was quickly dismissed by the fact that none of them wanted Teddy at the head of the table. But, she figured, at least one of them had a power-play plan in mind to take her spot.

Around 5:55, Teddy waltzed into the boardroom with an air of confidence. Already sitting down were Ricky, Jaymee, and Richard. All three of them were nervous. Ricky and Jaymee smiled at Teddy as he made his way over to his seat. Today was their day of reckoning as well. They knew Teddy must have prepared a persuasive speech if he was going to get Ralph or Richard to switch their votes. They did know that Jackie would never go against anything Gloria had put in motion. Deep down, Ricky and Jaymee were pessimistic about it. They saw no reason why anyone would switch to Teddy's side other than themselves. No one else would gain anything from it. Plus, they all knew that everyone hated him as well.

The boardroom doors were flung wide open. All eyes fixed on Jasmine as she and Ralph walked in the room. Jasmine glanced at

Teddy and turned her nose up at him. He smiled back. As she and Ralph sat down, Ralph noticed Ricky and Jaymee whispering to one another. Something about their exchange worried him. He nudged Jasmine on the knee.

"They turned," he whispered to her.

"That's not an issue to me. As long as we are deadlocked, nothing changes," she whispered back. She was very confident that was the worst-case scenario.

Yet when Jasmine looked across at Richard, he nervously smiled and turned his head away to avoid direct eye contact. She thought that was peculiar, but for Richard to turn against her would be like him turning against Gloria, which was out of the realm of possibility.

Teddy glanced around the long table, looking into everyone's faces. His imminent victory conjured up old memories of all the times Gloria had told him no. A joyous feeling overcame him.

"I guess we are ready to start," Teddy said as the clock on the wall turned to six.

"Hold up, where's Jackie?" Ricky asked.

***

Over at an abandoned cemetery in New Jersey, a badly beaten tied-up Jackie was thrown into a coffin by several Mafia goons that looked like they had once been defensive linemen. After closing the casket, the men nailed it shut and pitched dirt on it. Jackie struggled to get out, but couldn't. With his life hanging in the balance, all he thought about was killing Teddy and being at the board meeting. By the timing of this ill-fated event, Jackie came to the conclusion that it was planned out by Teddy. He just wanted one more meeting to wrap his hands around his neck.

***

Back in the boardroom, Richard looked in question at Teddy. Teddy just ignored him. If Jackie wasn't there, Richard knew something wasn't right. Jackie was the last person anyone expected to miss the meeting. Besides Gloria, Jackie was always the most punctual one of them all.

"He was well aware of this meeting. I say we proceed until he arrives. Is that an okay compromise?" Teddy was anxious to keep the meeting moving forward.

Everyone nodded. Ralph sent a text message to Jackie to hurry up, just in case.

"Let's wait for Jackie," Jasmine said, wary of his absence. She had spoken to him at noon, and he had said he was definitely coming.

Teddy deferred to Jaymee and Ricky, asking if they wanted to keep the meeting going forward.

"Hey, we made it. Jackie's a grown man. Let's keep going," Ricky pressed.

"Yeah, let's continue. Who knows when he'll get here? I got things to do." Jaymee smirked.

"Why the rush?" Ralph asked mistrustfully.

"Ralph, in case you didn't know, we have a business to run," Teddy huffed in irritation.

"Okay, go ahead," Jasmine said, annoyed by her siblings' and Teddy's actions.

"Good. Well, I called this emergency meeting today because it has been a hundred and twenty-one days, to be exact, since our dynamic leader was struck down by a vicious assailant. We can only hope that he will be brought to justice and be prosecuted to the fullest extent of the law." He sighed. "But back to business. This meeting was set because of this clause in the bylaws that states that if Gloria Dean is unable to function past that period of time, a suitable leader would be put in her place until she does recover."

"Get to your point, Theodore," Ralph angrily said. "Don't bore us with your propaganda. We all know how you truly feel."

Teddy looked at everyone except for Jasmine. "Okay... Well, since Gloria's departure and Jasmine's so-called reign, the business has fallen off substantially. I know Gloria meant well in having her as the replacement, but it's not working out as well as even I had thought. No disrespect, but this is not your local mom and pop store or some reality show. Our numbers have suffered. "

"And you're basing this on what facts? I've seen the books. They are the same as last year," Ralph said.

"Exactly my point. We should be making strides, not standing still while our competition leaps ahead of us. This business is about growth, not stagnation."

"So, you want to run the fashion company?" Jasmine asked. She was fed up with his foolish attempts to gain control. "Is that what you want?"

Teddy peeked over at Ricky and Jaymee. They sensed that Jasmine's eyes were upon them. They shied away from looking in her direction.

"Yes, only the fashion end of the business," Teddy replied back.

"You amaze me. You know that entity is the prize possession of our family. It has been run and controlled by a Dean for over fifty years. To you I say, go to hell!" Jasmine vehemently pointed her finger at him and glanced over at her siblings again, but they continued to avoid her eyes. "Are you two in on this?"

"Wait!" he said with deceptive calmness. "I have formed a triad with Ricky and Jaymee. We would run it together. It's the best for all of us. A Dean would still run the company."

Their betrayal hurt her deeply, and her emotions got the best of her. She stood up.

"You think he cares about you," she yelled. "Believe me, he's gonna screw the both of you to the wall. Wake up!"

"Jasmine, it's only business. We're doing what's best for the company. Don't take it personal," Jaymee huffed.

"What's best for this company is what Momma wants, not him." She pointed at Teddy. "He's a snake."

"Can I finish?" Teddy scoffed.

Ralph got Jasmine to calm down a bit. She sat back down, but it was hard for her to stay seated. Her emotional state made it hard to let this meeting continue.

"As I was saying before all of the interruptions," Teddy went on, "I feel that we as a unit can lean on the others' vast knowledge of the industry and turn things around. When Gloria finally wakes up out of her coma, her company will be on top where she left it."

"In order for that to occur, you need a majority vote. A deadlock means things stay as is," Ralph said. "Unless Jackie walks through that door and backs you up, this meeting is over." He started putting away his papers so that he and Jasmine could leave. The meeting now appeared to be a moot point.

"I hope everyone votes with a clear mind on what's best for the company." Teddy raised his hand high up in the air. "How many people feel that the Triad Group should officially step in and run the company?"

"Teddy, I need for you to tender your resignation. This attempt at a mutiny is bad for business," Jasmine said, pissed at the developments. "Whatever the fair market value is of your stock, we will pay you by the end of business tomorrow. We don't need you here!"

Just then Jaymee raised her hand. It took Ricky a little while longer. He had a change of heart, but knew that he had already signed a contract agreeing to be a part of this group. With only three hands up, Ralph moved to adjourn.

"Like I said earlier, a deadlock means nothing, Theodore. Nada," Ralph said as he closed his briefcase. "I'll have the papers sent to your attorney severing your ties with the Gloria Dean Company immediately."

"I'm not my mother," Jasmine said. "This business relationship is over."

Teddy locked eyes with Richard, who up to now had sat quietly. Everyone in the room noticed Teddy staring him down. Then, unexpectedly, Richard's hand went up in the air. It was like slow motion. No one imagined that Richard would sell out Jasmine. Even though Teddy had applied pressure on him, he still didn't have complete confidence that he would vote for his side.

Jasmine felt her stomach revolt with the sickest wrench she had ever felt. The thought of her father ripping her heart out was unbelievable. He was the only true and honorable man she had ever known. Her entire family had turned on her in front of her very own eyes.

She stood up to speak, but no words came from her mouth. Jasmine stared at her father who, shamefully, wouldn't face her. Finally she broke the awkwardness by bolting out of the room. Ralph gathered their things and went after her.

He stopped at the boardroom door. "You should really be ashamed of yourself. After everything that she has been through, you repay her like this. Her mother, her husband, and her past. She came back for you guys. The wonderful love for her family." He shook his head. "And Richard, I truly hope you burn in hell." Ralph went out the door, slamming it behind him.

Richard was almost in tears. Both Jaymee and Ricky, even though they had voted against their sister, looked down on him for what he had just done. They couldn't believe it. At no time in their lives had they ever seen him go against Jasmine.

"Richard, you made the right decision," Teddy said with a wicked smile.

Richard got up and stomped out. His work there was finished. Raising his arm had destroyed the relationship he had with his family, especially Jasmine.

Teddy reached down, grabbed his briefcase, and put it on the table.

He pulled out a champagne bottle and three flutes.

"It's celebration time. We did it," he said joyously.

Jaymee and Ricky were still flabbergasted. When the Triad was formed, they never believe it would lead to them gaining control. They just wanted their voice to be heard on changes, and thought Teddy would be the best vehicle for that to occur.

"How did you know that our father would side against Jasmine?" Jaymee asked curiously.

Teddy unwrapped the champagne cork, then popped it. The question she asked was one he had hoped to avoid.

"I figured that your father, being a brash businessman, would see that the company's needs were more important than hers. And he did. The one thing he loves more than Jasmine is your mother."

He poured champagne in the three flutes.

"Man, I can't believe this. He never has gone against her about anything. I could tell by the look in his eyes, it hurt him," Ricky said as he picked up his glass. "But it sure feels good to finally be on the winning end. Now we can make some real changes around here."

Jaymee also picked up her glass. She was still suspicious about the turn of events. "Teddy, I have to admit that I had doubts that you could pull this off. You are a genius in my book. The smartest man on earth. You are a legend," she said with a hint of sarcasm.

Teddy raised his flute to make a toast. "To the great future and the glorious past—may the Triad kick everyone's ass along the way."

Their glasses clinked and they sipped.

"I second that," Jaymee said with a smile.

"But the Triad is only until Momma gets better," Ricky added. It was important to him that the original reason for their union was kept intact.

"Well, let's enjoy the moment while it lasts." Teddy eyeballed them. "Remember, the future has no limits. We made history today."

Teddy and Jaymee finished their champagne. While Teddy poured more into their glasses, Ricky put his down on the table. An unsettling feeling overcame him. He felt terrible about what had just happened. Somehow he just knew the future of the company was about to change for the worse.

Jaymee noticed how weird her brother was acting. "Ricky, you okay? Don't worry. Everything is going to be all right. I got your back."

Ricky looked at both of them with disgust. He wanted to tell them to go to hell, but the thought of being in power outweighed his thoughts of guilt.

"It's not normal for Jackie to miss a meeting. Something must have happened," Ricky said, thinking hard about that. It was true—Jackie had never missed a meeting. He would either call in or be present. "Don't you think I'm right?" Ricky glanced over to Teddy, who ignored him and sipped his champagne.

"Well, there's a first for everyone," Teddy said, forcing a grin. "I'm sure he'll show up soon."

"Ricky, who cares? I'm glad he wasn't here anyway. He probably would have killed us…or at least Teddy." Jaymee laughed.

For a moment Ricky and Jaymee both forgot about Teddy's proposal to join forces with Randolph James. For them, all their goals had been achieved.

***

Stuck in the coffin underground, dirt started slowly seeping through the cracks. Jackie tried to remain calm as he attempted to get his cell phone from his boot. He was able to get his phone, but the battery was dying. Jackie figured he only had enough power for one call, but who would be available to take his call was a mystery.

CHAPTER **TWENTY**

Jasmine hadn't spoken to or seen anyone for nearly a week. She locked herself in the mansion and told the new security guards to not let anyone enter the premises unless authorized by her. And she didn't plan on approving any authorizations. The same prohibition applied to her calls as well. Anyone who called got her voicemail. Her siblings and father did attempt to come by and talk to her about what happened, but they were sent away like everybody else. Even friends like Ralph and Cleo were subjected to the same rule. The only exception was Jackie, whom she tried endlessly to contact. Besides him, she just wanted to close the whole world off. Her trust for people had vanished. Jasmine wanted to return to her own company, but not in defeat. So she fought off the urge to run away.

The only thing that kept her in New York was her mother. The thought of being the person who ruined the cornerstone of the family business haunted her. How she was going to explain it to Gloria when she woke up was the billion-dollar question with no answer. Jasmine knew her mother would never understand what happened. For that matter, she still hadn't got a grasp on the reasons for her own peace of mind. Especially the mystery of why her father had turned on her.

Her real test came in the first couple of days. Jasmine almost had a nervous breakdown from the pressure of trying to understand how she was wronged. But her inner strength wouldn't let her crack. To handle the pressure, she drank heavily. Jasmine hoped that it would help her get over the betrayal she felt.

When she got out of bed that morning, she felt weird. She couldn't explain why. It was an eerie feeling that came and stayed with her. Last night was like the others before it; she didn't get much rest. The bags under her eyes looked like someone had punched her. Her hair was wild and her hygiene was poor. She hadn't washed for the last day or two. And the hope of it happening today was a long shot.

Jasmine rolled over and grabbed her cell phone off the nightstand. She had missed seventy calls. She scrolled through them. About twenty calls had come from Maxwell. Seeing his name put a slight smile on her face. Her mind quickly shifted to their last night together. The unfinished business enticed her to call him. She found his number in her cell phone and dialed.

With slow groove music playing in the background, Maxwell came out from under the covers to see who was calling. He froze when he saw Jasmine's name on the caller ID. Not wanting to miss out on the opportunity to speak with her, he answered it.

"Hello," he said, nervously glancing down at the covers.

"Hey, it's me," she said enthusiastically. "Do you have time to talk?"

He made several strange faces before answering her. "Always."

"I miss you," she said, wishing he were holding her again. "I woke up this morning and started to come by and surprise you."

"Are you okay? I heard what happened. Is there anything I can do"

Her voice turned hollow for a moment. "I don't want to talk about that now. Let's just think about us. You remember where we left off?"

Her time in solitude only added to her ambitions with him. The only thing she wanted to discuss was what positions they were going to use.

Her remark shocked him. His eyes bucked wide open. "For real… that would have been fun."

"What are you doing right now? Got time for fun?" she asked with a big smile.

A woman came out from under the covers. She slowly crawled up his body, kissing his sweet spots along the way. He put his finger up to signal to her to be quiet. The woman complied but continued her pleasuring techniques. These techniques finally overcame him. Maxwell couldn't respond to anything that Jasmine was saying.

"Do you need me to call you back?" she asked with a bit of attitude. Jasmine wondered why he was not paying her any attention. Since they hadn't spoken in a while, she thought he'd be a bit more enthusiastic.

"No, no, I want to see you," he said.

His words brought a smile back to her face and a frown to the face of the woman on top of him, naked.

"Good. Why don't you come over to my mother's house?" Jasmine asked.

"Anything you want. Just give me an hour to get ready."

"See you soon," she said with a sparkle in her eyes.

Maxwell hung up the phone. He flipped the covers off, exposing their naked bodies.

"The booty was bangin' and the head was great, but I gotta kick you out, so please don't hate."

He got up out of bed and went to the bathroom to shower. The woman stared at him in disbelief. She thought she was all that and more. No man had ever pushed her to the side for another. She angrily got up and put her clothes on. Once she was dressed and ready to go, she grabbed the gold bottle of champagne they had been drinking and smashed his eighty-inch TV and any other breakables she saw. When she heard the shower cutting off, she ran out.

***

An hour later, Maxwell arrived at the mansion. He was in awe at the regal surroundings. The place seemed like a palace. Even though he had money and a lot of it, he still couldn't compete with the Deans' money. Ever since he got a subscription to the *Robb Report* magazine, he thought he knew every facet of luxury living. He never thought there was another level until today.

Approaching the front door only added to his awe. The castlelike doors stood twelve feet high. The gold-plated door handles amazed him. While he was examining the doorknobs to make sure they were gold, the butler opened the door.

"Come in, sir. Ms. Jasmine is expecting you," the butler said in a proper tone.

Maxwell stepped gingerly inside. His amazement continued. An art collection of timeless, million-dollar masterpieces hung on the walls. A student of the better things in life, he knew without a doubt that the artworks were originals. Everything he saw made his millions seem like nickels and dimes.

The butler led him to the living room, where Jasmine was waiting. When he appeared in the doorway, she rose and came to him. They embraced for a long while. Maxwell couldn't keep his eyes off of the antiques that the house held. Around the living room were also pictures of the family with past dignitaries from all over the world. From the queen of England and MLK to Obama, the Dean family was in all of the exclusive high-society circles.

"You feel good," she said, gripping his body sensually.

"Where's everybody at?" he asked, nervously looking around.

"I'm in my thirties. I think I can have company without permission." She laughed.

"You know what I mean. I don't want to be disrespectful."

She caressed his chest and laid her head against his heart.

Having him beside her eased her pain somewhat. His heart beat rapidly.

"You're nervous." His racing heartbeat shocked her. Jasmine had thought he was never fazed by anything. It tickled her to see him not as cool as usual. Maxwell in his own environment was king but now seemed like a pauper.

"I-I'm cool," he stuttered. "I'm worried about you."

She sighed. The last person she wanted to talk about was herself. Jasmine wanted hot, passionate sex with him, not pity.

Jasmine led him over to the couch and they sat down. Suddenly she was overcome by all that had gone wrong. She put her face in her hands. He rubbed the back of her neck to console her.

"I lost my mother's prize possession," she cried. "She will never forgive me for that."

Maxwell gave it to her straight. "Jasmine, you're an honest person in a dishonest world. Teddy doesn't play fair at all, but that's just like the rest of the business world. You've known him your whole life, so you knew what he was capable of. He's a mongoose in the world of snakes."

His attitude shocked her. Jasmine had expected a shoulder to cry on, not scolding. She took a deep breath and leaned back on the couch. "You're right. All those years my mother protected us from him and his power trips. As long as she held the majority, there was nothing he could do."

"I don't understand what happened. Why did Ricky, Jaymee, and your father go against you?" Maxwell asked, confused.

Jasmine wiped her eyes. "I don't know how it happened myself. I understand why my brother and sister did it, but my father, of all people. That has puzzled me since that day. It really makes no sense."

"Had you two been fighting?"

"No. The day before we had lunch, and everything seemed fine. He told me then that he thought I was doing a good job in my mother's place. It just doesn't make any sense."

"Maybe Teddy has something on him?" Maxwell asked with a raised brow.

"My father? No, I definitely don't see that as a possibility. Maybe he felt guilty and wanted Ricky and Jaymee to have an opportunity. I just wished he had told me beforehand. I would have stepped down before I let them share some Triad power situation with Teddy." She shook her head just at the thought of Teddy running the company.

"A triad? What are they, Chinese?" he asked. He wanted to laugh, but for her sake he contained it.

Jasmine did smile at his comment. "All I know is that all three of them supposedly are running the company together."

"For how long?"

"Until my mother gets better."

He rubbed her shoulders. "So, you haven't really failed. She'll still have her company when she returns. I'm sure she'll understand. It's not your fault."

She slit her eyes at him and chuckled. "You don't know my mother. She will question my leadership and want to have me hung from the highest tree."

"Well, if worse comes to worst, you could always work with me. I could use a person with your intelligence."

She laughed. "I just lost a power battle in one of the largest fashion companies in the world, and you think I would do your company some good. Please. The only reason I'm still here is for my mother's other holdings. You don't know how hard it has been. I hate this shit!"

He softly rubbed her arm. "I hope you don't run from me. I'd like you to stay around."

"I'm sure you tell all the girls that until the next one comes along." She playfully rolled her eyes.

"No. Seriously, I want to see where this can go. You're special to me," he said. In truth, she was. Normally, Maxwell would have already slept with her and been done with it. Yet now he imagined that they would have deep talks and romantic walks and get to know each other inside and out.

He leaned in and kissed her, then pulled back. Furtively, he glanced over his shoulder to see if anyone was watching.

She caught him looking around. "Believe me, my family is nowhere to be found. If they were, there would be fireworks."

Jasmine passionately kissed him. If there was any hold-ups on her giving in to him, they were now released. His arms wrapped around her. All the fear and tension disappeared from her face. She floated in harmony with every kiss and touch. When she unbuttoned his shirt, they stopped and stared into each other eyes. She saw that he was a little hesitant.

"Are you sure about this?" he asked.

"I think that's a question you should be asking yourself," she said as she stood up.

"I'm cool," he replied, trying to convince her that nothing was wrong.

"Let's cash that rain check," she giggled. "The bank is up two flights and to the left." She pointed up toward her bedroom.

Jasmine grabbed his hand and led him out of the room. His suspicions grew as they were heading to her bedroom. After his earlier sexapade, her bedroom was the last place he wanted to go. Maxwell had nothing left in the tank.

"Where are we going?" he asked, clearing the lump in his throat. He already knew what the answer would be.

"To finish what we started at your place before I left. You remember the whipped cream and strawberry dream." She laughed, but kept them moving out of the room.

By his facial expression, it was clear that he had some serious reservations. Jasmine noticed it.

"Don't go soft on me now. I got the whipped cream upstairs on chill." She winked at him. "Just how you like it."

Maxwell didn't know what to say. Making love to her was something he had dreamed of when he was a young boy in Brooklyn and every day since they had met. He wished he had something left in the tank, but his energy was spent. He had sex with the other woman four unbelievable times. The thought of faking it crossed his mind, then he realized she would know instantly by how soft he would be. Plus, he wanted to enjoy the lovemaking moments with her.

As they ventured up the stairs, she freakishly rubbed his crotch. It was very soft. If she weren't so horny, she would have questioned it. Jasmine figured that once they got in bed, that would change quickly.

"Don't worry. I'll make that hard for you." She playfully licked her tongue out at him.

"You got your foot hard on the gas today," he said.

"No need for brakes." She chuckled.

The pressure to perform was enormous for him. He didn't want to lose her this way. Though his sexual urges hadn't waited for her, he felt a strong connection with Jasmine. In his mind, she was the one. She had everything that none of the other women offered him: enormous amounts of money, intelligence, and glamour.

When they got to her bedroom door, he knew that he had to do something drastic in order to save the situation. Maxwell gently grabbed her arm to stop her from going inside. She turned to him. He decided to do something that he had never done in his whole life— turn a woman down.

"Jasmine, let's just hold each other. I don't want to mess this up between us. Plus, this is your mother's place."

"Even if she was here, I have my own wing," she said, frustrated. "Don't do this, Maxwell. I want you."

"I just think we should wait. I promise the next time we are at my place. No stops."

He saw the disappointment on her face. *She must think I'm a soft-ass punk. What kind of fool turns down some pussy from Jasmine Dean?* he thought.

"Okay, I'll grab some things and we can go back to your place. That works for me."

The loop she threw at him caught him off guard. That option hadn't crossed his mind. With the damage his date left, going back to his place was not an option.

He yawned. "I had a real late night at the studio. I just want to get in the bed with you and hold you."

She sighed. It was apparent that she wanted more than a warm body next to her. Looking in his face, he seemed sincere.

"You're nothing like what people say," she said, leaning into him for a kiss.

He glanced down at her body. *Man, I gotta hit this soon. If anybody finds out I turned this shit down, my street cred is through.*

He kissed her, and they twirled into the bedroom. She closed the door behind them, masking her frustration.

CHAPTER **TWENTY-ONE**

Two days later, in a discreet location in the Soho district, Teddy met with John and several of his business associates. His lawyer, David Overmeirer, was present as well. The meeting was taking place in a private loft that Teddy had for all of his little indiscretions and affairs. Nobody in the Dean family knew about it.

As they sat at the table, Teddy and David went through the contract. They smiled at each other, page after page. The terms were agreeable to both of them. When Teddy signed the last page, everyone smiled around the room.

"After you pay me that dollar, we can celebrate," Teddy said, standing up. "That's a bargain."

David handed him a dollar bill. "That was the bet. I still can't believe you pulled it off."

David grabbed the bottle of champagne that was chilling in the middle of the table. He popped the cork and poured champagne into the glasses.

John, who sat at the other end of the table, reached in his briefcase and pulled out a box of Cuban cigars. He grabbed one for himself and slid the box to the middle of the table.

"Ted, I want to be the first to say, I will never doubt your magic again. You, my man, are the architect of overthrowing a dynasty. Pure and simple," John said as he lit his cigar.

"Thanks, but remember it's your money, not mine's." Teddy laughed as he lifted his glass up. "Let's toast."

Everyone followed suit and lifted their glasses as well.

"May our business relationship stand the test of time. Long live the Gloria Dean Company," Teddy said with a chuckle.

They all tapped glasses with each other. Teddy walked around the table and grabbed a cigar for himself. John came over and lit it for him.

"Make sure the money is wired to my account before tomorrow morning," Teddy whispered in John's ear.

"I'll have my people do it right now." John walked over to one of the guys at the table and started talking to him.

David came over to Teddy and pulled him away from the others.

"So, what are you going to do when the news breaks tomorrow morning?"

"Don't be concerned. The Dean family is not a problem anymore," Teddy said smugly.

"Are you still going away?" David asked.

"A month in fabulous Switzerland. Nobody needs to know my whereabouts. I'm sure the brother and sister combo will be going berserk trying to figure out what happened. I can hear them right now, crying, how can I get my mommy's company back?" He laughed. David still seemed a little tense. "David, you have to loosen up. We scored one of the biggest deals in history. Nobody thought this was ever possible. I did it!"

David smiled. "You sure did." His confidence started to reappear. "You enjoy that time away. I will keep everything under control."

"That's what I like to hear." Teddy sucked on the cigar. "I'm about to be the new King of New York."

John came back over. "Teddy, you're forgetting something?"

Teddy didn't think he forgot any detail of the deal. "What's that?" he laughed.

"Jaymee Dean."

"Were you really serious?" Teddy asked.

John glared at him angrily. "No Jaymee, no deal."

Teddy looked at David for some help. David was just as dumbfounded as him. "Jaymee is in, but we have to wait until the smoke clears."

"You told her?" John asked.

"Yeah, of course," Teddy lied. "Jaymee will be a valuable asset."

"Good, I will be in contact with her soon."

"Are you sure about her?" Teddy tried again. "She does come with baggage."

"Yes."

"But why? There has to be a good reason."

"Teddy, your money will be deposited tomorrow. Enjoy your trip," John said as he walked off.

CHAPTER **TWENTY-TWO**

The next morning when the *New York Times* hit Jaymee's doorstep, she was at the kitchen table with Brittany, eating breakfast. She didn't have a care in the world. Her mind was now at ease since the formation of the Triad Group with Teddy and Ricky. With Jasmine out of the way, no one could stop her, or so she thought. From the kitchen window she saw the paperboy walk away. Getting the newspaper was last on her list of things to do. Normally, she didn't read it anyway. As the paper sat on the ground, she went to take a shower. When Jaymee got to her bedroom, she noticed her cell phone vibrating. It was her brother.

"Ricky, it's too early for your mess," she said to the phone as she put it back down. "I am not about to let you ruin my day."

She took off her pajamas and got into the shower with a smile as big as Texas on her face.

About twenty minutes later, she stepped out of the shower, naked. She was to find Ricky seated on her bed in tears. She quickly covered up her body with a towel.

"What's going on?" she said in a panic. "Why are you in my bedroom?"

"He fucked us. He fucked us good," he whimpered. "Momma's gonna kill us!"

"Slow down! What are you talking about? Who fucked us?"

"We lost Momma's company."

"I didn't lose anything!" she said.

"So, now you're going to act stupid?"

An alarm was starting to go off in her head. "What did Teddy do?"

He wiped his eyes. "He sold the company yesterday."

Jaymee slumped down on the bed next to him. She was totally nonplussed by what had happened. The main thing on her mind was how could she spin this around so that Ricky took the blame.

"I'm sure you're wrong. He can't do that without our approval. We run the company together as one. The Triad, remember."

He swung his head back and forth. "Nope. I called my lawyer and he said that he was in his rights to sell the company if an adequate offer was made. And that's what he did."

She leaped to her feet and grabbed her phone. Jaymee wanted answers, now. She started to make a call.

Ricky grabbed her hand. "No need. I've tried calling him myself. I even called his lawyer. He said something about Teddy being out of the country. I just want to kill him."

Outraged, Jaymee threw the phone to the floor. "How dare he?" she cried.

Brittany came to the door. "Momma, are you okay?"

"I'm sorry, baby. Momma got a little excited. Go back to getting ready for school. Your dad will be here soon."

Brittany left the room.

"So, what are we going to do?" he asked, begging for a way out.

She folded her arms together. Tears began racing down her face just as they did Ricky'. Her stomach did cartwheels. Jaymee couldn't believe the mess they'd made. The first person to come to her mind to call was Jasmine. With the way they treated her at the board meeting fresh on her mind, though, she knew that call would not be an easy one.

"Maybe we should call Jasmine," Ricky said, bringing her up himself.

Jaymee acted miffed. "Please. She's not going to talk to us. I hope she doesn't find out about this until we figure out a way to get the company back."

"How do you figure that's going to happen?"

She broke down crying again. "I don't know. But I know one thing, if Momma wakes up, and she finds out what happened, there will be hell to pay."

Ricky took some deep breaths. "You know, when the decision was made to form the Triad, I remember having reservations about it."

"How many people know about this?" Jaymee asked.

He stared at her like she was crazy. "Jaymee, it was on fuckin' CNN! The whole damn world knows what we did. We're toast."

He threw the newspaper at her. Headlining the front page was the sale of their company and a picture of Teddy smiling with a dollar bill in his hand.

She fell back on the bed and stared up at the ceiling. "Everybody knows by now. I think I'm going to be sick."

Jaymee got up and went to the bathroom. When she got by the door, she shot Ricky a disappointed look. He shot her one back. Somehow, some way, she had to blame him for this debacle.

***

At the mansion, Jasmine was still sleeping like a baby. Her body was curled up under the covers. Since the other entities of the Dean empire were self-sustaining, she didn't really have any work to do, so she had nowhere to go and no time to be there by. Since her departure from the fashion entity, this schedule had been working pretty well for her.

The home phone next to the bed started to ring off the hook. She buried her head in the pillows to muffle the sound. Her thought was, *I have no responsibilities and no one cares what I do, so it can't be for me.* She ignored the calls, but they persisted. Jasmine pulled herself up and glanced at the caller ID. It was the hospital calling. Jasmine snatched the phone up off the hook.

"Hello," she said, still half asleep. "What did you say?...She what?... Oh, my God. I'll be right there."

She quickly got out of bed. Still wobbly, she dragged herself to the shower.

***

John settled in nicely at his new office at the Gloria Dean Company. Which was Gloria's office. Around the whole building he had movers boxing up personal belongings of all the employees that had been fired. Downstairs at the entrance, he had the guards turn away the old designers and staff. He was making way for his own team to come in. He sat back in Gloria's chair with his feet propped up on the desk. In his mouth was his customary fat cigar. Everything seemed to be going perfectly until Ricky and Jaymee entered the office through the private entrance. The security guard caught them right before they entered Gloria's office.

"Mr. Lincoln, there's a Ricky and Jaymee wanting to see you," the security guard said.

The situation presented a dilemma. Talking to them was not on the top of his list. He figured that they would be coming, so he had prepared himself. Taking over this company was an act of revenge for him. He'd told no one, but years ago his father and grandfather were run out of business by Gloria and her father, Jack. He welcomed the faces of the defeated.

"Yes. I'll see them." He smiled.

Jaymee and Ricky stormed into the office. Seeing John with his feet on the desk perturbed them. Ricky quickly went and pushed his feet off. The armed security guard grabbed him and threw him to the ground.

"Now, if you are going to be in this building, you have to respect me," John said, staring at Ricky. Jaymee was cool, to some degree. She knew that the roughhousing act that her brother started was not the way.

"Ricky, calm down. We just need our questions answered." She looked at John in hopes that he would instruct the guard to let go of her brother.

As Ricky calmed down, John signaled to the guard to let go of him, and he did. Ricky and Jaymee sat in the two chairs opposite their mother's desk.

"I don't know you, but after our attorneys get through with you and Teddy, you'll be begging for yesterday. You need to vacate the premises," Jaymee said.

John clapped his hands arrogantly. "Bravo, bravo, you almost had me scared." He took a puff of his cigar and put it down. He then leaned forward. "This transaction is final. The Dean family has been paid handsomely. More than market value." John turned up his nose and smirked.

"Where's Teddy?" Ricky asked, fuming.

The pain of losing the company was written all over their faces. Now, having gotten his revenge, he realized that they were just pawns, but reversing the damage was not an option.

"I don't know Theodore Hicks's whereabouts. I figure you should. You three were running the company together." John smiled. "My lawyer has the documents and proof of the sale. This company is now the property of the Randolph James Company."

Ricky and Jaymee both thought back to Teddy's offer to join him in partnering with Randolph James. Neither one wanted to expose that secret now. And since they hadn't talked to Teddy, they felt the deal was a farce in the first place.

Jaymee put her hand up to stop him from saying anything else. "Hold up. How did you buy our company? We never agreed to a sale."

"Actually, you did indirectly. Theodore showed me the contract that he had you guys sign, and from what I read, it definitely gave him the right to sell on your behalf."

"That don't make any goddamn sense," Ricky said, raising his voice.

"I'm just the buyer, not the seller. It makes perfect sense to me. Look at it this way—you guys made a fortune off me."

Jaymee snarled, "What was the sale price?"

John smiled. "Call your accountant."

"This is bullshit!" Ricky and Jaymee both said.

Ricky growled at him, looking like he wanted to jump across the table and rip his throat out. "What will it take to get our company back?" he asked. "I'll give you half a billion on top of what you paid."

John hated to be rude, but that was the only way he felt the meeting would end. "That's not going to happen. Sorry. I suggest you take up any more complaints with Theodore Hicks. I plan to run this company forever, and there's nothing you can do about it."

"You're not using the Gloria Dean name?" Jaymee asked.

"Of course, that's what I paid for."

"I will be back," Ricky said as he stood up. "You better watch your ass, bitch!"

John laughed. "Are you threatening me? You, of all people. I will crush you like the bug you are."

Feeling hopeless, Ricky stormed out of the office. Left alone and with nothing to say, Jaymee looked like a deer in headlights.

"Is there anything else, Ms. Dean?" John asked with a smug smile on his face.

She cleared her throat and stood up. "Everyone has a price. What is yours?"

"Is that what your mother would say?" He chuckled.

"I will get this company back."

"I'll be right here when you don't," he replied sarcastically.

Jaymee walked out of the office looking like a wounded animal. She was confused and didn't know what she was going to do.

***

At the hospital, Jasmine came into Gloria's room with mixed feelings. Seeing her mother conscious was emotionally lifting. Yet it also meant that she would be pushing on to other things. She had declared that she would leave once Gloria got better since her arrival, but now with the end near, she didn't want to go. Though she denied it to family and friends, Jasmine liked being back in New York City. Her only problem was the mutiny in the boardroom and telling her mother about all the events.

Gloria's face lit up once she saw Jasmine. This was the first time she had seen her daughter in years. With her near-death experience, the moment was big. She struggled to open her arms so that her daughter would come over and hug her. Jasmine slowly made her way over, and they embraced.

"Momma, I love you. I'm so glad you made it," she tearfully said.

Not even fifty percent recovered, Gloria could barely talk. Her speech was weak and slurred, but that didn't stop her from trying.

"They didn't kill me yet. I've got a couple of more miles left in me."

Jasmine sat down in the chair next to the bed. *After I tell you what happened, it's my miles that I'm worried about,* she said to herself.

"Momma, we have so much to talk about. I don't want to fight with you anymore. With your recovery in sight, I will be leaving so that you can go back to running your company." She grabbed her mother's hand. *Damn, I shouldn't have said anything about the company,* she thought.

"Where's Jackie and your brother and sister?" she mumbled. "I hope you all haven't been fighting."

The memories of that boardroom meeting came back to her. The festering wound was opened again. She wanted to kill everyone who'd double-crossed her, most of all her father. Jasmine knew the truth would be too tough for her mother to take in her fragile state. She started to mention Jackie, but realized she hadn't spoken to him either. Jackie's disappearance was an unsolved mystery that Jasmine didn't want to think about. In the back of her mind, she figured he might be dead. But she kept hoping that he was somewhere looking for the person who attempted to kill her mother.

"I don't know. We haven't talked," she said, avoiding eye contact.

Gloria slurred. "How's the business doing? I know I put a tremendous amount of pressure on you to run the company, but I trust you the most. I know there's only one person who can run that part of the business like me." She forced a smile.

Jasmine didn't want to continue the conversation. The last thing she wanted to tell her mother was what they all did to her. Not that she wasn't going to tell, but today just didn't seem ideal.

"I see you're talkative today. Shouldn't you be resting?" she said with a raised brow at her mother. "You need to rest."

Though she was very weak, Gloria looked like she had questions she wanted answers to now. "Where's your father?" she asked, probing for more information.

"I don't know. I haven't talked to him either." Once the words left her mouth, Jasmine knew she had screwed up. It was like jumping out of a plane without a parachute. The floating in the air may be bad, but the fall would be deadly.

It was a struggle, but Gloria turned her head to stare at her. She was used to Jasmine not speaking with her siblings. For her not to have talked to Richard meant something had happened. Richard and Jasmine, in her eyes, were almost inseparable, two peas in a pod.

Jasmine tried her best to ignore her mother's eyes burning the side of her face.

"You're not leaving here until I get an answer," Gloria demanded.

"Answer to what?" Jasmine replied evasively.

"Don't play dumb. Something happened, and I want to know what, and I want to know right now. Don't play with me, Jasmine Marie Dean!"

Her mother's words were very slurred, but Jasmine heard her clearly.

Her mother was getting weaker. Delivering bad news was not her specialty. She wanted to escape the situation, but knew her mother would only keep persisting. Jasmine knew telling her mother what happened was only going to make her hit the roof. And not telling her really wasn't an option.

She coughed and turned to her mother. "You need to get your rest. I'm going to leave." Jasmine stood up.

Gloria slit her eyes at her. "Jasmine," she growled. "Sit your ass down."

"Momma, you need to rest."

"What do you think I've been doing? Tell me what you're hiding!" Gloria demanded as forcefully as her weak body would allow her.

Jasmine dropped her head. "I lost the company."

Gloria looked dumbfounded. That was the last answer she expected.

"Explain," she whispered as her oxygen level decreased.

"Jaymee, Ricky, and Richard all voted against me. Ricky and Jaymee formed some triangle leadership with Teddy. They are supposedly running the company until you get back."

Gloria breathed an audible sigh of relief. As Jasmine well knew, the company was all her mother ever knew. It was the legacy she wanted to leave. "I understand Jaymee and Ricky turning against you, but Richard?"

"That hurts the most," Jasmine admitted.

"I'm sure there's a reason."

"I don't care. He could have come to me. Whatever it was, we could have worked it out."

"We'll fix that once I get back. How was the company performing?" she asked, looking curious.

"Sales were the same as last year. Yet the new group said that they could easily triple sales. Their argument was that I was bringing the company down," Jasmine said, peeved by the memory. Rehashing the incident stirred up more hatred for her siblings and her father. "I don't want to see them ever again."

Gloria flinched at the sight of her daughter's pain. "Don't worry. Momma is back now and we will fix all this drama. Teddy will be gone from the company. That's a guarantee."

Jasmine didn't care. She wanted out of it all. For her, family meant everything, and hers had committed the ultimate betrayal.

"Once you get out of the hospital, I'll be leaving. I think I'm going out West to open up some Jazzie stores in L.A., Oakland and San Francisco. That is, before I set off to conquer Europe and Asia."

Gloria leaned her head back on the pillow. Jasmine saw her mother almost in tears, and she didn't know what to say. Her principles had been violated. She had tried to work things out with her brother and sister. The reason her father turned on her was still obscure, but she didn't care at this point. As far as she cared, they could all go to hell.

"Will you call your brother and sister?" Gloria asked, wiping some tears from under her eyes.

"Sure. When I'm on my way out."

"So when will you be leaving?" Gloria asked plaintively.

"Don't worry, Momma, I have some unfinished business to resolve before I leave. Payback will be painful."

Jasmine started to grab the remote and turn on the TV. She glanced over to her mother and noticed that she had ebbed back into sleep. She then put the remote down and closed her eyes as well.

***

In a dark corner at Starbucks, eating croissants and drinking caramel macchiatos, Ricky and Jaymee were trying to think of a way to locate Teddy. This Starbucks was one that Teddy frequented. While waiting, they had called almost everyone they knew with connections to him, and no one to this point had a clue to his whereabouts. With their mission failing, they knew that sooner or later they would have to call Jasmine for help.

When Ricky got off the phone, he was pissed off and frustrated. The people sitting near them could tell something had really gone wrong for them by their erratic behavior. Nothing made sense to Ricky or Jaymee. With no one to turn to, they just sulked and exchanged harsh looks with one another.

"Maybe we should call…" She paused to think about it a little bit more.

"Jasmine," he said, finishing her sentence.

"We're family, right? She wouldn't ignore our calls, would she?" Jaymee had a desperate look on her face.

"I don't know. I would, but she's a better person than I am. She understood the business way better than we did. Man, we fucked up. I don't even want to think about what Momma would say," Ricky said with a frown.

"Thank God, we have time to think of something before she finds out." Jaymee had the same kind of pinched frown on her face as well. "So, what do we say to her?"

His cell phone rang. He glanced at the caller ID.

"Jasmine," he said, shocked to see her calling him.

Jaymee saw his frozen look. "Ricky, what is it?"

"It's Jasmine calling me…Do I answer it?" he asked, perplexed by the decision.

"She must know. Damn!" Jaymee said. "Answer it. We need her

help."

"You sure?" he asked with his finger on the talk button.

She nodded for him to do it. He did.

"Hello," he said with desperation in his voice.

Jasmine was at Gloria's hospital door, getting ready to exit. Her eyes were fixed on her mother, who was still sleeping.

"Ricky, I just called to tell you…"

He interrupted her. "We fucked up. I know what happened wasn't right—"

She cut him off. "I didn't call to talk about that."

"Just let me finish," he begged. "I need your help." He looked at Jaymee sitting across from him. "We need your help."

Jasmine could tell by the crackling sound of his voice that he had done something wrong. Her first instinct was to tell him about their mother and hang up. Yet the protective sister mode in the back of her mind came forth.

"What is it, Ricky? I don't have much time," she said, maintaining an attitude.

He sighed. "We lost the company."

A stunned silence followed. "What the hell do you mean by 'lost the company'?"

"Teddy tricked us into signing some documents that gave him the power to sell the company. I swear when we read the papers he didn't have that kind of power."

Disbelief colored Jasmine's voice. "This can't be happening. Tell me he didn't sell Momma's beloved company, did he?" she whispered into the phone.

Ricky was hesitant to respond. The answer was simple, but the repercussions were deadly. He handed the phone to Jaymee.

"Hello," Jaymee said, clueless to what had been asked.

"Jaymee, did Teddy sell the company? That's all I want to know." Her tone rose to a frightening pitch.

Seeing that there was no way to avoid the question, she answered with a simple but sad "Yes."

After a moment of collecting her thoughts, Jasmine put the phone back to her ear. "You don't know how bad your timing is. I'm at the hospital because Momma just came out of her coma."

"She's dead?" Jaymee cried.

"When she finds out about this shit, you will wish that she was."

Ricky snatched the phone from her. He had heard Jasmine's muffled voice.

"Can we see her?" he asked.

"Yes. Come on up. Of course, when she saw me, the first thing she asked about was her precious company. I told her what happened between us in that boardroom coup, but what you have to tell her is going to start a war."

"What do we do?" Ricky asked, his voice warbling.

"My opinion, you should try telling the truth. If you don't tell her up front and she finds out later that you were lying, you're toast."

"Will she stay so that we can tell Momma together," Jaymee said in the background.

"Tell her no. I gotta find Jackie. Something must have happened to him."

"He always disappears," Ricky said.

"He normally calls in," Jasmine said.

"We need you right now!" Ricky pleaded.

"I'm not a part of this shit anymore. You two have to ride this one out all by yourselves. Bye." Jasmine hung up the phone.

***

In the cemetery where Jackie was buried alive, some kids were playing soccer near him. The ball rolled on top of the coffin. One of the kids noticed the coffin in the ground. He called over his friends. Out of morbid curiosity, they opened it. Once the lid was open they saw the gruesome remains of a man. By the look of things it would take some DNA samples to identify his body.

***

At home, Jasmine looked up Jackie's car's GPS location. As she studied a map of where the car was, she realized it was in the Hudson River. She called the police and told them her suspicions.

CHAPTER **TWENTY-THREE**

The police and Jasmine watched as Jackie's car was pulled from the Hudson River. Given her mother's present condition, she had held back from telling her anything about Jackie possibly being dead or even missing. As the car rose skyward, Jasmine started to think how she was going to break the news of his death to her mother. Telling her that Jackie was dead would be devastating. She knew Gloria considered him like one of her children.

When the car, shedding water on all sides, touched the tarmac, several police officers walked over to it. She anticipated the worst when she saw the bullet holes in the front window of the car. Yet by the reaction of the officers, she could tell that they were perplexed.

"There's no one in here," one of the officers yelled back at them.

She let out a sigh of relief, until she realized that his disappearance was now even more mysterious. He must have been kidnapped or his body had been stashed somewhere else. She grabbed her cell phone and started to make a call.

***

At a nearby coffee shop, Jasmine sat sipping a cup of coffee. She had been waiting for over an hour and her waitress was getting upset. All

Jasmine had ordered was a cup of coffee while other customers waited to be seated. She could care less about making the waitress mad. Her concern was focused solely on the person she was meeting. When she saw a burly black man in a sleek black suit with a black shirt come in the door, she cracked a smile.

As he made his way over to her table, she stood up to welcome him with open arms. They embraced and sat down together.

"Chris, how are you?" she asked.

"The question is, how are you? You sounded desperate over the phone." He gave her an assessing look. "What's going on?"

Chris Daniels was an old friend and former police detective. At one time, he was Jasmine's personal bodyguard. Now he was a private investigator.

"I shouldn't be doing this, but it's not for me," she whispered.

"I heard about the company. That Teddy is crazy. You got to get him for that. What can I do, though, that Jackie can't do?"

"That's the problem. I haven't seen Jackie for days. He didn't show up for that board meeting, and that's the last time any of us have talked to him. Yesterday, I found out his wife and son had disappeared as well."

"Damn, I'm sorry to hear that. He's good people."

"He might be dead," she said sorrowfully. "Look, I need your help. My mother loves the company and I got to get it back. I'm sure all of this has something to do with Jackie. Everyone knows that he is my mother's lifeline."

"Where is Jackie's stepbrother, Bronco?"

"Going crazy trying to find his brother."

Chris smirked. "I bet the murder rate is going up in New York. Bronco ain't wrapped too tight."

"Would you expect any less?"

"OJ didn't either."

They both laughed.

"So, are you in?" Jasmine asked.

"I don't know, Jasmine," Chris said, sounding fearful of taking on the challenge.

"What's the hesitation?" she asked, not sure of why he didn't want to help.

"I'm going to be real with you. You muthafuckas are wealthy. When you have that kind of money, people come up erased like they never existed. It's a whole different world. The law can't even touch you. And the people who crossed you probably got just as much money as you. I got to think about my family. I happen to love breathing."

She reached over the table and took a hold of his hand. Jasmine was the kind of woman men had a hard time saying no to. Chris was no different. As she looked at him, he melted.

"Whatever you need, I'm there for you," Chris said.

She smiled. "Thanks. I need to figure out what happened. I've called Ricky and Jaymee's attorney, and they told me that the contract to form this Triad Group was the way it was. Teddy had to have worked an angle to weasel the company away from them. They are stupid, but not that stupid." She took another sip of her coffee.

He thought for a moment. "So they formed this group and voted you out with the help of your father. Then Teddy turned around and sold the company based on the Triad contract, giving him power of authority to do it. Is that about right?"

She nodded.

"What do you want from me?"

"I need to know how the sale went down and with whom."

"Where are the two geniuses at now?" he inquired with a smirk. "I'm gonna have to talk to them eventually."

She shook her head. "Right now they're at the hospital seeing my mother."

"What about Ralph? Maybe he can shed some light on the situation."

"I called him before I called you, but I got no answer. I was thinking about dropping by," she said.

"What about your father? Where is he at in all this stuff?"

"I haven't talked to him. He's dead to me," she said with conviction.

Chris looked her dead in the face. "I'm sure Teddy had something to do with it. Out of all people, your pops would never turn against you," he said with certainty. "You need to talk to him."

"I don't care. He could have come to me. Things didn't have to get this out of hand." She rolled her eyes. "There's nothing he couldn't have come to me about." She motioned her hands as if she was choking someone. "He wouldn't even look at me!"

Chris knew she didn't have the nerve to deal with her father, so he moved on. "I'll look into what happened with your father and I'll contact Ralph. You worry about your mother. Expect a call from me later tonight." He got up from the table and left.

She pulled out her cell phone again and dialed Ralph. Once more, all she got was his voicemail. Jasmine sensed something wasn't right. Ralph was not the kind of person who would continue to ignore calls, especially ones coming from the Dean family.

***

When Ricky and Jaymee arrived at Gloria's bedside, they were happy to see that she was sleeping. They brought in two dozen red roses and enough balloons to fill up half the room. They were hoping the flowers and balloons would hide the guilt their faces showed. They looked pitiful as they approached her. Both of them prayed she wouldn't wake up while they were there. They did find solace seeing the TV turned off, which to them was a good sign, because they really weren't ready to tell her about losing their mother's prized possession.

Jaymee crept over to the other side and gently kissed her mother on the forehead. And Ricky kissed her on the cheek. Without saying a word, they started slowly back backing out the door. They were just moments away from escaping the room without having to explain anything when one of the balloons popped.

Gloria was startled out of her sleep. She saw them creeping out.

"Where are you two going?" she asked, still groggy.

The culprits looked at one another for an answer.

Gloria laser-eyed them to compel them to talk.

Frightened by the look on his mother's face, Ricky blurted out, "We didn't want to disturb you."

Still weak, Gloria motioned with her hand for them to come closer. Ricky obeyed quickly. Jaymee saw the same look in her mother's eyes as she had seen many times before. It was a look of disappointment. She walked over at a very slow pace, like a child about to get spanked.

With both of her children by her side, Gloria reached over to the little table next to the bed and grabbed a cup of water. Gloria pulled herself up on her bed.

"What the hell did you two do to Jasmine?"

Neither one wanted to answer her question. They knew they were wrong. There were no words to justify their actions. Like school kids, they wanted to blame someone, but no one came to mind. This time around, they had painted themselves into a corner.

"Somebody is going to answer me," Gloria demanded. "Jaymee, what happened?"

"I, we, helped Teddy run Jasmine out of the company. He promised that we would all run it together." She said it in a way, hoping that her mother would have mercy on her.

Gloria shook her head with disappointment. "I have always told you two that family is important. I'm sure Jasmine could have done the same to you, but she didn't! No matter how mad you made her, she wouldn't desert you. That's why I left her in charge during emergencies like this."

What their mother had said was the truth. If there was one thing about

Jasmine that they all knew, she would always be loyal to her family.

"I'm sorry, Momma," Ricky said. "I never thought Teddy would do us like that. We trusted him."

Her eyes scanned both of them. "What exactly did he make you do?" she asked. Her fist balled up, showing her white knuckles.

They stared at one another to see which one was going to speak up. Ricky cleared his throat. Jaymee took a step backward so that she wasn't within Gloria's reach.

"We formed this Triad Group, from which we would run the company together. Then last night..." Ricky stopped to take a deep breath. He also slightly stepped away from his mother's grasp. "He sold the company."

Gloria was mystified. "What company?" she asked.

"Your company," Jaymee replied. "Isn't that what we're talking about?"

An intense flame came to Gloria's face. Her hand reached out to grab one of them. They were barely out of her reach.

"When I get my hands on you, I swear I'm going to kill you," she said with her breath shortening. "Who did he sell to?"

"Some John Lincoln guy," Jaymee said, somewhat under her breath.

"Who?" Gloria asked, wanting her to speak up.

"John Lincoln," Ricky replied.

"Are you sure?" Gloria asked with a perplexed look.

"Do you know him?" Jaymee asked.

Gloria froze for a second. "No. How old is this Lincoln?"

"Might be around fifty," Ricky said. He found his mother's reaction unusual.

"I know the name quite well. John Lincoln's father, John Senior, was a competitor back in the late seventies and early eighties. Your grandfather destroyed the Lincolns' business by undercutting the sales of their top lines." Gloria's blood pressure and heart rate shot up. Her monitors went off and the nurses raced in. Ricky and Jaymee were escorted out the door so that they could attend to Gloria.

While in the hallway, they could see that Gloria still had her eyes fixed on them. Seeing that the nurses needed to restrain Gloria with straps saddened them. They moved away from the door and walked down the hallway.

"What are we going to do?" Jaymee asked. "She hates us."

He glanced at her in disbelief. After all they had done, he couldn't believe that Jaymee thought anyone loved them. Even if they hadn't lost the company, they were heading for a chastising just for questioning her authority by having Jasmine removed.

"I hate us. All we can do now is hope that Jasmine helps us," Ricky said, dispirited about the outcome.

Jaymee smirked at his comment. She didn't want her fate to depend on Jasmine's generosity, but she really had no choice. Ricky's face filled with tears as they dragged themselves out of the Intensive Care Unit. After all these years of wanting to protect his family, it had turned out that he betrayed the family.

CHAPTER **TWENTY-FOUR**

Early the next morning, Chris arrived at Ralph's house in Darien, Connecticut. From outside, everything looked okay. He knocked on the door several times, but never received a response. It was strange that the lights were on and Ralph's car was still in the driveway. Chris started to leave but decided to call Ralph's cell phone. He heard his phone ringing from inside. He strolled around the back of the house. The back door was ajar. Foul play was the first thought that ran through his mind. He rubbed his bald head, apprehensive about what he might find, then pulled out his gun from the small of his back. Chris quietly opened the door and let the gun lead the way.

Upon entering, Chris vaguely heard country music playing upstairs. He checked the first floor thoroughly. As he crept up the stairs, a foul odor came from a room down the hallway. Not wanting to be surprised, he inspected each room along his path. When he got to the room with the smell, he covered his mouth and nose. He slowly turned the doorknob. The door slowly opened and he saw Ralph hanging from the ceiling fan. By the look of his body, he had been beaten and tortured before the hanging.

Chris did not flinch. Dead people were a part of his business, and though Ralph looked bad, he had seen worse. It was painful for him because he knew Ralph through the Dean family. From his back pants pocket he pulled out some rubber gloves. Chris put them on and got up on the bed. He checked Ralph's pants and his shirt.

In his shirt pocket, Chris found a business card with John C. Lincoln's name on it. He remembered the name from the newspaper as the guy who bought the Gloria Dean Company. He put the card in the inside pocket of his jacket. He studied Ralph's fingernails. There was some blood and skin under them. It led him to believe that Ralph had fought for his life.

Chris pulled out his small forensic kit and took samples. Once he finished, he searched around the room for any other clues. In Ralph's closet he noticed that his safe was wide open and empty. With no more clues in sight, he went out the same way he had come in.

When Chris got back in his car, he pulled out his cell phone and dialed.

"Hello," Jasmine answered.

"You might want to sit down for this," Chris said, starting up his car.

"What did you find out?" she whispered.

"It's Ralph. He's dead. I found him hanging from the ceiling."

Jasmine was speechless as the phone dropped from her ear. It crashed to the floor. Gloria noticed what happened. Seeing the anguish on her daughter's face convinced her that things were not going well. Jasmine picked up the phone and tried to return to some sort of normalcy.

"Chris, I'm sorry."

"It was not something I wanted to tell you. This situation is already getting out of hand. Who are these people?"

"I don't know. So, what do we do next?" she asked.

"Ralph must have had something that someone wanted. There was definitely a struggle. I need to find out what they got from him. They cleaned out his safe."

"Now I have to break that news to my mother. What a welcome back to life this has been for her. Shit!" Jasmine was mad at herself. "I'm in over my head."

"Just hold it together. I promise I'll get to the bottom of it all," he said confidently. Chris wanted badly to help Jasmine.

"Please, call me when you know more."

"Let your mother know I'm on top of it, okay? I'm sorry."

***

After he hung up the phone, she continued to hold it up to her ear. With Gloria in her sight, she didn't know how to tell her that Ralph had been killed and how he had been killed. The secret longing that Ralph and Gloria had shared for one another was no secret to her. Jasmine had known about it back when she was a little girl. Though nothing ever came from it, their friendship still blossomed. He was Gloria's best friend, which made delivering the news all the more difficult.

She inhaled and exhaled slowly as she walked into the room. Her mother read the pain on her face. Jasmine embraced her mother and kissed her on the cheek, then sat down in the chair next to the bed. Gloria looked at her with tears in her eyes. Seeing her mother's tears made her eyes water as well. She grabbed them both a Kleenex off the table next to the bed. Jasmine wiped her nose.

"What happened now?" Gloria asked with gloom on her drawn face.

Jasmine sensed Ricky and Jaymee had come clean. "I take it Ricky and Jaymee talked to you about what happened."

Gloria slanted her head. "That's the least of my worries. We'll get the company back."

"I guess that's one good thing." Jasmine dropped her head, still not sure of how to deliver the news.

"Jasmine, what is it?" Her mother coughed, trying to catch her breath. "What could be worse than losing the company? Has anyone talked to Ralph or Jackie? I want to see them as soon as possible." She glanced at Jasmine's depressed face. "Why are you looking like someone died?"

"Momma, it's Ralph. He's dead," she said slowly.

Silence filled the room. The look of dread filled Gloria's face. Her heart plummeted to the ground and cracked. Hearing the news put her back in a depression. *I loved him so much*, she thought to herself. This was worse. She loved him deeply. The thoughts of things never said or acted upon flashed through her mind like sand passing through an hourglass. She wished that she could have done something to reverse all of the events. Everything seeming so surreal, it made her numb. In the back of her mind, she couldn't help but think the root cause of all the terrible events led back to something she had done.

Jasmine felt her mother's pain. She hugged her mother. They cried together for the first time in their lives. For her mother to cry over anything was big. The last time she had seen her cry was at her grandfather's funeral, some thirty years ago.

Gloria pulled away from her. "How did he die?" she asked. Gloria stared directly into her eyes. She wanted answers no matter what the details might be.

"Chris said he found him hanging."

The imagination of him hanging hurt deeply, but the thought of it being suicide was complete nonsense. "He wouldn't do that. It's murder."

"Chris found evidence of a struggle. I'll know more when he calls me back."

"What about his files?" Gloria asked nervously.

"His safe was cleaned out," Jasmine said. "Whoever did this knew exactly what they were doing. None of this is random. I want to know what they got out of his safe."

"This is all my fault." Gloria's hands covered her face. Things were already going downhill, but by her facial expression, it was about to get worse. Jasmine noticed a more stressed-out look on her mother's face than ever before. Her mother had never been tested like this, ever in her life. She normally had all the answers, but now she only had questions.

"What's wrong?" Jasmine asked. "Should I get the doctor?"

"That was my only hope of getting the company back. Several months ago I drew up some papers to make sure that if I was ever to die or be in a comatose state that the company could only be sold if all the Dean kids signed off on the deal. It replaced my death clause."

"Damn, that's what they took. How would they know about that?"

"That's the only thing stopping us from getting the company back. Ralph must have found out about the sale and went to Teddy about it. Once he told Teddy about the clause, they figured they'd get rid of him fast and destroy any proof that it ever existed."

"Maybe he had a copy somewhere."

"The one in his safe was the copy. I'm sure they hit his office at the same time."

The monitor measuring Gloria's heart rate started to rise. She looked like she was about to go into shock. She scared Jasmine, who pushed the call button for the nurse.

The nurse on duty came in with some medication and a cup of water.

"Is she okay?" Jasmine asked.

The nurse checked her vitals and gave Gloria some medication to take. She took it without disagreement.

"You need to take it easy, Mrs. Dean," the nurse said to Gloria. "You have to relax."

"I lost it," Gloria yelled. Her roar scared Jasmine and the nurse.

"Momma." Jasmine started to say that they would get the company back, one way or another. Her fear was that that might be a lie, so she stayed quiet. Jasmine hopelessly leaned back in her chair. Seeing her mother suffer was hard on her. This was uncharted water. At no time in her life had she ever seen her mother in such a vulnerable state.

Gloria commanded her, "Go and find Jackie!"

Jasmine wanted to say what she thought about Jackie's disappearance, but knew that news would only be more crushing. Gloria had always depended on Jackie being there when she needed him. Now, in the worst crisis of her life he was nowhere to be found.

"Momma, Jackie has dropped out of sight," Jasmine said softly.

"Don't say that," Gloria cried.

"I hope not, but we haven't heard from him in awhile. I fear Jackie might have been killed too."

CHAPTER **TWENTY-FIVE**

The loss of the family business foundation gave Gloria many sleepless nights, agonizing about what happened and why. For her, the money meant absolutely nothing. She hated to have things stolen from her. Even if it took the rest of her life, she vowed, the culprits would pay a price that money couldn't touch.

What bugged Jasmine was that no one had heard from Richard. For a man who she held in such high esteem, he was now the scum of the earth to her. Gloria had asked about him several times, wondering why he hadn't come over. Everybody gave her the same answer: "I don't know where he is." It was understandable why he hadn't come to see her. Richard was well aware of her attachment to the company.

Needing answers herself, Jasmine decided to do something about it. Remembering his pattern of appointments, Jasmine ventured over to his Thursday two p.m. appointment with Dr. Lee, his chiropractor. Dr. Lee had a private practice in Brooklyn, just over the bridge of the same name. Knowing that her father rarely locked his car doors, she got into the backseat and waited with a blanket covering herself. She wanted to make sure he had no way of escaping her.

Richard came out, holding a white bag with his prescription in it. When he got in his car, he didn't notice her in the back. Not until he started the car and adjusted the rearview mirror did he see her rise up. He jumped.

"You almost gave me a heart attack. What are you doing here?" he asked, scared.

She gave him a nasty scowl. Jasmine didn't want to be there, but she had to know the truth about why he double-crossed her. Though Richard turned to face her, he looked away in shame.

"How is your mother doing?" he asked. Richard seemed genuinely concerned. She cut straight to the chase. "I'll ask the questions. What the hell is going on? And I don't want to hear any more lies."

Richard's face gave away the pain of his betrayal. Yet he didn't know where to begin or what to say.

When he remained silent for too long, she went on. "I thought you were my father. A man of integrity. What a joke," she said, opening up the car door to get out. His face made her sick to her stomach.

"Wait. I'm sorry," he cried. "I don't want to lose you."

She stopped to hear what he had to say. His outcry seemed sincere enough to warrant two more seconds.

"It's no excuse, but Teddy blackmailed me into voting with him. I had no choice."

"You had a choice. You could have come to me and just told me what he was up to. Look at things now. It didn't have to go this way."

"I never thought Ricky and Jaymee would join him. I promise you, I didn't know that."

"Your promises don't mean shit! You told me that you would never cross me. Of all the people in the world, I would have never expected that from you." She opened the door a little wider. "As far as I know, you could be in this with Teddy. For that fact, everything you've ever said was probably a lie."

Tears slowly dropped from her cheeks. Her father had hurt her in ways she had never imagined. He had been the closest to her since she was a child. Their relationship was more than being father and daughter. They were truly friends. They confided in one another. His integrity and honesty was something she had always admired about him. His qualities were what she looked for in men. Until now Richard had been her hero.

He sat there quietly, thinking of what to say. Apparently, nothing came to mind that would make the situation any better.

"Say something! Say something, damn it!" she yelled. "What the hell did he hold over you that you couldn't tell me about?"

Using his shirt, he wiped away some tears from his own face. "Jazzy, I did something I wasn't proud of years ago. There was a woman named Vanessa who I had a relationship with."

"So?" she said, not understanding where it was heading. "You cheated on Mom. That's no reason to turn your back on me!"

"She died. I mean, someone killed her. I walked into her apartment, and she was there lying there dripping in blood. I tried to help her, but she died in my arms. I knew that if I called for help, I would be blamed for her murder, so I called Teddy." Jasmine huffed. "He always said that he knew people who could get rid of any problems. I put my trust in him." He hit his head against the steering wheel. "I know I messed up. I was scared. I was cheating on your mother and got caught up."

She knew that he was telling the truth. Jasmine had wanted her father to suffer, but seeing his pain made her think she was no better. Thinking about all the times that he had been there for her, she felt it was only right that she move forward and forgive him, even though it wouldn't be easy.

"Mom's fine," she said gently. "She asked about you. You should stop by and see her. She deserves to know the truth. Just don't expect roses and candy."

***

In Gloria's old office, John sat back in his chair, smoking a cigar. With his feet propped up on the windowsill, he was admiring himself. So far everything had gone as planned. With the Gloria Dean Company in his hands, he figured that he would now rule the fashion and cosmetic industries.

His secretary barged into his office, waving a piece of paper at him. It startled him. He almost fell out of his chair.

He jumped out of his chair to regain his balance. "What the hell is going on?" he asked.

"They filed an injunction to stop the sale and us doing business," she said, almost out of breath. "Are you going to jail?"

His eyes bulged. "When?" he asked as he put the cigar out.

"Today. Read." She handed the paper to him.

He read every single line of it. His mood changed the more he read. The admiration he felt for himself was now depleted, replaced by fear. The blood in his face disappeared as he stood, speechless.

"Should I tell the board?" she asked.

He tried to weigh the consequences. "No. I have to find a way out of this first."

"A freeze is going to be put on our accounts. They think we're doing something illegal," the secretary said, exasperated. "Are we?"

"Shit! Calm down. Let me worry about it," he shouted. "Don't let anybody know about this. You hear?!" He gave her a scary look to enforce his words. "Nobody!"

The secretary nodded tightly and eased out of the office.

When the door closed behind her, his phone suddenly rang. With great regret and hesitation, he answered it.

"Hello. How are you doing?" he asked in an upbeat manner. John wanted to appear unfazed by the injunction.

"You think I don't know about the injunction? There's nothing I don't know about this family," a woman said on the other end of the line.

"I've got it under control," he said, hoping to project confidence.

"That's what scares me," the woman sneered.

"I promise you, they have nothing. It's a mere stall tactic. There's no link between us and Teddy Hicks," he said with confidence.

"What about the lawyer's files and contracts?"

"Everything has been destroyed. They have nothing. The Gloria Dean Company is all ours."

"You better be right. I have everything at risk here."

"We're in this together," he said.

She chuckled in the phone. "You really believe that, don't you? You're nothing but the face," she said. "If you mess this up, I don't have to tell you what you can expect. My husband is much more easygoing than I am! How come Jaymee Dean isn't with you? My instruction were simple enough even for you."

What she said about him being the face was true. She held all the cards. John wanted so badly to say something back, but he feared what that may cost him. He also didn't understand why Jaymee was so vital.

"I'll take care of it," he sheepishly replied.

"So, what are you going to do about our loose end?" she asked.

"I guess he's terminated."

"Now you're talking like the puppet I know. Bye, Johnny boy," she said before hanging up the phone.

John scratched his head. "I wonder who she really is," he asked himself. "If worse comes to worst, I'll have to use my backup plan."

He reached in his briefcase and pulled out the document that Gloria and Ralph had put together.

He smiled. "This is all the insurance I need, bitch!"

***

A few days later, after a memorial service for Ralph, the Dean family returned home. Even though she was warned by doctors not to come, Gloria was with them. She insisted that she would attend her best friend's service. They all wore black as they stepped out of the long black stretch limousine, and the media hovered. They wasted no time in rushing inside. When they got into the house, Chris greeted them. He walked up to Jasmine and pulled her away.

"We have to talk," he whispered in her ear.

Jasmine turned to whisper something to her mother, and Chris helped Gloria down the hallway to the office. With everyone else gone, Ricky and Jaymee felt left out. Understanding his predicament, Ricky went into the kitchen to grab a drink. Jaymee, on the other hand, went down the hallway anyway. She was determined to know what was going on. Jaymee boldly walked in the office where they all were gathered.

"Is there something going on?"

"Not now, Jaymee. We are trying to clean up the mess you made," Gloria said angrily. "Wait outside."

"I'm sorry. I thought we were still family."

"Hell, I know you're sorry. You should have been careful. How dare you decide who the fuck should run my company! Get the fuck out!"

Everyone in the room was at a standstill as Jaymee stood there, stunned by the way her mother laid into her. It wasn't the first time she had talked to her like that, but it was still embarrassing. She turned and walked back out of the office without saying another word.

As Jaymee passed the kitchen, Ricky saw her determined, angry look. He went to the doorway. "Where are you going?"

"Ricky, I want to talk to you seriously."

"About what?"

"We can start our own fashion company, but make it better. People have contacted me. They want me to run their company. We can do it together."

"What people?"

"I'm not totally sure," she admitted. "They couldn't tell me all the details when I met with them, but they seemed legit."

Ricky rolled his eyes. "Seriously, what are you talking about? You want to leave Momma now?"

"It's not like she cares about you and me. It's always been about her precious little Jasmine. Fuck them."

Ricky pointed down the hallway where the private meeting was occurring. "That's the team I'm on. Hey, if I got to ride the bench for a minute, then so be it. Sorry, but I'm not leaving this family, not now."

"You are so stupid. Who cares about Gloria Dean and her damn dynasty? I'm glad she got taken down. We need to be applauding Teddy instead of ridiculing him." She kept her eyes fixed on the office door. It still hurt her that she wasn't allowed to sit in on the conversation and the way her mother spoke to her.

Ricky opened up a beer. "Calm down, cowgirl" he said. "What else do you expect? We caused this problem. You think Momma trusts us to help fix it? Please. I wouldn't trust us for nothing right now. We're not going to be back in the game for some time."

"Speak for yourself," she huffed. "They're never getting the company back."

"I put money on it that Jasmine, Momma, and Chris will get it back. I heard them talking about something they had a lead on."

"What lead?" she inquired.

"Some guy," he said, turning unsure.

"What guy?" she demanded. "Jackie's back?"

"I don't think so, but ask Momma." He laughed. Ricky knew that would get her goat.

"Fuck you," Jaymee said. "Jackie did the smart thing. He left before the ship sank. I suggest you do the same."

"Jaymee, get it through your thick skull; we caused this shit. We are in the wrong. When you finally realize that, come and talk to me. I don't want no part of your pity party."

With her heels clacking loudly in the silence, she stormed out the front door.

"The nerve of some people," Ricky said before he gulped down his beer.

Back inside the office, Jasmine and her mother sat listening to Chris.

"Now, what do you mean, Teddy will be coming back to the United States on Friday?" Jasmine asked. "In his G6?"

"My overseas contacts tracked him to Switzerland. He's been in Lugano all this time. He has a ticket to come back on Friday," Chris said. "Flying commercial."

"Sneaky bastard. That only gives us the weekend to get him to come clean. Hell, he may extend his trip." Jasmine rubbed her head in frustration. It was hard for her to believe that they only had one opportunity to get the company back. "Man, that injunction only lasts until three p.m. on Monday. Can we get an extension?"

"No. With no shred of proof, they won't grant it."

"Is there a contingency plan?" Jasmine asked. She knew how unpredictable Teddy could be. If he was enjoying himself somewhere, he might stay there forever, was her thought. With the company on the line, she wanted more insurance that besides them depending on him coming back to United States.

"Yeah, what about the authorities grabbing him?" Gloria asked.

"They can't. He hasn't committed a crime."

"What do you mean? He stole the company from up under us."

"In the eyes of the law, he would have to be wanted. We don't have any proof. At this point he's just like any other traveler on vacation," Chris said, clearing up any misunderstanding that they had about Teddy's criminal status. "Until proven otherwise, legally he had the authority to sell the company."

"Bullshit!" Gloria turned to Jasmine. "That rat is going to pay."

"I got Bronco looking for him," Jasmine said, expecting her mother's disapproval.

"You know I don't like him," Gloria griped.

"You may not like him, but the one thing you can count on with Bronco is, he's going to avenge his brother's death."

CHAPTER **TWENTY-SIX**

The sun broke through the clouds and shone upon the city like a return to glory, but nothing was as bright as Jaymee's smile when she exited her home resembling Jackie Kennedy Onassis with dark sunglasses and a black scarf wrapped around her neck. Parked out front was a limousine. She waved toward the limo as she approached. The chauffeur opened the door for her. She smiled at whoever was inside as she got in. The car then sped off through downtown.

***

With only the weekend left, Teddy's arrival was on the top of everyone's agenda. At the airport, waiting for his plane to land, were John and some of his Mafia cronies, along with David, his lawyer. David kept out of sight of John and his people. Teddy had chosen to fly commercial to hide amongst the hoi polloi to save his own ass. He figured the deal might have some hiccups, but based on what David had said, things seemed a little more screwed up than anticipated. Teddy knew he needed to escape whatever trap waited on him.

When the passengers deplaned, all the men stood up to make sure that they didn't miss him. Passenger after passenger got off the plane

216 | d. E. Rogers

and still no sign of Teddy. As the crew left the plane, the only people left standing around were John and his cronies. David had disappeared. Unknown to John, Chris had remained out of sight as well, but he was just as disappointed.

After a few awkward minutes of waiting, John and his people left. They figured that if he did come in another way, he had to go home or to his hideaway where the deal was finalized. They were confident that they would reach him before anybody else.

Chris talked to a crew member standing by the exit door. He wanted to know if Teddy could have eluded him some other way. The crew member said no, that all the passengers came through the same exit point. Chris walked away, thinking. His mind was set on going to his home to wait and see if he appeared. For him, Teddy's appearance meant everything. At this point, the entire fate of the Gloria Dean Company rested on them finding Teddy.

***

In his sky-blue Maybach with dark-tinted windows, David sped out of the airport parking lot. When he merged into traffic at the highway entrance, Teddy rose from the backseat. He held a worried look. If David hadn't tipped him off about John and his people, he would have been caught. Being gone for almost a month had left him uninformed of what had transpired in the meantime. Paying off the crew members to let him go out the employee exit definitely helped him avoid them. What puzzled him was why they were there waiting for him in the first place. Their business was done, at least as far as the sale was concerned. It did put a snag in his silent-partner plans. He feared going to the office to meet John might be a deadly mistake.

"What has happened in the last couple of days?" he asked nervously. The one thing he did cherish more than money was his luxurious, easy life.

"I don't really have an answer for you. As far as I know, everything has gone as planned. Even the Deans' injunction isn't a reason for great concern. It was expected of them to do so." David continued, sounding puzzled. "I don't know. Without the dossier, the Deans have nothing." David tried to consider another angle. "Nobody's seen Jackie. Some people think he's dead."

Teddy rolled his eyes. "That's to be expected. I'm more concerned about John."

"Jasmine has called my office, constantly threatening me. I really think, she might be worse than her mother. "

"David, what I do know is that they weren't there to welcome me home." Teddy raised his brow. "Jasmine is the least of my concerns. I think John and his people want me dead."

"Something doesn't feel right. What do you know about this John guy anyway?" David asked, glancing at him through the rearview mirror.

Teddy shrugged his shoulders. He didn't see how that made a difference. To him, a sell was just that, a sell. He was never one to question his decisions. But doubt kept creeping into his mind that he had made a grave-digging deal with the wrong people.

"Mid-forties, yuppie. Family has billions," Teddy continued, thinking as he talked. "You've seen him."

"I did a little research on him actually. His family only has millions and they cut him off some ten years ago. He's been living off a trust fund. There's no way he could have afforded to buy this company. Some major players are lurking somewhere in the background."

Teddy shot him a look in the rearview mirror. David's *I told you so* tone annoyed the hell out of him.

"Where do you want me to take you?" David asked.

Teddy thought hard about the question. Part of him wanted to sleep in his own bed. The other part was unsure whether or not he would survive the night there. It also crossed his mind again that he had made a huge mistake in selling the company the way he had.

"Take me to the other location," he told David.

"They've been there before. Are you sure?" David squinted his eyes at him in annoyance.

"That's the last place they will look. Also, I need to get something for this migraine." Teddy rubbed his head.

"Forget that notion. We're going to the boat. They don't know about the boat," David said with a demanding tone. He figured Teddy wasn't thinking clearly. "Did you ever contact Jaymee?"

Teddy leaned back in the seat. He had totally forgot about the inclusion of Jaymee. Her part in this deal was still a big mystery. He felt like he had walked back into the lions' cage. His time in Switzerland had been joyous. He'd attended swinger parties and slept with a different woman almost every night. The thought of what was going to happen next worried him.

David shook his head. "I knew it was going to be a bad idea."

"Just drive," he said, infuriated by David's comment. He knew he was right. Before all this happened, his life was footloose and fancy-free. Now, with people on his tail, he was a fugitive.

***

It still bothered Chris that he'd miscalculated Teddy's arrival. His sources had even told him that he got on the plane. It puzzled him as he drove down the street. The possibility of Teddy slipping past him seemed ridiculous. He had people posted around the airport and no one saw any signs of Teddy. Weary, he held off calling Jasmine and Gloria. He wanted to provide them with some good news, and the news he had now was far from good. When he drove past Teddy's house, he noticed no activity. He parked down the street. Chris pulled out his phone to call one of the people on his team. Before he could dial, an incoming call from Jasmine appeared on his screen. He paused to muster up some courage.

"Jasmine, I got nothing right now. I just pulled up in front of his home." He grimaced.

"So what happened at the airport?" she asked, confused. "I thought your people saw him get on the plane in Switzerland."

"It's like he turned into a ghost. I had men posted all around the airport and no one saw him. I even looked in the plane."

"So, what now?" Gloria asked in the background. Her aggressive tone spoke of her frustration and anger.

Jasmine brought their point home.

"Chris, we need real results. Right now we have nothing. I need something."

"I don't know what to say," Chris replied, disappointed at himself.

A long moment of silence came over the phone. Chris didn't have any bright ideas for finding Teddy.

"Chris, don't give up. I got a feeling that something will turn up soon. Teddy can't hide forever," Jasmine said.

"I'm doing my best," he said, defending his poor results.

"And continue doing that. I know this isn't an easy one. I'm not worried about the injunction. As long as we get Teddy or find some proof that it was illegal, then that will reverse things in our favor."

She spoke so confidently that Chris bought into what she was selling. His confidence rose just listening to her. Her calm demeanor made things seem like a practice drill instead of a real-life situation.

"I'll call you when I hear more," Chris said.

A lightbulb went off in Jasmine's head. "Where's David, his attorney?" she asked.

"Why?"

"If Teddy disappeared, then I know for sure only one person could make that happen for him, and that's David."

"I got someone at his house, but he's been out of town on business the past couple of days."

"Damn, I wish you would have told me that earlier. I bet money they're at Brewer Yacht Haven East."

Chris's ears perked up. "That's in Long Island, right?"

"Yeah, David has a boat out there."

"Thanks. I'll check it out." He hung up the phone.

***

Gloria looked over at Jasmine to see if her confidence was for real. Jasmine sensed her looking, so she smiled. The last thing she wanted was another outburst of yelling from her mother.

"If I find Teddy, I don't know what I might do," Gloria said. "Well, to tell the truth, I do have some ideas. I need Jackie."

Jasmine nodded, but she had no answer to the Jackie request. Having not heard from him, she assumed the inevitable, that he was dead somewhere. Though nothing was said, she knew Gloria thought the same.

"No matter what, we always got Plan B," Jasmine said.

Whatever Plan B was, it brought a devilish grin to Gloria's face.

"Now, that's what I'm talking about."

"No one knows, right?" Jasmine asked.

"Not even Ricky."

***

It was quiet and serene at Brewer Yacht Haven East. The waters were calm, the sun beamed. Today would have been a perfect day for a nice sail at this exclusive spot. The place was a yachtsman's dream. With its great protection, large docks, and wide-open fairways, yacht owners coveted it. The well-manicured grounds only added to its allure. Regarded as the finest marina in the New York metro area, it housed some of the most expensive boats, owned by some of the wealthiest people in the world.

David, being of blue blood, was a true yachtsman. He had been sailing since his childhood. In his family, owning a sixty-foot boat was commonplace. His father had one, as did his grandfather. For David, it was his escape from the madness of his work and his pristine, nagging wife. His yacht, which he loved more than anything, had seen a lot of action. He held parties there, and on occasion it hosted his extramarital affairs.

Inside the boat's cabin, David sat down. He leaned across and grabbed the bottle of brandy and two glasses. He poured two drinks as if Teddy would be joining him soon. David downed his glass in one throw and poured another one for himself. He peered at his watch and then the clock on the wall. Seeing that it was four-thirty, he was a little upset. That drink went down just as quick as the first. David had a feeling that things weren't going to end right. Seeing a clock radio over to the side, he grabbed it.

"I need a song that will take me away from this," he said with a smile.

He turned it on and the radio exploded, killing everyone inside the boat.

***

Rolling down the Long Island Expressway back to Manhattan in his maroon-colored 458 Spider, John played Mozart on his Bose car stereo. The crisp sound made it seem like a mobile concert hall. Suddenly his hand moved to the steering wheel and hit the mute button. He pushed the talk button on the car system's voice-activated, hands-free telephone.

The system's voice was of a woman. "Who would you like to call?"

"The Falcon," he said with a smile.

"Dialing the Falcon," the system said.

The phone rang several times. No one answered. The voicemail came on for the Falcon. A computer-generated voice instructed him to leave a message.

"She makes me sick," he said before it beeped for him to leave a message. "The trash has been taken out. So there are no more roaches infesting the house. You are now the new Dean at the school," he chuckled. "I hope you're happy now."

He hung up the phone.

"I want to know who the hell she is," he said. The thought of being in the dark about her made him furious. Inadvertently, he swerved across the interstate, eliciting a blast of a horn. Nothing made sense to him, not even her connection to the Dean family. He figured his only leverage was to understand what they meant to her, and why she had such a vendetta.

CHAPTER **TWENTY-SEVEN**

Later that day, at a corner bar in Brooklyn, after several pick-me-up drinks Richard mustered up enough liquid courage to do the most undesirable thing he could ever imagine. Telling Gloria about the part he had played in the downfall of her company made him sick to his stomach. The alcohol might have calmed his nerves, but his face still showed the fear and pain of what was to come. He and Gloria had faced many situations, but none like this one. Even the fact of his deep, dark affair didn't compare to the expected reaction she would have once he told her the truth. He figured that once Pandora's box was open, a shit storm of problems would be coming his way.

When Richard arrived at the mansion, he walked up the steps to the front door as if on eggshells. If he was a suicidal person, that would have been the best route to take. Knowing how volatile Gloria was in these types of situations made the idea of him leaving on a stretcher believable. As he came through the door, he found Ricky and Jasmine in the family room watching TV. He stopped in the doorway.

"Where's your mother?" he asked, slurring his words.

"She's upstairs in her bedroom," Jasmine said, pointing at the ceiling. "Are you okay?"

He nodded.

Richard took the direction and went upstairs slowly. He looked like a dead man walking. He crept up the three flights of stairs, dreading what was coming. Ricky and Jasmine glanced over at the elevator and laughed. They both wondered why he didn't catch the elevator up to the third floor.

"So, what's going on with him?" Ricky asked. "I know you know something."

She sighed. "I don't know, really. He wouldn't tell me."

"He needs to be repenting for what he did to you and Momma." Ricky smirked.

Jasmine scowled. She couldn't believe his gall. Not taking responsibility for his part agitated her.

"And what should you be doing?" she asked angrily. "Kissing Momma's feet."

Richard reached the top and stopped, glancing back down the stairs as if it was the last time his feet would be coming up them. He pulled out a bottle of Red Irish Rose wine from his back pocket. With one gulp, the pint was done. He stared down the empty hallway leading to Gloria's bedroom. As his journey toward her door started, old memories flashed through his mind of when they were together—some good and some bad. One moment that stuck out the most was Gloria and him fighting, and she accidentally had pushed him down the stairs. He got to the door and knocked softly, twice.

"Hey, Glo, it's me, Richard," he said as his voice cracked.

Gloria had been sleeping. Hearing his voice woke her up immediately. She jumped out of bed, smoke practically coming out of her ears. When her feet hit the ground, the first thing she did was look in her end table drawer to make sure that her gun was still there. She stared at the gun for a few seconds before closing the drawer.

"Come on in," she said.

He went inside with a sorrowful look on his face. What he wanted to say still hadn't developed in his head. Seeing her sitting on the side of the bed, looking beautiful, made him think of what he had lost.

She trained her cold eyes on him. He saw no love, only hatred

"What the hell do you want?" she demanded. "You took it all!"

Richard took a deep breath, hoping that would work. His oxygen seemed cut off as he gasped for air.

"I know...I'm the reason you lost the company," he blurted out.

"Tell me something I don't fuckin' know." She glared at him. "You idiot!"

For the longest time there was complete silence. He couldn't bring himself to tell her why. Then Gloria went back in her drawer and pulled out a gun. She stood up and pointed it at his head.

"Why?" she asked. "Of all the things in the world you could take from me, why this? What did I ever do to you to deserve this?"

He was speechless. She walked over and slapped him across the mouth. Her diamond ring, which was turned to the inside, cut his top lip.

"You are going to answer me right now or I swear I'm going to put a bullet in your cranium." She took the safety off the gun. Alarmed, he backed up into the closed door. There was no escaping his punishment for defying her authority.

This was a side of her that he had never seen. Through all their years of marriage and fights along the way, Gloria had never shown such loathing. Her face made it clear that she was not bluffing about shooting him in the head. And even if he believed otherwise, the cocking back of the trigger changed that thought.

"I was blackmailed by Teddy," he said desperately, seeking forgiveness.

"What does that have to do with my company?" she asked with the gun still aimed at him.

Her unsympathetic state scared him. *And I taught her how to shoot a gun*, was the thought that crossed his mind.

"Teddy said if I didn't vote for him, he would have me arrested for murder."

"You should have gone to jail!"

He didn't know how to respond to her statement. She had given him a life that others could only dream of, and he had repaid her by sacrificing her business for his own safety.

She waved the gun at him to finish the story. "Get to the point! What did he have on you?"

"Back before we got our divorce, I had an affair with a woman. She ended up dead one night, the night I ended up going to see her. I panicked and called the only person I thought could help me..."

"Teddy," she said, completing his sentence. Gloria sighed and looked off toward the window. "Murder?"

"Yeah," he said regretfully. "I didn't want to vote for him. I never thought that Ricky and Jaymee would also join him. I hated doing that to Jasmine."

"Richard! You fucked me over!"

"I'm sorry," he cried.

"Was it for the money?" she asked.

He couldn't believe she asked him that question. His mouth was wide open. In all their years together, he thought that she knew at least that much about him.

"I know you're broke. Richard, there's nothing in this world I wouldn't do for you, but I have to know—was it for the money?"

"No! It wasn't about the money," he shouted. "Please put the gun away. I just want to talk to you."

"Shut the hell up. You don't order me to do shit!"

"I just want to talk. I know I was wrong," he pleaded.

"Damn right, you are wrong!"

All the same, Gloria slowly dropped the gun to her side. Tears welled up in her eyes. The love she still felt for him was revealed in how her eyes shone in her disappointment.

"I knew about you and Vanessa way before she died. Teddy had nothing on you. He showed that information to me back when we were getting a divorce. He wanted me to use it in court during our proceedings. I told him no and to destroy it."

"But he had pictures and other evidence that he said would link me to the crime scene. I saw it."

"You know Vanessa was once my friend, and you destroyed that."

Richard had no answer for that. "It was all my fault. Vanessa was a good person."

"Sometimes, bad things happen to good people."

Richard was baffled, but sensed Gloria knew something. *She had Vanessa killed*, he thought. *I'm such a big dummy.* With the gun removed from the direction of his head, he felt a little bit better. Reading what Gloria was thinking was the mystery.

"I'm sorry for everything," Richard repeated.

"I remember the police questioned me about her murder." Gloria sighed. "But I had a solid alibi."

"What does that mean?" Richard asked. It didn't matter what was said from this point forward—Richard was convinced Gloria was involved in Vanessa's murder.

"Nothing. I don't want to talk about your past. If you killed her, then so what?"

"I didn't kill her," Richard said, defending himself. "The murderer is still out there."

She was speechless, mainly because he actually fell for Teddy's trick. He was too naive to call Teddy on it. Looking at his pitiful face, she knew that he had to be telling the truth. Gloria stood there thinking of what to do with him. She had only loved three men her whole life—Richard, Ralph, and her father. With the latter two gone, losing him wasn't what she wanted.

At last, she went over and hugged him. The gesture scared the living daylights out of him. With the gun pressing up against his back, he wasn't sure if this was her way of saying good-bye to him or what. Not knowing what would come next, Richard held her gently.

"I forgive you," she muttered out from his chest.

"I have hated myself since that day."

"I know you have. Maybe losing the company was a good thing." She pulled away and looked up at him.

Do I even know you? he said to himself. Richard didn't know what to make of her strange behavior. He didn't want to die, but that was more in line with what he had expected. For Gloria to say that maybe losing the company was a good thing was beyond his comprehension. Instead of asking any questions or saying anything that could possibly ruin their moment of bliss, he stayed silent and held on to her like the days of old.

"I'm not going crazy. I'm just scared," she said tearfully. "Someone tried to kill me. Maybe that person was Teddy, but if it wasn't him, then who was it? I know I haven't been a saint."

Richard held her tightly. He wanted Gloria to feel the power of his love. It had crossed his mind several times that Teddy might have been involved in running her down. The reasoning behind him doing it now made no sense. Teddy had had plenty of opportunities throughout the years. And with all the recent deaths centered on the business and the family, red flags went up for him as well.

"Maybe I can move back in until this madness is sorted out?" Richard asked.

"I don't mind, but you have to stay in the room down the way," she said, pulling away from his chest.

She walked back over by the bed and put the gun in the drawer. Gloria turned around to see what his thoughts were.

"You mean, my old room, where I had to go when things weren't going right." He let out a little laugh.

"It's better than the one I had planned for you in the ground," she said, killing his happy face. By her directness, he knew he wasn't totally out of the woods with her.

"You know," she added, "since my accident and time in the coma, I've learned something. Losing the company doesn't make me happy, but what I really want is to make sure our family situation improves." He was dumbfounded as she paused, gathering her thoughts. "More than anything else, I realized that the true reason behind the company being lost wasn't Teddy. It was the poor relationship between all our family members."

Downstairs in the living room, Ricky and Jasmine were now engaged in an intense game of chess. Neither one was speaking to the other. Ricky's cell phone rang. He grabbed it from his hip. Seeing that it was Jaymee at first made him not want to answer it. But when Jasmine checkmated him, he saw no point in not answering.

"Hello," he said. "I'm surprised you're calling me."

Jasmine mouthed to him, "Who is it?"

He mouthed back, "Jaymee."

Jasmine rolled her eyes and got up. Just the thought of Jaymee made her sick. She had not forgiven Ricky for his part in what happened, but at least they had talked it out. Plus, he had apologized repeatedly. Jaymee, on the other hand, still pointed the blame everywhere but at herself.

Jasmine sat on the couch across from where they had played.

"Where's Jasmine?" Jaymee whispered into the phone.

"What am I, your navigational system now?" he quipped.

"I got some news I heard about her man Maxwell," she snickered.

"Just leave it alone."

Ricky didn't want to be in the middle of any more of her mess. Up until now all of Jaymee's scheming had gone to hell.

"So, you want your sister getting dogged out by some player?" she asked in a sarcastic tone, egging on a response from him.

Jaymee knew that was his weakness. Ricky always felt that with his father gone from the house, he was the man of the family. Protecting his mother and sisters from doggish men was his job, even though Jackie did the real protecting.

"What is it?" He quickly glanced over at Jasmine.

"Maxwell got that supermodel Zoë Tate pregnant."

"Damn, he hit that?" Ricky said, impressed. Zoë Tate had been on his wish list for years. His reputation as a womanizer, though, had ruined his chances with her.

"Tell her when you see her," Jaymee said. "I'm sure she'll get a kick out of it."

"How do you know for sure?" he asked, not a hundred percent sure that Jaymee knew what she was talking about.

"The girl is three months pregnant. It's in the paper. He didn't deny it when they asked him. If it wasn't his baby, then I'm sure he would have denied it."

Ricky shook his head. Seeing Jasmine sitting on the couch in her own little world made him feel bad that he was going to be the one to puncture her balloon. He figured by the amount of time that she and Maxwell had spent together, their romance had blossomed.

"I'll tell her."

"Good. Tell me how she likes them apples." Jaymee smiled.

"You're a trip. Bye," Ricky said, hanging up, disapproving of his sister's last comment.

He couldn't believe the pleasure his sister took in tearing Jasmine down. She was so childish. It amazed him that his sister wanted to run a major company.

Ricky went and sat next to Jasmine.

"By the look on your face, that bitch has some more bullshit," she said, raising her voice. "She needs to grow up!"

Ricky sighed. He regretted having to do it. "It's about Maxwell."

"Not another 'he's dating this or that girl' report. Save those, 'cause I don't want to hear it. I got a company to get back, and that's the important thing right now. It should be Jaymee's as well."

"He got a girl pregnant!"

By the look on her face, that was a different kind of report than she expected. She stared off into space, trying to make sense of it. She and Maxwell had spent so much time together confessing their feelings that the thought of him being with another woman didn't seem plausible.

"Who is she?" she asked, clearing the lump in her throat.

"Zoë Tate."

She reflected back on a time at his house, and by accident she saw that he had five missed calls from her. It angered her that she had fallen for another player.

"I don't care," she said, falling back into the couch. "Just another man being a so-called man."

Jasmine did her best not to let her hurt show. Yet Ricky sensed that she was in pain. His mind was set on giving that same pain back to Maxwell.

He leaned forward. "I'm gonna have a talk with him," he said, balling up his fist.

Jasmine glanced at him. She knew he meant well.

"No, I'll handle it." Jasmine stood up. "I want him to deny it in my face."

"I'll come with you," he insisted.

"No!" Jasmine said.

"I'm going," Ricky demanded.

"You can go only if you stay in the car," she insisted.

Ricky didn't want to agree, but he figured that was the only way he was going to get to come.

"Okay, but if you're not back outside in ten minutes, I'm coming in blazing."

She grinned at her little brother's fierceness. "Let's go."

As Ricky and Jasmine headed to the garage, coming downstairs were Richard and Gloria. Gloria saw them heading out the door. She turned to Richard.

"Now what?" she asked, worried.

CHAPTER **TWENTY-EIGHT**

When John arrived back in Manhattan, he went to a secluded coffee shop over in the Village. Once inside, he sat down at a table where another man was waiting. He wore dark sunglasses and a brimmed hat covering up his head and forehead.

"Damien, what did you find out?" John asked with a sparkle in his eyes.

"This Falcon, I found out, is from the Marconti family. Her name is Meagan Cunningham. Her father is a well-to-do mob type who made his money by being a silent-but-deadly partner in the casino business. He's worth about ten billion. The daughter, on the other hand, is married to some Frenchman. He's a steel baron, net worth twenty to thirty billion. From what I can tell, she's loaded. The problem is that she is one of the most unseen people in the world. There's not one picture of her."

John didn't see an angle. It seemed like she was on the up and up. The puzzle still didn't come together in his mind. He knew that something was missing. His curiosity got the best of him. *Why would she hide her identity?*

"So, what does this steel baroness, daughter of the Mafia, want with this company?" He realized he could see himself in the man's mirrored sunglasses.

Damien laughed. "Now, that's the funny part. She was a classmate of Jaymee Dean during their prep school years and even in college."

"So Jaymee's in on this already?" John asked, becoming even more confused. If Jaymee was involved he wondered who else was part of this takeover.

"No. Apparently they feuded from the time they met up until Jaymee stabbed her in the rib cage. Meagan needed forty stitches," Damien said as he picked up his coffee and took a sip. "I heard she could have died."

"So, what can I do? I need an edge with this woman. Ruining the deal doesn't put her out at all. Buying and selling is probably a daily activity for her."

Damien stared at him over the cup. He could tell that John was thinking about doing something stupid. "Don't do something you'll regret. Just leave it alone. You are in a perfect situation. Don't fuck it up," Damien commanded. "You're the front man. Did you ever contact Jaymee?"

"No," John replied.

"That's your first problem. Maybe she has the answer."

John sat speechless and humbled. He wanted to challenge what his associate said. In his mind, he knew that Damien was right. Going up against anyone with unlimited funds was never advisable. Meagan would crush him five times over without even a pause.

***

Jaymee had just pulled into her driveway when her cell phone rang from her purse. She quickly answered it.

"Hello!"

"Jaymee, how are you?" a woman's voice said. She sounded much older.

"Who is this?" Jaymee asked, trying to place the voice.

"I think it's time we meet."

"Who are you?" Jasmine asked again.

"You spoke with one of my associates recently. I also know Teddy told you about me awhile back."

"Yeah, all I know is that Randolph James is involved. I do want to be part of your team."

"Sorry for the delay, but Rome wasn't built in a day. I would love for you to work with me."

Jaymee's voice started to falter. "Are you Randolph James? He's a man, right?"

"That's good you think so. But I am him."

Jaymee didn't know how to respond.

"Jaymee, don't go quiet on me now. We both have dreams that can be fulfilled if we help each other. I want you to be a leader."

"How? What is this really about?"

"You," the woman replied. "I know you have unlimited potential."

"Me?" Jaymee was at a complete loss as to what the woman was talking about.

"I want to discuss your future and some secrets your dear mother has kept from you."

The mention of her mother was enough to set her off. "Don't waste my time," Jaymee snapped.

"I won't."

"Let's meet tomorrow."

"Why not today? I'll have a driver by your home in an hour. It will be a history lesson for you. "

Jaymee paused to think about what the woman really wanted to tell her. "Is this about me running your company?"

"It can be."

Jaymee smiled. "Okay."

***

It took almost an hour and a half for Jasmine and Ricky to get over to Maxwell's place. Jasmine parked at a meter down the block. She turned off the car, but kept the stereo playing softly. Ricky cracked his knuckles.

"You sure you don't want me to come in with you?" Ricky asked. He hit his fist into his hand. "He ain't gonna disrespect my sista! I don't roll like that. He's a cockroach in my book. Imma peel that cap back with my nine millimeter."

"I'll be fine," she said, looking at him out of the corner of her eye.

It was kind of cute to her, seeing how protective he was trying to be. The fact that Ricky did have a gun seemed ridiculous, but she appreciated his dramatic effort of support. Ricky didn't even know how to use a gun.

Jasmine stepped out of the car slowly. When she got to his building entrance, her cell phone rang. She saw that Chris was calling and answered it.

"Yeah, Chris, what is it?"

"And now his attorney is dead," he said in a dejected voice.

"What about Teddy?" she asked. "Weren't they together?"

"Right now that's the only body they identified. A witness said that they saw two men get on the boat earlier. Supposedly, a couple of hours before the explosion."

"What happened?" she asked, for clarification.

"Someone blew up David's boat."

The news damaged her confidence. Jasmine went and sat on a park bench near the building's entrance. She held the phone away from ear while her emotions calmed. If Teddy did die on that boat, she was certain that their claim on the company had gone up in flames with it. In any other situation, her wish would have been to have Teddy killed. His greed was the real root of their demise.

"I don't know how my mother is going to take this bit of information."

"One of my associates told me that the person who bought the company is really a Meagan Cunningham. Does that name mean anything to you?" he asked.

"Meagan Cunningham..." A light went on. "A skinny white girl who hated everybody. She's behind all this?"

Jasmine stood up from the bench. She paced in front of the entrance. Her blood boiled with anger.

"What is she about?" Chris asked, needing to see how the pieces all fit.

"She hated our family. Most of all she hated Jaymee. They fought all the way from prep school to NYU." Jasmine fumed just thinking about Meagan doing this to them. "So, she tried to kill my mother?"

"Hold on. Let's not jump to any conclusions," Chris said.

"Where is she?" she demanded. "And don't lie, Chris."

"Jasmine, I don't know. Her addresses vary, from the Hamptons to Manhattan to Rome. I put some men on it before I called."

She glanced up toward Maxwell's penthouse suite before turning to walk away. Saving the business was far more important than their relationship. She had developed feelings for him, but now was not the time to be weak for love.

"Chris, I'll call you later," she said.

"Don't do anything until you talk to me first. Okay?" he stressed.

"That woman is not going to bring down this family." She hung up the phone and stomped back to the car.

When she got inside the car, Ricky looked at his watch, then at her. It amazed him how quick she took care of business. Examining her face, he saw no tears or signs of emotion.

"What happened?" he asked.

"Meagan Cunningham is what happened," she snapped.

He leaned his head back, thinking. "Why does that name sound familiar?"

"She's the person that bought the company, not John Lincoln. Apparently, he works for her. I knew this had something to do with the past. It always comes back to bite you."

Ricky finally realized who Meagan was. "Isn't that the girl Jaymee stabbed?"

Jasmine nodded. "Now it's my turn."

She started the car and they drove off.

***

At the Gloria Dean Building, night had descended. John, sitting in Gloria's old chair, admired her huge picture on the wall as he looked over his shoulder. He hadn't taken long to see the bigger picture. Not being a brave or courageous person, he was scared to death of Meagan. All the deceit and murdering that had taken place made him only wonder if he would be next if he didn't play his role.

I'm the new king of fashion and cosmetics. No one can touch me, he said to himself. He gazed out the window and embraced the panoramic view of Central Park. The broken ties between him and his family meant nothing now. He felt like he was on top of the world. He grabbed the picture of Gloria by the sides with both of his hands.

You're nothing, he repeated several times before hurling the picture across the office.

***

That night the Dean family, minus Jaymee, sat by the Olympic-size swimming pool. It was refreshingly warm and beautiful stars lit up the sky. Everyone was exhausted from talking about the situation over and over again. How and why Meagan would do something like this didn't make sense. Financially, she had access to more money than them, and it seemed suspicious how she had resurfaced after all these years.

This kind of pressure had Gloria agonizing. She kept thinking about her exchange with Richard earlier in the day and what she had said about losing the company maybe being a good thing. Never in her life had she ever had to work this hard at anything. Her prospects of them winning were low. She felt hopeless, glancing at everyone around the table by the pool. Holding back her feelings about things was not her strong suit.

"I just want to say that I thank you all for your help," she said, grimacing behind her mask of confidence.

"Momma, we're in this together," Ricky said.

Gloria slit her eyes at him. *We wouldn't be in this situation right now if it wasn't for you and Jaymee joining up with Teddy*, she thought. Not wanting to cry over spilled milk, she moved on.

"Thanks, Ricky. You and Jasmine have been so strong in this. I don't think I could have made it without you."

Jasmine could hardly contain her astonishment. It was definitely a different day and time. Gloria looked nothing like her old self. Her demeanor showed the defeat of a person holding on to the little life she had left. It was a terrible sight for her to take. Her mother had always been a barracuda. Gloria was the strongest person she had ever known. She wanted so badly to give her a hug. To do that in this situation, though, would only aggravate Gloria. She would perceive it as a pity hug. The thing she hated most in this world was pity. Everyone knew taking the fashion business away wasn't about money or power—it was about principle. Gloria's other holdings were performing well, if not better, than her clothing line. The connection to her parents was what made the loss hard to swallow.

"Momma, this is nothing. We'll be back on top in no time," Jasmine said confidently. That wasn't the point. Gloria still had billions upon billions, enough to last ten lifetimes. The Gloria Dean fashion empire was the one thing her parents loved and told her to never sell. It was the crown jewel of their accomplishments that led to all the other riches.

The strength Gloria saw in Jasmine comforted her. She knew that her daughter was only trying to be positive. The Gloria Dean Company was slipping away fast out of their hands and they had no way of holding on to it.

"Where's Jaymee at? I haven't seen her for awhile now. Tell her I'm not mad anymore," Gloria asked. "Any word on Jackie?"

Jaymee's disappearance wasn't out of the ordinary. With her strained relationship with Jasmine, they could only stand to be around each other sparingly. But her whereabouts were unknown to everyone, even Ricky. Jackie, on the other hand, was still a mystery. Though everyone expected that he might be dead, they tried to keep hope alive.

Gloria gave Ricky a significant look. If anyone knew where Jaymee was, it would be him. But he shrugged his shoulders, indicating he had no idea.

"I wanted to tell you all, but this couldn't wait." Gloria glanced over at Richard. He froze. "No matter what happens on Monday, I'm stepping away from the business. There's more to life than this."

The circus could have dropped an elephant in the pool, and no one would have noticed. Everyone was shocked to hear Gloria say that there was more to life than her company. With their mouths wide open, they tried to figure out if this was a joke, but she never laughed.

"Are you sure about this?" Jasmine asked. "Momma, you're the one who said there's only three ways you leave any business: standing, on your knees, or dead on your back. We can still win this."

Gloria nodded sadly.

"If we get the company back, then who will run it?" Ricky asked.

"Boy, that's not important right now," Richard said, interrupting him. "Let your mother talk."

Gloria didn't want to answer the question because of the timing.

Seeing Ricky lick his chops, salivating over the possibility of running the company, she knew it was best to put him in his place.

"I had a long talk with Jasmine, and she has agreed to stay and run the new company. She will be the next me," she said without hesitation. "I'm handing everything over to her."

It took a moment for the news to sink in with him.

"Oh," was the only word he could come up with.

"I will sit on the board, and you and Jaymee would run your own divisions, but you will report up to Jasmine."

Ricky's eyes lit up. The chance to run his own shop was a dream come true.

"Thanks," he said. "I'm sure Jaymee will like that as well." He went and gave her a hug.

"That's all I have to say." Gloria pulled away from him and headed back into the house.

Richard smiled at her as she passed.

Turning over the reins of the business to her children was always her intention. It just had come sooner than she had imagined. Since coming out of her coma and watching Jasmine in action, Gloria felt that she would excel in the leadership role. Putting Ricky and Jaymee in the position of running their own fiefdoms would give them the experience they needed, and Jasmine would take care of any financial hits they took.

*** *** ***

Early the next morning, Jasmine wandered into the kitchen for a snack. Like any other day, her choice was Raisin Bran. As she sat at the kitchen table munching away, Ricky came rushing in from the hallway. He pointed to the monitor.

"I can take care of this nigga for you if you want," he said in his roughest voice.

Jasmine saw Maxwell's Bentley coupe at the front gate on the security monitor. She quickly got up and went to the phone on the wall. She pushed the button for the security.

"You can let him through," she said, gritting her teeth.

She hadn't planned on talking to him anymore. Her mind was set: he was guilty of cheating on her while they were dating, and that was it. Jasmine didn't see what more needed to be said.

"He's beneath you!" Ricky said.

Advice from her playboy brother was not what she needed right now. She asked archly, "Don't you have all his CDs?"

"We're not talking about me. You're my sister and that's what makes this different."

"Thanks, Ricky. But I got this."

She left the kitchen and went upstairs to fix herself up a little.

***

Jasmine showed Maxwell to the back garden. Maxwell didn't know where to start, and his silence irked Jasmine. She felt as if she was wasting valuable time.

"You wanted to talk, so talk," she said, rolling her eyes at him.

"I've been calling you like crazy, and you haven't returned any of my calls. I just want to know what's up. What did I do?"

She gave him a black look. His audacity gave her chills. *How dare he play the innocent role with me?*

"Huh. I know about her and the baby," she said, getting up in his face. "You must think I'm stupid."

"She told you about that?" he asked, caught off guard. He missed the baby remark.

"I don't want to see or hear from you anymore. To think I almost slept with you," she said, disgusted.

Maxwell replied quietly, "I wanted to tell you, but she told me not to." He had the most pitiful look on his face. "I'm sorry. I know it doesn't change what happened, but I met her before us. Believe me, I want you. I think we have something special. That was a different time and a different me. Jasmine, I'm deeply in love with you. I don't want to lose you."

Jasmine started to walk away. The "she told me not to" statement stuck out like a sore thumb. She turned back to him.

"Why wouldn't she want me to know?" she demanded.

"Because you're sisters," he said, almost like her question was stupid.

Her mouth dropped to the ground. She stood there dumbfounded. Maxwell reached out to her, but she pulled away.

"I thought you knew," he said.

She slapped him across the face once, then attempted to do it again. He grabbed her by the arms to contain her.

"That's old shit. We messed around almost eight years ago."

She snatched her arms from his grasp. Jasmine studied his face. Now she saw all the similarities.

"So, you're Brittany's father?"

Maxwell stood there tongue-tied. He didn't know anything about a Brittany. His face scrunched up, trying to understand where she was going with her questioning.

"What are you talking about?" he asked. "Who's Brittany?" To Jasmine, the resemblance was now uncanny. The big dark eyes matched. They also shared the same dimples and the full lips. His clueless act seemed real to her.

"That was years ago. Jaymee said she had an abortion," he said, not a hundred percent sure that it happened that way.

"And what about this Zöe Tate situation?"

"I did not get that girl pregnant," he protested. That's just the media creating a story. Believe me. I stopped seeing her before I even met you. Jasmine, I only want to be with you."

Jasmine rubbed her forehead. It was like a nightmare. She knew

Jaymee could be evil, but to lie to , and make Kenny think the baby was his was just so wrong. And the way she treated Kenny so badly only made the situation worse.

"You need to have a conversation with Jaymee," Jasmine said, walking away. "I can't handle this right now."

"Come back, Jasmine. I love you," he said.

She wanted to turn back around, but things were now too complicated. Her feelings for him did run deep. The missed opportunities to make love to him crossed her mind as she walked closer to the house. Yet how she could be with a man who had fathered a child with her sister?

CHAPTER **TWENTY-NINE**

The setting sun beamed into Kenny's bedroom windows through the venetian blinds. He turned over and caressed Jaymee's naked body. He kissed her on the neck passionately. By the look on her face, his attention perplexed her.

"I'm glad you came over this afternoon," he said with love in his eyes.

There was no one on this earth he loved more than her, not even his own mother. Even when she treated him badly, he never wanted to leave her side. Being the mother of his child only strengthened that bond. Kenny desperately wanted her to love him the same way.

"Yeah, I'm glad I came over too. You don't mind if I stay over here the next couple of days?" she asked as she looked over at her cell phone light blinking.

He saw her look at it.

"Someone was really trying to reach you earlier."

She ignored his statement. "So, can I stay?"

Jaymee took a deep breath and turned around to face him. She kissed him on the lips and rubbed his chest hairs seductively. She played on his weaknesses as she batted her bedroom eyes.

"You can stay as long as you like," he replied, enjoying the sensuous feeling that she gave him.

Her phone vibrated. They both glanced over at it.

"So, who are you hiding from?" he asked.

"What makes you think that I need to hide from anyone?"

"This is me you're talking to. You want to come over here and stay for a couple of days, which you are more than welcome to do, but it's not like you've been beating down my door to do that in the past. What gives, baby?"

Jaymee seemed to make a decision. With the constant phone calls, she probably felt she had to say something.

"I was going to tell you later, but I'm through with my family. My mother is an overbearing ape that wants all the bananas. She doesn't care about anybody but herself. It's all about the Gloria Dean Company and her reign. Fuck that shit. Fuck her and Jasmine." She smirked. "I wish she had never adopted me."

"What are you talking about? You're not adopted."

She gave him a weird look and huffed. "I just want to be away from them."

"You still need your family."

"So, now you're taking their side of things!"

Her anger, the one attribute that he hated the most, started to surface. He kissed her to bring her rising emotions back down. It worked a little, but she was still annoyed.

"I know your mother can be a pain, but to divorce yourself from them is kind of deep."

"But I'm divorcing them and getting back to us. I don't need her to be in this fashion business. I'm better than them. I don't want to be a Dean anymore."

He saw the seriousness in her eyes. Her breaking the ties with the company was a great step for their relationship chances, but the aspect of shutting out her family was scary to him. He knew it was something going wrong in her life that she held close to her heart. Kenny was determined to find out what it was and to protect her from harm's way.

"Whatever you need, I'm here for you. This is your home as well as Brittany's."

She embraced him. "You're so sweet."

***

Across the city, at the Dean mansion, Gloria, Richard, Jasmine, and Ricky ate dinner as a family at the boardroom-style table. It had been a long time since they had sat down and had a meal together. With every chew, Gloria kept her eyes glued to the empty seat in which Jaymee normally sat. It angered her that she had disappeared so suddenly.

"Where the hell is your sister?" Gloria asked Ricky.

"I haven't heard from her. I called her several times yesterday and this morning."

Gloria thought her actions were very weird. With all the events that had transpired, he knew that she was upset, but this seemed extreme, even by her measures.

"I'll go by her house later," Ricky said.

"You know, I called her myself yesterday, and she didn't call me back either," Jasmine said, curious about her sister's disappearance. "Something's not right. She hasn't contacted you Ricky?"

"No," he replied defensively.

"Damn, first Jackie, now Jaymee. Who's next?" Gloria asked, getting upset. "Is she that mad at me?"

"Momma, if Jaymee wants to stray now then let her. We need to stay focused. Are you with me?"

Gloria nodded in agreement.

Ricky noticed that his mother kept looking in his direction. "Why are you looking at me?" he asked defensively. "I'm just as clueless as everyone else. I haven't seen or heard from her in days."

"So you have no idea why she's not coming around?"

"No," Ricky replied, though he looked like he was withholding a secret.

"Really," Gloria said.

She saw the beads of sweat forming on his forehead. She had more questions to ask. Jaymee was the weird child out of the bunch, but always kept in touch. That was the thing that bothered her the most. The last couple of exchanges between her and Jaymee played vividly in her mind. She started questioning her tough-love act that was force fed on her kids. Being the more delicate one, Jaymee always took criticism the hardest. Ricky and Jasmine always rolled with the punches.

"If any of you do speak with her, tell her to come home. I want her to know I love her," Gloria said. "I love all of you."

"Momma, where the hell do you think Jackie is?" Ricky asked. "You don't think he's behind this, do you?"

Gloria glanced over at Jasmine, then started eating like the question had never been asked. Imagining Jackie being dead was too painful.

"I'm sorry," Ricky said. "He hasn't shown up. Where the hell is he at is all I want to know?"

Jasmine snapped at Ricky, "Have you lost your mind? Leave it alone. All of us need to be focused on what's important. That's getting the company back. I don't care at what expense."

***

For Chris, the day had moved like a bullet. One after the other, every single lead turned up nothing. The news still hadn't reported finding a second body, and eyewitnesses said they saw another man. Chris went back and forth, seeking any leads that would prove that Teddy was still alive. With no signs of Teddy returning to his home, Chris started to believe that maybe he was dead. It was hard to believe that he was that elusive.

By the time the morning rolled around and the birds sat on the ledge chirping, the Dean family, all having had a rough night of sleep, woke up collectively paralyzed. No one went down for breakfast. They all stayed in bed, pondering the outcome of the day's events. Each one of them questioned his or her own future. Not that they didn't know today was going to come—it just came sooner than they had imagined. Would they really lose their prestigious place in the fashion and cosmetic industries?

Jasmine stared at the ceiling, praying. Even her optimistic mood had swayed to hopes that her prayers would be answered. As far as she was concerned, her only care was that her mother be okay. Though Gloria gave that speech to them about handing over the company to her, and giving Ricky and Jaymee their own divisions to run, she didn't buy it. Deep down, Gloria was a winner who hated losing. If Jasmine knew anything about her mother, that was it. With no evidence to back up their claim, it was certain that the sale would stand. That was the part she feared her mother wouldn't be able to handle.

Her cell phone rang; she turned her head toward it. She didn't want to answer it but couldn't afford not to. Her arm reached out for it and grabbed it.

"Hello," she mumbled.

"Girl, are you asleep?" her friend Cleo asked.

Jasmine took a look at the clock on the wall. She saw that it was 9:30 a.m. Her hand wiped the matter from her eyes as she stretched her arms over her head. She then brought the phone back to her ear.

"What's going on?"

"Have you seen the news this morning?" Cleo said in a somber tone. "Jaymee is a trip."

Jasmine was still half asleep and didn't really pay attention to what Cleo had said.

"Why?"

"Turn on the TV," Cleo said. "That will make you know that I'm not playing."

Jasmine searched around the super California king bed trying to find the TV remote. She finally found it under the covers near her feet. She clicked the on button.

"What channel?" she asked.

"Fifty-six."

She turned to the channel. At the podium was Jaymee. The caption on the TV read, The new CEO of the Gloria Dean Company. The headline jolted her out of the bed.

"Cleo, I'll call you later."

Jasmine ran out into the hallway; coming toward her was Gloria. By the mean look on her face, she figured that her mother had seen it herself.

"I guess you know," Jasmine said softly.

"I swear if I find that bitch today, I'm going to strangle her to death. I promise you that much." Gloria fumed. "This ain't no fuckin game! This is the last straw."

"I'm going to get to the bottom of this. Jaymee's going to regret this," Jasmine said, pissed at Jaymee's betrayal of their family.

"I just don't get it." Gloria said. "We're missing something."

"I get it. That little heifer double-crossed all of us. She had this planned from the beginning. I know she did. She convinced Meagan Cunningham to buy the company for her so that Teddy wouldn't be suspicious. Meagan in turn had this John guy deal with Teddy so that she was left out of the picture."

Gloria looked impressed that her daughter analyzed so quickly the moves that Jaymee took to pull this off. "Call Chris and tell him to locate her," Gloria said.

"Jaymee better have some real answers."

"The gall of her. It all makes sense now. My accident, Tommy being killed in the house, and Ralph's death. See, they killed David and Teddy to shut them up. It's obvious that whoever she is connected to fears that Teddy knew something and would eventually break."

Jasmine had a hard time buying that scenario. "Momma, Jaymee's not a cold-blooded killer. She's your daughter. And I'm not sure Teddy is dead."

Gloria paused for a second to think about her choice of words. "You don't know what turns people into killers. I do."

"Am I missing something?" Jasmine asked, hoping to clear up the confusion. She saw some darkness appear in her mother's eyes. "Are you not telling me everything?"

Jasmine knew there was something definitely on Gloria's mind that was deeply disturbing her, but she refused to share it.

"Never mind me," Gloria said.

Jasmine said tentatively, "It's got be someone who knows our family well. They knew how to get in the house and when to get in the house. It's someone who has something to gain by seeing you humiliated. If Teddy is dead, then who? Momma, only you know who wants you dead. Think! Who wants you dead more than anything else in the world?"

Gloria had so many enemies, so much history of crushing people's dreams, that the list of people would run off the page. Jasmine could tell that she didn't know where to start.

"I still think Jaymee holds the key," Gloria said.

"And you are probably right!"

It was like a light bulb came on in Jasmine's head. She remembered a question she had wanted to ask her mother since she came out of her coma. The one question that they never got a straight answer to: What was Gloria doing that early morning before her accident? Jasmine thought of ways to not offend her mother by questioning her about that day, but right now it was the six-hundred-pound gorilla in the room. So, she had no option but to be direct.

"Why were you jogging over at that park in the early morning hours?" she asked suspiciously. "I know you said a business meeting, but what kind of meeting?"

Gloria froze in surprise. Then a guilty look came over her face.

"Momma, what were you doing over there?" Jasmine demanded.

The butler came to the top of the stairs. He got their attention.

"Madam, Theodore Hicks is here to see you."

Jasmine and Gloria simultaneously turned to face one another. The last person they expected to see was Teddy.

"Wait right here," Gloria said before she rushed to her room and came out with her gun.

She returned to where Jasmine waited. They heard a loud commotion coming from downstairs. Both of them raced down the three flights of stairs. When they got to the bottom, the butler was trying to pull Richard off Teddy. Jasmine jumped in as well. She did her best to pry her father's hands off Teddy's neck.

Gloria got close enough to Teddy and shot him in the leg, just above the knee. He toppled to the floor, shrieking in pain.

The loud gunshot instantly ended the squabble. They all turned to her. She pointed the gun at Teddy. He held his leg as he lay awkwardly on the floor.

"Right now I got nothing to lose. Killing you doesn't mean a thing to me. Most of the newspeople think you're dead anyway," Gloria said, coldly staring at him. "I hope you got the answers I'm looking for."

***

With all the heat on the street and the murder attempts on his life, Teddy felt that coming clean to Gloria was the best thing. He knew with their history, all she wanted was her company back. Killing him wasn't at the top of her list.

"I'm going to kill him with my bare hands," Richard said, trying to get by the butler and Jasmine.

"Daddy, no!" Jasmine yelled.

"Killing me won't get your company back. I can help you," Teddy cried.

"Just tell me why?" Gloria asked as she slowly cocked her gun.

Staring down the gun's barrel with Gloria's menacing face aimed at him, Teddy knew that he better give her something that she could sink her teeth into. He licked his lips slowly.

"John Lincoln isn't the guy behind all this. It's Meagan Cunningham."

He acted like the information was golden. An air of confidence came to his face. He felt that would buy him the time needed. Gloria cocked her gun back.

"Is that all you know?" Jasmine asked. "Teddy, you are so stupid."

Teddy froze. His safety net had a big hole in it and he was falling through it, fast. The only thing that seemed to be a good sign was Gloria dropping the gun to her side.

"Teddy, we don't have much time. You need to get it together soon. Your future depends on what you tell us," Jasmine said.

Teddy squirmed on the floor, holding his bleeding leg. His impression of which route was safer changed a lot. Gloria appeared to be crazy. He had never seen this side of her.

"I'm sorry. I didn't know this would happen. I'm here to help," he begged.

Jasmine huffed. "You let Jaymee beat you at your own game. That's pitiful."

The pain was excruciating, but the comment puzzled him. He glared at her to explain. She saw his confused look, and it almost made her laugh.

"You really don't know." Gloria smirked. "Stupid, stupid, stupid!"

"Know what?"

"Jaymee is now the new CEO of the Gloria Dean Company,"

Jasmine said. "Funny turn of events."

That outcome was unfathomable in his mind. *How could I have been beaten by her, of all people?*

"That's impossible. She was totally ignorant of what was going on," he snapped back at them.

Yet Teddy realized that it must be true. He sat there in agony, wondering what went wrong with his plan.

"Oh, my God," he replied.

"Like God wants to help a snake like you," Richard said. "It was better when we thought you were dead."

"Do you have the file that Ralph had in his safe?" Gloria asked.

A glum look came over his face. "No. I destroyed all three of the copies and his computer."

"I know there's another copy out there and I bet someone has it," Gloria shouted. "Why did you do this? I have always been good to you."

"I'm sorry," Teddy cried in fear.

"And where the hell is Jackie? I know you know something."

She held the gun up toward the direction of his head. By the grimace on her face, his next answer was going to determine whether or not he lived.

"Answer me!" she yelled, watching his reaction.

He immediately responded, "These people are crazy. I begged them not to kill anybody. They wouldn't listen. They killed Jackie and Ralph."

Gloria was in total shock. She didn't know how to react to hearing that Jackie was dead. Her eyes stayed on Teddy as her hand clutched the gun. Jackie was her treasured partner in crime. He had been the better half who did the dirty work. Her heart plummeted.

Seeing her mother almost incapacitated, Jasmine stepped in. She coldly stared at Teddy. "It's ten now and we need a miracle by three p.m. Teddy, if I don't find what I need by that time, you better have one helluva confession to make."

The pain of the gunshot was excruciating. Teddy was willing to do life in prison if it meant getting him some medical attention. "I'll do whatever."

"I'll call Chris right now," Jasmine said.

"Call me a doctor, please," Teddy begged.

Gloria raised her nose at him, like she wanted him to bleed to death in front of her eyes.

"I'll get Baker to come over and check out his leg," Richard said.

"If I don't get back what's mine, Teddy, you are going to wish you were dead. And if you run, I will have someone hunt you down like the dog you are and scalp you," Gloria said as she walked off toward the downstairs office.

CHAPTER **THIRTY**

At the Gloria Dean building an hour and a half later, Jaymee, John, and several executives walked into the boardroom. Jaymee took her seat at the head of the table. A position that she had dreamed about taking for years. Everyone seemed to be savoring the victory of taking over the company except for John. He was unclear of his future role.

One of the men with them was Vincent Marconti, a notorious mob figure. He was a burly man who stood six feet tall. Five years ago he supposedly had gone legit, cutting his mob ties. More times than not, the FBI still followed him expecting him to return to his roots. From time to time, he still made calls to eliminate obstacles that stood in the way of doing business his way. He now had a sixty-five percent stake in the company, but he had put up all the funds to purchase it. Oddly, to everyone around them, he had given Jaymee thirty-five percent.

The other person at the table was the infamous Meagan Cunningham. She was a beautiful Italian princess, with a slender figure and dark brown hair to match the elegant style she possessed. She hadn't spoken with Jaymee in years, but when she was approached with the deal by her father, it was a no-brainer. Everyone in the fashion and cosmetic industry knew that the Gloria Dean Company each year turned a profit. Normally, Meagan was more cautious about the people she did business with, but the persistence of her father made the decision easy. No one said no to him.

As Jaymee, Vincent, and Meagan settled into their seats, John opened up a bottle of champagne. While he poured the bubbly in the glasses, Vincent and Meagan both gave Jaymee a weird stare. She acknowledged their look with a slight grin. John handed everyone a glass. He stood up behind his chair and raised a toast.

"I want to congratulate Queen Jaymee for pulling off this spectacular deal. Here's to a bright future and to us running this company," he said.

He drank the champagne in his glass, then took a seat. Jaymee knew it was time to put him in his place. She understood that John was a puppet. Plus, she hadn't forgotten how cavalierly he had treated her and Ricky after the takeover. Paying him back would be enjoyed.

"Thanks, John. I really appreciate your confidence behind me being a good leader. I also want to thank Vincent and Meagan for the tremendous part that they have played in this saga." She smiled. "Now, for the future of this company. I plan on leading it up to such a high plane that we will be untouchable. I think the future I have planned for this company is brighter than anything you could imagine."

The *I's* that Jaymee kept saying caught John's attention. He glanced at everyone else, but no one looked at him.

"That sounds terrific. I can't wait to see people's faces when we put out the next line," John said.

Jaymee stretched her neck. The room was cool, but she was hot. This was her first official situation she had to deal with. She had no business acumen, but that was the last thing she wanted them to know.

"The new line is definitely going to be something the world will be proud of. Our customer base deserves something fresh and appealing for both the older generation and the younger generation."

"I have some great ideas already. I can't wait to show you," John said.

Vincent coughed. "Hey, give the woman a chance to finish what she's saying," he said in an ominous voice.

John shut up pronto. Vincent nodded at her to proceed.

"That brings me to my next issue. John, your role as president is over, effective this minute," Jaymee said.

John was shocked. "What? You've got to be kidding me! We're all in this together."

"John, there are other roles you can play in this company," Meagan said, glancing over to Jaymee. "You can be a vice president or something. We'll find a place for you."

"Fuck that!" John cried, but then he saw how swiftly Vincent turned toward him. "No disrespect, Meagan and Vincent, but I was promised this."

Jaymee cleared her throat to speak. Vincent put up his hands to signal that he was going to handle this one.

"Son, the first thing about business you need to know is that it is constantly changing. You need to adjust daily. If I got paid for how many times someone broke a promise to me, I'd be able to support every person in the room for the rest of your life. I would be lying to you if I said I wanted you to be president of this company. No disrespect, but I don't fuckin' know you." He pointed at John. "The name on the outside of this building says the Gloria Dean Company, and my money is behind a Dean, not a Callahan."

"Lincoln," John said, correcting Vincent.

"Smart kid! You get my fuckin' point," Vincent said with a devilish grin. "Unless you have money to bring to the table, your name doesn't mean squat."

John dropped his head in shame. He couldn't believe how they were playing him. All the dirty work he had done and promises made to him were now diminished to nothing. Though he felt it was in his best interest to leave, his bravado wouldn't let him.

"Here's how it's going down. I want it in writing that I will be the president of this company by the end of the day. In addition, I want a hundred million dollars for all of my troubles. Let's just call it a signing bonus."

The outrageous demand stopped all three of them for a moment. Then Vincent laughed.

"The balls on this son of a bitch. You have some nerve telling us how it is going to be. You best hope you make it out of the building. If you know what I mean."

John grinned at Vincent. "You don't scare me, mob boss. Try that Tony Soprano shit on somebody who's scared."

Vincent flared up. Meagan grabbed her father by the arm to contain him. He waited to see where John was going with his point.

John knew what he was doing was gutsy. Making it out of the building wasn't a guarantee. He figured that Vincent wouldn't make a move to harm him in the building. For now, he felt comfortable playing the cards he had in his hands. Tomorrow wasn't a concern as of now. He wanted revenge on the Deans and his cut of money as well.

"Why would we want to do that?" Meagan asked.

John looked over at Jaymee.

"What are you looking at me for?" Jaymee asked in a pissed-off tone.

"I have the document in my possession that will stop the sale of this company. It's all the evidence your mother needs to stop all of this. You all know what I'm talking about. We wouldn't be here now if you didn't." John leaned back in his chair, pleased by his newfound position of superiority.

Everyone's attention now turned to Jaymee as they waited to hear her response.

"Teddy destroyed all of them. He's lying," Jaymee said, calling his bluff.

"He destroyed all but one, and I have the original with your mother's wet signature on it. I bet she would give me what I want." He smiled at her.

"Hey, cockroach. This is bigger than all of us in the room. You're making a horrific mistake!"

"Give me what I want," John demanded.

Vincent chuckled at the absurdity of his threat. "It's not going to happen," he said with killer eyes. "You're a dead man."

"Oh, really?" John smiled.

***

When Jasmine came out of the kitchen, the only people she saw were her father and Teddy. Richard was trying to stanch the flow of blood from Teddy's leg.

"Where'd Mom go?" she asked, looking at them.

"She went upstairs right after you went to make a call and hasn't come back down," Richard said. "I think the situation is getting to her."

Taking a break during this crucial time was not characteristic of Gloria. No way was she walking away. Jasmine could tell something wasn't right. She dashed up the stairs and ran down the hallway to her mother's room. She wasn't in there. Jasmine checked her dresser where she kept the gun. The gun was missing. Jasmine rushed out of the room and back downstairs. Richard saw the panic of her face.

"Is she all right?" Richard asked.

Jasmine shook her head.

"Make sure you get Teddy to the courthouse by three p.m.," she said, grabbing some keys off the wall.

"What's going on?" Teddy asked. He figured that Gloria wasn't upstairs.

"Mom went to see Jaymee."

"That sounds like a good thing. That girl has a lot of explaining to do." Richard fumed.

"I gotta go. Call Ricky and tell him to meet me at the courthouse." Jasmine ran to the back of the house where the entrance to the garage was located.

***

It was a bittersweet moment when Gloria entered her old office. She went inside slowly. Slung over her shoulder was her handbag. Seeing that her self-portrait was now replaced with one of Jaymee only added gasoline to the fire burning inside her. And even though this was not a planned meeting, she had dressed impeccably as if it was. Her face wore the pain of betrayal. If she had to, she was ready to shoot Jaymee to get her prize possession back. Once inside the office, she searched around the room. No one was there. In fact no one was even on the floor. She then edged over to the boardroom. It was just as empty as the rest of the floor. Gloria took a seat at the head of the table. She reflected on the golden times at the company when her parents ran it together. Not until her cell phone interrupted those memories did she come back to the present. Gloria hurried and answered it.

"Hello...what did you find out?...It can't be! If that's the case, then she can have the company. I don't want to, but we have no choice. Who told her? Carry out Plan C...Don't question my judgment! Just do it!" Gloria hung up the phone. She got up from the chair and dragged herself out of the room.

At the elevator, the doors opened and Jasmine ran into her mother. Seeing the defeated look in Gloria's eyes made her think that she had might have shot Jaymee. She looked around but didn't see anyone.

"Mom, where's Jaymee?"

"I don't know," Gloria replied without raising her head.

"We don't have much time now. I have to get you to court. I told Dad to have Teddy there by three." Gloria was so despondent, it was if Jasmine was talking to herself.

Jasmine linked their arms together and helped her mother get on the elevator. After Jasmine pushed the lobby-level button, Gloria took one more look out into the office. It brought tears to her eyes, thinking that this was her last time there.

"I guess this is good-bye," Gloria somberly said as the doors closed.

All Jasmine could do was hold her mother as the elevator went down. It crossed her mind to ask Gloria about the run in the park again, but she decided it wasn't the right time.

"Momma, we will be back."

***

In the judge's chambers at the courthouse, Jasmine, Gloria, Richard, Ricky, and Teddy sat with Gloria's new attorney, Peter Samuels. Peter was an old friend of Ralph's. He was a sharp dresser, but he was a little on the chunky side.

Across the table was Donald Riff, the attorney representing the new Gloria Dean Company owners. Donald was a high-paid lawyer from Wall Street. A Harvard grad with connections throughout the New York City court system, he was known for winning the impossible high-profile cases. He had also been suspected of illegal payoffs and bribes.

Teddy had just finished telling the judge what happened. Though bandaged up and holding a cane, he seemed to be too willing to help. Jasmine and Gloria were still suspicious about his motives, because Teddy never did anything to help someone out with leveraging some financial gain for himself.

The judge, Marlene Kennedy, maintained an icy demeanor throughout. By the look on everybody's faces, other than Donald, they didn't have much hope that things were going to go the way they wanted.

"Now, Mr. Hicks, your story, as compelling as it is, still doesn't mean anything," the judge said sternly. "And this document that you all mentioned, the one that states that in order for a sale to go through, all of the members of the board must sign off, hasn't surfaced, at least to my knowledge."

"He's admitting to stealing my company from me," Gloria shouted. "And that doesn't count for anything?"

Her attorney tried to quiet her down.

"Samuels, please keep your client quiet, or I'm ending this now."

Jasmine put in, "No disrespect, Judge Kennedy, but my mother is right. Our company was stolen, not sold. No one agreed to this sale."

Donald smiled. All signs pointed to a victory for him. With no document to present, the Deans' case was dead in the water.

"Marlene, my goal is to make it clear that we did nothing wrong on our part in acquiring this company. The allegations made by Mr. Hicks are new to me. He was at the original meeting, where we finalized the deal. All the papers were in line at that time," Donald said. "My clients have suffered. They are losing millions while we wait to legitimize a foregone decision."

The judge briefly considered the cases that they both had presented. She leaned back in her chair and removed her glasses.

"In all fairness, Mrs. Dean, I believe that this document does exist, but without it being present there is no way I can uphold any injunction. I must side with Mr. Riff that the sale must go through."

Mr. Riff pumped his fist in the air. "Yeah, thanks Marlene." He stood up to leave.

The whole Dean clan sat in disbelief.

"Hold on, Mr. Riff. I am allowing you to inform your clients that they can start operating the daily business as usual, but I am granting the Dean family a thirty-day extension to find this mystery document."

Gloria smiled at the judge and turned her head up toward the ceiling. "Thank you, Jesus," she said to herself.

"That's not fair," Mr. Riff cried. "This is ruining the business at a critical stage."

"That's my ruling. If you're so sure that this document doesn't exist, then why should you care?"

"Judge, hold up for a second," Gloria said, getting the attention of everyone. "On second thought, tell Jaymee Dean this is my gift to her. I'm not going to contest it any further."

"Momma," Jasmine said with concern. She wanted her mother to think about what she was saying. "This is a bad decision."

Yet Gloria nodded to affirm what she had said.

Everyone was stunned by the new twist. Had Gloria gone off the deep end?

"Are you sure?" the judge asked as the others waited on Gloria to answer.

"One-hundred percent sure."

"Momma, what are you doing?" Jasmine and Ricky asked simultaneously.

"I'm being a mother."

"I guess this case is over," the judge said with uncertainty. "Are you really sure?"

Gloria waved her hands in a sweeping motion. "Definitely."

"I'm not crazy," she said to all of them. "Jaymee and I are far from being done. She's just a little misguided at this time. Just watch, she'll realize that she who wears the crown carries the responsibilities of the people she leads. There's a lot of pain at the top."

"So, we have to start over?" Ricky asked.

"I'm not rolling over that easy." Jasmine was fired up. After all they had been through, she wasn't going to give up.

Her comment brought a surprising smile to Gloria's face. "I give it less than two years, and we'll buy back the company for pennies on the dollar."

"I'm thinking less than a year," Jasmine said with utmost confidence.

Gloria rose and walked out of the judge's chambers with Jasmine by her side. Jasmine looked at her phone and read a text message. She leaned over and hugged her mother.

"She's over at the office. Let's go," she whispered in her mother's ear. "Let's get to the bottom of this."

"How do you know?" Gloria asked, curious to know who her daughter's source was.

Jasmine cut her eyes at Gloria. "I know."

Ricky looked around as if someone was missing. He began to panic a little. "Where did Teddy go?"

Jasmine rolled her eyes. "You find him. We're going to pay Jaymee a visit."

CHAPTER **THIRTY-ONE**

Back at the Gloria Dean Company headquarters, Jaymee sat back in Gloria's old chair, basking in the victory. Her face was filled with joy and self-admiration as she looked out the window. Defeating her mother brought such a great feeling of joy. After years of being under her mother's thumb, she was now the big dog. How she got to the top meant nothing. Being at the top and staying there was all that she cared about. Through all the secret meetings revealing details of her mother's sordid past and shady dealings, never did Jaymee assess or question why she was really chosen. Arrogantly, she believed she deserved it, especially after learning about her mother's biggest secret of all.

Her office phone rang. She turned around to get it.

"Hello," she said with a smile. "Jaymee Dean."

"It's done," a voice said before the phone was hung up.

As she put the phone back down, Gloria and Jasmine both barged in. Jaymee wasn't fazed. She pushed the silent security button on the floor. In many ways, this was how Jaymee wanted to see Gloria and Jasmine, in her office and on her terms.

"I've been waiting on the two of you to come and congratulate me," Jaymee snickered. "I couldn't have done it without you."

Gloria flew around the desk and slapped her in the face several times. Jasmine pulled her mother off.

"You tried to kill me for this. After all I gave you," Gloria cried.

"I didn't try to kill you. I had no part in that. That was all Teddy's doing," Jaymee said, trying to defend herself. "Just be glad you lived."

Gloria went after her again, but the security officers came in and stepped between Jaymee and her mother. With a busted lip, Jaymee still mustered up a smile. This was the proudest moment of her young life. For the moment, she was the queen.

"Are you okay, Ms. Dean?" one of the security guards asked Jaymee.

"They were just leaving. Make sure that they don't return without my approval." Jaymee winked at her mother and Jasmine.

"Jaymee, you don't know what you have started. I'm still going to bring you down. I hope you know that when things go wrong, your partners are going to ask for your head on a platter. Are you ready for that?" Gloria tried to go after her once more, but Jasmine held on tight enough so that she couldn't get close.

"This is not a game. If you hate me, then I'll leave, but don't turn your back on Mom like this," Jasmine pleaded. "We're family."

"I had a great teacher, so you should know that all the bases have been covered," she said, glaring at her mother. "The pupil trumps the teacher. Such an epic victory. I see the headlines now."

Gloria's anger grew exponentially. Hearing Jaymee gloat turned her stomach. She wanted so badly to beat some sense into her. "You might be at the top right now, but you don't know diddly about staying there."

"Good point. Security, you can leave. We have some private family matters to deal with." Jaymee slit her eyes at Gloria. "I know more than you think. Why don't you tell your precious Jasmine why you were in the park that day running like a crazed woman?"

"It was you? You tried to kill me?" Gloria's anger grew.

Jaymee chuckled. "I had nothing to do with any of that. That was all Teddy. He was the one blackmailing you."

Jasmine was feeling like she was a couple of steps behind Jaymee and her mother. "Then, how do you know?"

"See, Teddy wanted mommie dearest gone really bad. He was work-ing with some *New York Times* reporter on digging up your secrets. Found some interesting shit."

Gloria cleared the lump in her throat. "So! Get to the point!"

"So, I had nothing to do with your accident or Tommy's death. That was all of Teddy's mess. He's such a good planner, but his execution stinks."

"But why all of this?" Gloria asked.

"I only want to destroy you," Jaymee said with venom.

"You have really lost your mind," Gloria replied.

"Me? I'm not the one with a million secrets."

Gloria paused to think about what her daughter was threatening. Jasmine's eyes went back and forth, looking at them both. She had no idea what was going on.

"Should I call you sis or mom?" Jaymee smirked. "How much do you think I know now? Or am I still losing my mind?"

Jasmine's eyes bucked. All her life, she had known Jaymee as her sister and never thought anything else.

"Jaymee, what the hell are you talking about?" Jasmine asked think-ing it was nonsense.

This secret was something Gloria had hoped to keep hidden for-ever. How Jaymee had found out, however, was puzzling to Gloria. Only a few people knew the truth, and none of them were still alive besides her. Instead of dropping her head in shame, she stayed poised.

"I love you like you were my own child. Your birth mother was go-ing to put you up for adoption. I took you in. I'm your mother."

Almost on cue, a beautiful Puerto Rican woman in her late fifties came in the door behind Jasmine and Gloria. She wore a silk white dress with a black belt wrapped around her waist. With the woman were two burly black bodyguards dressed in dark suits different than the uniformed guards who had just left.

"That's where you are wrong," the woman said, adamantly pushing past them to go to Jaymee's side.

"Alexis," Gloria said, shocked like she had seen a ghost. "You're dead."

"You wish," Alexis said with a smile. "Your plane explosion didn't kill the right people."

"It was you all along," Gloria said, putting all the pieces together. "Where is he?"

"One thing at a time."

Gloria fumed, knowing where the story was heading.

"I just hate that the job wasn't done right. You stole my daughter from me."

Gloria huffed. "You didn't even want her. All you wanted was the company."

"And now we have it," Jaymee sneered. "I always knew you were treating me differently. Just guilt!"

"Jaymee, don't do this. Think about what you are doing. We're family. It doesn't matter if we disagree with each other. You're my sister," Jasmine pleaded. "I love you."

"So poetic and sad at the same time," Alexis said. "Your father said taking you out would be hard. You did throw me for a loop, surviving the hit-and-run, and you brought Ms. Jazzie back." Alexis looked over at Jasmine. "I must admit, you're not a bad businesswoman."

Jasmine said, seeing red, "Say another word about me, and you're going to need more security in here."

Gloria stood there just listening and fuming. In her mind, it seemed surreal that Alexis could have survived the plane's explosion. She kept envisioning the plane's explosion in the sky over and over in her head.

"Jasmine, you might want to join me. My sister, Gloria Dean, is going down," Jaymee said with smirk.

"Jaymee, don't believe her lies." Gloria tried to urge Jaymee to think about her actions. "I love you."

"The book of G.O.D. As told by Gloria Odessa Dean. So funny. See, Jasmine, Mommy dearest over there tried to kill me and her own father. After hearing she would have to share the company, she took it by force," Alexis said. "Ran her own father out of the company he built. She killed Jackie's parents and almost killed us."

"I didn't have anything to do with that explosion," Gloria said with sadness in her heart.

"You are one evil bitch. You killed the pilots and Jackie's parents all to get my daddy away from me."

"Jaymee and I are the victims here," Alexis said, rolling her eyes.

"Stop lying." Gloria couldn't take it anymore, and she reached out to grab Alexis. The guards wouldn't let her even come close.

"Yeah, we got off the flight. Your father told the pilot to take off without us. We were going to take another plane to meet Jackie's mother and father in Puerto Rico the next morning. Jack was so optimistic in thinking you wanted to make amends with us. I knew you had plans to get rid of me, but that was extreme." Alexis smiled. "We saw you rushing onto the runway. When the plane exploded, we knew that you would never give us peace. I wanted you dead, but Jack was so resistant, so we just disappeared."

"I had nothing to do with that explosion. I called and you didn't even let me speak to my father. I should have killed you. I built this company up, not you. You think I was going to let some piece of trash destroy my family? My plan for you was personal, like a bullet to the head."

"Such harsh words. I am still your stepmother. Show some respect."

"Where is he?" Gloria asked, anticipating a showdown with her father was near. "I can't believe he bought all of your bullshit for this long."

Alexis looked at her and grimaced. "Well, he won't be joining us. Your father, the good man that he was, didn't have the stomach to take his daughter down. I tried and tried to convince him, but he wouldn't. At least not the way I wanted. He wanted to just live off the millions he had hidden and go on with his life. I wanted revenge. I wanted blood."

Gloria realized the truth with horror. "You killed my father!" She did everything in her power to get to Alexis, but the guards were way too strong for her. Gloria simmered in anger as they restrained her. After a few moments of struggling, she submitted and calmed down.

"I'm not a beast like you. I loved Jack." Alexis smiled.

Gloria looked over at Jaymee. "You can have the fashion company," she said. "I don't want it. Jaymee, I love you. Don't believe her."

Alexis started laughing, and then Jaymee joined in.

"What's so funny?" Gloria asked as she got angrier.

"You think that's all I want? I'm coming for it all," Alexis said. "I am going to destroy you. I want you nailed to a cross."

"I'll sell it all before that shit happens," Gloria said vehemently. "You will pay for my father's death."

"How many more people have to die?" Alexis asked.

"You had Ralph killed?" Gloria asked. "I should have known that if Meagan was in the picture, her father wouldn't be too far behind."

"Just calling in favors. Poor John Lincoln. Like father, like son," Alexis said with a wink. "Your father kept great information on everyone. He knew people's weaknesses in such detail. We could have ruled the world together if it wasn't for you."

"Why?" Gloria pleaded to know the answer. "Just tell me why?"

"He was an obstacle in the way of progress. Just like everyone else around you. I eliminated them to clear my path to you."

"What about Jackie?" Jasmine asked. "Where is he?"

"Another victim of progress," Alexis said somberly. "I did like his mother."

"Jaymee, if you ever need me, I'll be there for you," Gloria said, almost in tears. "Alexis, your ending will be brutal."

Alexis rolled her eyes. "The great ones always end on their knees. I wish I could put a bullet in this bitch!"

Gloria rolled her eyes at Alexis and her comment. "I never thought of you as a coward," Gloria said, egging her on. "You better kill me now."

"Coward? This is the Jack Dean way of business. Just that Jack Dean isn't here. It's a shame. Jack was such a great teacher. I loved his marquee saying: 'If you're not innovating, you should be generating.'"

Gloria wanted to wrap her hands around Alexis's neck, but knew there was no way that was going to happen with the guards present. "I should have known you were Randolph James," Gloria said. "I know I have not been an angel, but I have always done what was best for my family."

"Funny thing is that Randolph James was your father's creation. He just didn't want to take you out."

"This company was always half mine, and you acted like I had to prove myself to you." Jaymee spit at Gloria in disgust. "All things in the dark come to the light eventually."

Gloria wiped some of the spit from her face. Spitting in her face was the worst move Jaymee could have ever made. For Gloria, their relationship was now at a point of no return.

"Please escort them out," Jaymee scoffed to security. "And make sure they don't return...ever!"

"Don't do this," Jasmine said. "I know about Maxwell and Brittany."

"And?" Jaymee rolled her eyes. "Be gone!"

Jaymee turned to face the window as the security guards escorted Gloria and Jasmine out of the office.

Gloria looked at Alexis and smirked. "See you in hell."

Alexis sneered at Gloria. "Been there, done that. I loved the malls."

After Gloria and Jasmine left, Alexis sat down in Gloria's old chair as Jaymee took her familiar seat across from it. Alexis stared over at Jaymee. She sensed Jaymee was a little bothered about what had just happened.

"Are you okay?"

"I'm fine." Jaymee couldn't look her in the eye.

"This is my personal vendetta. If you want out I would understand."

Jaymee took a deep breath. "No, I'm in. But…"

"But what?" Alexis asked. "What do you want to know?"

"Did you kill my biological father?"

"No. Of course not. Your father, Jack Dean, was extraordinary, inspirational, and the greatest love of my life."

Jaymee cleared her throat. "How did he die?"

"Jaymee, focus on how he lived, not how he died. Your father would be very proud of you."

Jaymee smiled.

Yet Alexis thought back to Jack Dean's death. It had been five years on the fourteenth of February.

Jack was at his desk with the phone to his ear as Alexis walked in. By the look on her face, she disapproved of whatever he was doing.

"Why bother?" she asked from behind him.

Jack quickly hung up the phone and turned around to face her. "What's wrong with you?" he asked as his temper rose. He could tell whatever she was about to say was a recurring argument that he wanted to avoid.

"You have called and hung up every month for the past ten years. Just to hear her voice. For God sakes, she tried to kill us."

"I still love her. And if you remember correctly, she was really trying to kill you."

Alexis fumed. "She should pay!"

"Can't you leave it alone?"

"Look at our lives," Alexis said, smirking.

Jack huffed as he glanced around at their multimillion-dollar surroundings. "We live in a castle in the hills of Rome. We have servants galore and want for nothing."

"We are in hiding. To the real world, we have been dead for twenty-five years."

He threw his hands up in the air, tired of the disagreement. "What do you want from me?"

"I want her to pay."

"How?" he asked with a hint of sarcasm.

"You know."

"She's not ready!" Jack scoffed.

"She's our daughter," Alexis yelled.

Jack shook his head. "Why now?"

"She's always been our daughter."

Jack dropped his head, trying to figure out how to end this argument once and for all. "Alexis, you didn't want her. I begged. You said you didn't want a child. You gave her up for Gloria to raise, without hesitation. Gloria has raised her and taken good care of her."

"For what she did to us, Jaymee deserves to run the whole company. I want Gloria out. That's all."

"I'm not going to be a part of that."

"I thought you loved me."

Jack rolled his eyes. He couldn't believe she was trying to question his love in this dilemma. "Really! Are you going to be a kid about this?"

"Jack!"

"Alexis, no. And this is the last time we're going to discuss it."

"Vincent is willing to help out."

Jack angrily stood up. "Damn, woman! Leave it alone. Vincent is my friend, not yours."

Alexis's eyes watered up as she became extremely emotional. "I understand."

"Good." Jack raised a brow, yet he was suspicious about her willingness to give in.

"I need a drink. Do you want one?" she asked.

Jack calmed down and sat back in his chair. "Yeah."

"I'll get it for you. Two Jack Dean specials." She smiled at him as she slowly walked out of the office.

When Alexis left the room, she went over to the bar in the living room. She made the drinks. The Jack Dean special was a full glass of Jack Daniels neat. After she finished, she poured a clear liquid from a vial that she'd secreted in her pocket into Jack's glass. Looking at the drink, she burst into tears. She wiped the tears away and headed back into the room. When she walked back into the office, she handed Jack's drink to him and sat on the couch across from him.

"Thanks," he said.

"No problem," she replied.

"I hope you understand where I'm coming from. I'm old and I just want us to live a good life. I'm tired of talking about Gloria."

"Don't worry. We will never discuss it again."

Jack smiled. "Good." He then took a sip of his drink. "This is just what I needed."

Alexis smiled over at him. "Anything for the great Jack Dean."

Alexis snapped out of her flashback. She noticed that Jaymee was staring at her.

"Are you okay? Jaymee asked.

"I'm great. I just thought about a time when your father and I were vacationing in the south of France. It was a beautiful time."

"You know she's going to come after you."

"Gloria is nothing without Jackie," Alexis said with confidence. "I'm more concerned about that Jasmine. She's a bright girl."

Jaymee flared with jealousy at the comment. "She's nothing special. We'll bury both of them."

Alexis wasn't thinking about Jasmine anyway. "We need to bury Teddy Hicks. He's still an owner."

Jaymee frowned. "What do we do?"

Alexis rolled her eyes. "What do you think, baby? He has to go the hard way." Alexis saw the worried look on Jaymee's face. "Don't be afraid to get your hands dirty."

CHAPTER **THIRTY-TWO**

Later that evening after all of the craziness had died down, Jasmine was so stressed out and exhausted from the drama that she ran to the only person who could help her right now, Maxwell. When she got to his door, he was surprised and elated to see her. In his eyes, Jasmine saw the warmth and love she needed to feel. Jasmine had thought that she didn't want to deal with him anymore, but her heart said differently and guided her to his front door. No matter what obstacles they faced, she was willing to work with him so they could stay together.

When Maxwell opened the door, she fell into his arms. A great relief overcame her soul. This was the right place, only place, for her to be at this moment. Maxwell held her tightly and kissed her on the forehead. He stared deeply into her dark brown eyes and melted. Jasmine saw what she needed to see: she was the woman who made him weak and human. She was his kryptonite. Now she knew what he had said was true: he had never loved another woman even close to his feelings for her.

After the warm welcome, they walked into his media room. Jasmine noticed that he had been watching *Iron Man 3*. He paused the movie as they sat down. At first she kept a social distance from him, but after one look into his eyes she bolted onto his lap and kissed him with all the passion her body had to give. Jasmine ripped the buttons off his shirt and began kissing his neck.

"I love you, Jasmine," Maxwell moaned.

Suddenly Jasmine stopped. She pulled away so that she could look him in the face as she spoke.

"Maxwell, I'm in love with you," she said. He was about to interrupt, but she placed her index finger over his lips so that he would wait. "No man has ever made me feel this way. I'm not expecting a ring or anything like that, but I'm willing to do whatever it takes to make us work. You are not perfect, and neither am I, but if we work together, our flaws won't be an issue."

"Can I speak now?" he asked, grinning.

She playfully rolled her eyes. "If you have too."

"Jasmine, I'm with you on us taking it slow, but I'm not going to sit here and lie. My end goal is for you to be my wife. You are an amazing lady. You're brilliant, sweet, intelligent, and tender. You are this boy's dream come true."

Tears formed in Jasmine's eyes. She leaned in and kissed him.

"How slow are you talking?"

"I don't know."

"Short but slow?" She laughed.

"I do have that raincheck up in my bedroom." He winked.

"The bank is open to put cash in and out...slowly."

"You're nasty." He smiled. "But I like that."

"You better."

He lifted her up in his arms as he stood up from his chair.

"So what happened with your company?"

She shook her head, dismissing the subject right at the start. "That's a conversation for breakfast in the morning."

"Okay," he replied as he swept her out of the media room, heading to his bedroom.

Once they lay down on his huge bed, their clothes quickly disappeared. Their naked bodies tangled together like beautiful strokes of a painting. Chills went through their bodies as they touched one another. His seductive eyes hooked her soul. Maxwell lit an internal flame within her that burned as hot as the sun. Their lovemaking was so incredible that she couldn't remember any other time that her body felt so good, so soon. The way he held her, caressed her, sucked on her, did unbelievable things to her body that she wanted it to last a lifetime. Just the thought of his luscious lips touching her neck made her quiver.

If they had any doubts about their relationship being true, this night definitely erased them. And as they lay holding each other, Jasmine was thinking about making love three or four more times.

She got her wish. They continued to make love until the sun rose up the next morning.

Maxwell looked over at her and smiled. "You are incredible."

She smiled. "I know. You're not that bad yourself."

"So are you ready for breakfast?"

Jasmine looked at him with excitement. "I'm glad you asked." She rubbed his chest.

He laughed out loud. "You are so greedy."

"Blame my huge appetite for you. I just want have you inside of me forever."

Just hearing her say that turned him on. Maxwell pulled her on top of him. "This is the last time and then we are going to have breakfast…for real."

She winked at him. "For sure, sweetie."

CHAPTER **THIRTY-THREE**

E arly on a Sunday morning two weeks later, Gloria was in the kitchen, sitting at the counter reading the *Wall Street Journal* and sipping a cup of coffee. She was dressed for church, wearing all white. Her hair was up and her makeup was flawless. On the counter by the door was an oversized white hat. She seemed peaceful, like her world was in the palm of her hand. Though she had lost her crown jewel, she was still the queen of all things fabulous.

She was in such deep thought about everything that had transpired, she didn't realized for a few moments that someone was knocking at the door. When she saw the butler walking that way, she got up and followed. Seeing that it was the guard, she went to the door as well.

"What's that?" she asked him.

The guard shrugged his shoulders. He handed it over to the butler.

"It's for you, Mrs. Dean," the butler said, handing her the nine-by-twelve yellow envelope. "It came by messenger yesterday while you were out."

What could this be? she wondered as she tore the envelope open. Her eyes bulged. It was the newest Gloria Dean Company fall catalog. A little note was attached. It read:

"'Now that you're out of the way, the Gloria Dean Company can grow. You are the greatest liar of all times and I hate you. I hope you die a terrible death. Thanks for nothing, your sister, Jaymee Dean.'"

Gloria sat for a long time in a daze. She couldn't believe the strange turn of events and how Alexis had planned the plane explosion. As she walked back to the kitchen, Jasmine and Ricky both were coming down the stairs. They were dressed for church as well. Jasmine noticed the envelope.

"What's in the package?" Jasmine asked.

Gloria looked down at it and smiled. "Nothing," she said, continuing on into the kitchen. "When did you get in?"

Ricky and Jasmine followed.

"What do you mean?" Jasmine smiled.

"I saw you leave last night," Gloria said in a gotcha type of way.

"Really," Jasmine smiled again.

"You were with Maxwell last night?" Ricky asked like he was upset.

"Ricky," Jasmine said to quash his concern. "We are an item."

Gloria saw the love in her eyes. "Leave your sister alone. She's happy."

"So, what's new for today?" Ricky asked, looking at his sister and mother.

"Same as yesterday. Our goal is to be back on top by the end of next year. Who needs the old company? I like the sound of the Dean Family Incorporated," Gloria gleamed. "It feels good, starting from scratch."

Jasmine noticed a difference in her mother's behavior. She was more at peace.

"Sounds like a plan." Jasmine smiled.

"Isn't it gonna be funny when we take down the Gloria Dean Company?" Ricky laughed.

As they all let it sink in, it got funny to them, also. Everyone then busted out laughing.

"No matter what happens in the coming year, Jaymee is still part of this family. But the business part of it all will not end nicely for her," Gloria said.

Everyone looked at each other, absorbing Gloria's words. They all knew it would be a volatile situation, battling Jaymee.

"Let's get to church," Jasmine said. "Today's sermon is about love and family."

"That should be an interesting one," Gloria said.

The Deans pulled up outside the church and got out of their limousine. As Gloria, Jasmine, Ricky, and Richard walked up the long stairs, they noticed Jaymee, Kenny, and Brittany getting out of a limousine as well. The two groups glanced at each other. Brittany attempted to run over to them, but Jaymee held her back.

As Jasmine entered the church, she was immediately met by Maxwell. They shared a long kiss. Then they joined the rest of her family as they walked down the aisle to a front pew. Jasmine looked at her text message. The number was listed as unknown. The message said, "I'm in position." Jasmine quickly texted, "Do it now." Once they were seated, Jasmine leaned over to Gloria's ear.

"I have a secret I want to share with you after we get home."

At that moment, Chris came in the church and walked over to them. They huddled around him.

"They found Jackie's body over in Jersey," Chris said sadly.

Instantly, Gloria cried and Ricky held her. Jasmine stared over at Jaymee. As they locked eyes, they both knew their rivalry was truly just beginning.

***

Poolside at a private resort in the French Riviera, in a waiter uniform and cap, Bronco walked up to Alexis and Vincent Marconti sitting in the shade of a cabana, enjoying the sun and drinks. Vincent looked up and saw the menacing newcomer. Alexis was unaware of what was going on.

"I guess there's no way out of this," Vincent asked with a smile while Bronco stood there silent. "She killed your parents. I have nothing to do with this. Just business."

Alexis's heart stopped once she realized what was going on. She saw the murderous look in Bronco's face and feared for her life. She couldn't help but think, Gloria had outsmarted her. "How much money do you want?" she begged. "Gloria's the monster."

Vincent grimaced. He hated that she brought money into the picture. One thing he knew about Bronco's type was that no amount of money in the world would make up for the loss of his parents and his brother.

"Is there anything I can do for you?" Vincent stared dead in his eyes, hoping to find some kindness in the killer before him. "I'm a powerful man."

"She killed your parents," Alexis cried out, sensing their end was near.

"And who killed my brother?"

People by the pool took notice of Alexis and Vincent's strange expressions. It was obvious that they were intimidated by the waiter.

"So, there's nothing I can do to change this moment?" Vincent smirked as he slowly tried to reach for his gun under his towel. He knew begging wouldn't help.

Bronco shook his head, which Vincent expected anyway. "You got them on the plane, but then you got off. In my book, their lives are on you. Then you killed my uncle Jack and my dear brother. I don't know you and don't trust Gloria, but Jasmine tells me you planned that explosion and had my brother murdered. I believe her."

Seeing no way out, Vincent quickly came to the conclusion that this was it. "Well, we're all going to hell someday," Vincent said, grimacing.

Bronco stood there, staring them down. "Some sooner than others. Tell Lucifer I sent you.'"

Vincent went for his gun but was too slow. Bronco shot two bullets. Both of them were hurled off their chairs. He ran off into the bright sunlight as the poolside commotion went wild. As Alexis died, she grabbed her cell phone and pressed the number two on the speed dial.

Jaymee answered. "Hello, hello, Alexis," she said. In the background, she heard the screams and the ruckus. Jaymee knew by the mayhem that Alexis was probably dead. The only question left for her was what would be in store for her.

***

Thousands of miles away, near South Bend, Indiana, Teddy stopped to have breakfast at a local diner in the wee hours of the morning. The only people at the diner were him and a truck driver who was being served. Though Gloria showed no signs of retribution against him, he figured that it would only be a matter of time before she would come after him. Thinking it was the best move, he decided to escape New York City and hit the road to live a quiet and safer life in rural America instead of another country. He figured Europe and South America would be his enemies focus on finding him. Teddy wanted to get as far away from the fashion world as possible.

After he finished his breakfast and paid his bill, he walked outside, feeling good about his new life. Teddy noticed the truck driver leaving the diner and heading over to his truck. The truck driver opened the back of the truck and let out his ramp. Teddy got into his car. Right after he started it, a deep-voiced man spoke from the backseat as he pointed a gun into Teddy's neck.

"You didn't think it would be that easy," the voice said to him.

"Is there anything I can do?" Teddy begged. "Do you have a price?"

"Drive forward into the back of the truck."

"And if I don't?" Teddy asked as his heart beat hard and fast.

"Either way, your life is over. You make the choice."

"We can make a deal," Teddy said with hope. "Who sent you?" Teddy had created so many enemies for himself that he was clueless to who might actually want him dead.

"A deal! That would mean my boss would have to trust you. Now that's funny."

Teddy looked around, hoping to see anyone who might be able to help, but it was like a desert. He slowly drove into the back of the truck as tears raced down his face. The truck driver closed the doors to the back. In complete darkness, Teddy let out a loud hollering cry. The passenger door opened, and the lights in the back of truck came on. To Teddy's surprise it was John Lincoln.

"Oh, Teddy, we meet again," John said with a grim look on his face. "You screwed me." John pulled out his gun and pointed it at Teddy.

Teddy began to sob.

John laughed. "No need to cry, my friend. I hear death is beautiful."

EPILOGUE

A few days later after Jackie's memorial service, Gloria and Jasmine sat quietly as the limousine journeyed through the streets of Manhattan en route to the mansion. In their own way they both felt responsible for Jackie's death. Gloria for the life she had him live by being her personal fixer and Jasmine for never stepping in to stop him. Though they both knew that in the end Jackie had been who he wanted to be. He enjoyed the fashion life and the hurt he had to inflict on people at times. But they both felt they should have done more.

Out the corner of Jasmine's eye she stared at her mother with intrigue. Though it was clear that Jaymee was now the owner of the Gloria Dean Company, she still had a lot of unanswered questions.

"Momma, I want to know the truth. No bullshit!"

Gloria raised her brow and wiped her tears away. "What do you want to know?" she asked softly.

Jasmine saw a different, more defeated person than normal. To Gloria, Jackie had been her backbone for years and now without him she was alone. He had done what she wanted and when she wanted it. His skillset was irreplaceable. To put it simply, she was the money, Jackie was the power, and that combination gave her enormous respect.

"Everything, but let's start with the plane crash." Jasmine stared directly at her. She didn't think her mother had done it, but she still had her doubts.

Gloria took a deep breath. "I didn't have anything to do with that explosion. It kills me just thinking about how evil she was. My father should have never married that hustling tramp. I told him from the beginning never trust a hungry stray dog."

"I don't remember much, but I do remember you and Alexis not getting along. Why?"

Gloria rolled her eyes. She was miffed by the question. "Really, Jasmine!"

"Momma, I just want to know these things for myself. I'm with you until the end of the earth."

"She gave up her daughter like she was throwing out trash. We were in the hospital happy for her and she tells us that she's giving up the baby to be adopted. And when my father went along with her reason of just wanting to be with him, I knew he would do anything that woman asked. I am surprised that he ran away with her, and that hurts deeply. She must have told him one hell of a lie about me blowing up that plane with his sister and brother-in-law on it. That's the only way my father would have disappeared. He loved me too much."

"Did you ever think about telling Jaymee the truth?"

"No, never. She's a Dean. My blood is her blood. From that day in the hospital to now, she is my child. I love her like I do all of you. That's why I was at that park that morning."

"Trying to keep it a secret?"

"Yeah. Funny thing is that my biggest flaw is loyalty."

"Teddy should have never been trusted."

"I know, but his father was good to us."

"I got Bronco out trying to find him," Jasmine said with confidence.

Gloria rolled her eyes. "Don't trust him. Just remember when the grass is cut the snakes will show."

"You do know we're going to get the company back, and that means destroying Jaymee."

"That's business."

Jasmine smirked. "For Jaymee it's all gray."

"She was always the most delicate one who took things so personal. I wish she would have connected better with you."

"Momma, it will get ugly." Jasmine looked over at Gloria so that she understood the gravity of what she was talking about.

"Jasmine, I don't want anymore deaths."

"I'm not you, Momma. I only make it to where people wish they were killed. Smart business is my weapon."

"So what happened with Alexis?" Gloria quipped.

"Mitigating circumstances that needed a more permanent solution."

Gloria grabbed Jasmine's hand and looked in her eyes. "Baby, don't become me. You're better than that."

"Thanks Momma, but I'm just protecting my family," she replied as the limousine pulled into the mansion's gate.

AUTHOR'S NOTE

When I was thinking about writing this book, I thought deeply about what family really means to me. Though *The Dark Side of Money* is a about a wealthy family on the brink of disaster, it addresses what makes any family weak or strong, and how it must move forward when faced with adversity. And despite the fact that the characters are fictional, I think we can all relate to the flaws, triumphs, failures, and personal characteristics that might seem to some like looking into a mirror. While I have written a multitude of stories about numerous subjects, I must admit that writing about the inner workings of family more deeply intrigues me. Just looking at the different dynamics of how people connect, love each other, and fight for and against one another is compelling material within itself.

In my mind, family is not what connects you by blood, but more by the sisterhood and brotherhood of friendships that you make throughout your journey in life. It's about common shared ideas, dislikes, likes, and a profound appreciation for what is important. Though close friendships and family relations are never perfect, you should always hope and pray that your relationships are built on a foundation of love, trust, honesty, and forgiveness. I believe the DNA of relationships is made of those four key ingredients. If your relationships have them and you reciprocate, there is nothing in the world you won't be able to accomplish.

In my life, family has been very important in my development, taking me from *who I was* to *who I have become*. They will also be the ones to get me to *where I need to be*. Many of my accomplishments in life couldn't have been done without family carrying me along my path in life. Their energy and strength have been a source of guidance, love, and support. I hope all people have the support of loved ones who truly care about their existence. The love of your family, no matter how it's developed, is a strong bond that cures, heals, and enlightens the mind and heart. I believe one of the wonderful things in writing about family is that every person has a distinct viewpoint of the family that he or she is part of or has created. Though similarities may exist, these stories are unique in their own right (excluding plagiarized stories). And best of all—family stories go on forever, enhancing the fabric of our great society.

CPSIA information can be obtained at www.ICGtesting.com
Printed in the USA
LVOW12s0949210114

370272LV00016B/248/P

9 780970 880864